Dorothy Uhnak and The Murder Room

›› This title is part of The Murder Room, our series dedicated to making available out-of-print or hard-to-find titles by classic crime writers.

Crime fiction has always held up a mirror to society. The Victorians were fascinated by sensational murder and the emerging science of detection; now we are obsessed with the forensic detail of violent death. And no other genre has so captivated and enthralled readers.

Vast troves of classic crime writing have for a long time been unavailable to all but the most dedicated frequenters of second-hand bookshops. The advent of digital publishing means that we are now able to bring you the backlists of a huge range of titles by classic and contemporary crime writers, some of which have been out of print for decades.

From the genteel amateur private eyes of the Golden Age and the femmes fatales of pulp fiction, to the morally ambiguous hard-boiled detectives of mid twentieth-century America and their descendants who walk our twenty-first century streets, The Murder Room has it all. ››

The Murder Room
Where Criminal Minds Meet

themurderroom.com

Dorothy Uhnak (1930–2006)

A native New Yorker, born and raised in the Bronx, Dorothy Uhnak attended the City College of New York and the John Jay College of Criminal Justice before becoming one of the New York Police Departments first female recruits in 1953. She wrote a memoir detailing her experiences, *Police Woman*, before creating the semi-autobiographical character of Christie Opara, who features in *The Bait*, *The Witness* and *The Ledger*. Opara is the only woman on the District Attoney's Special Investigations Squad, and applies the same cool, methodical approach to hunting down criminals as she does to raising a child on her own and navigating complex relationships with her colleagues. During her 14 years in the NYPD Uhnak was promoted three times and twice awarded medals for services 'above and beyond'; she also earned the department's highest commendation, the Outstanding Police Duty Bar. Her writing was equally highly regarded: *The Bait* was widely praised by critics, and won the Edgar Award for Best First Mystery of 1968. Dorothy Uhnak died in Greenport, New York, and is survived by her daughter Tracy.

The Ledger

Dorothy Uhnak

An Orion book

Copyright © Tracy E. Uhnak 1970

The right of Dorothy Uhnak to be identified as the author of this work
has been asserted in accordance with the Copyright, Designs and Patents
Act 1988.

This edition published by
The Orion Publishing Group Ltd
Orion House
5 Upper St Martin's Lane
London WC2H 9EA

An Hachette UK company
A CIP catalogue record for this book is available from the British Library

ISBN 978 1 4719 0652 7

www.orionbooks.co.uk

With love to Mildred: my sister and my friend.

1

Christie Opara tapped her fingers lightly over the typewriter keys as she tried to phrase the next sentence of her report. She glanced at her notebook, filled with cryptic notations which, translated, provided the Dun and Bradstreet rating of one of the city's major construction companies. It was just one of ten similar reports to be handed over to Chief Supervising Assistant District Attorney Casey Reardon, and since he had ordered the investigation, there was probably a perfectly valid reason for the hours of dull research.

Christie picked up the telephone receiver on the second ring. "Special Investigations Squad, Detective Opara."

"Tom Dell here, Christie. Tell the Man his chariot awaits."

It was three-thirty. If Tom Dell had Reardon's car ready, that meant she'd get an early break. "Okay, Tom. I'll tell him you're impatiently awaiting."

"Tell him that, kid, and we're both in trouble."

Detective Bill Ferranti neatly tapped the pages of his report together, stapled them and stood up. "Christie, if you're going into Mr. Reardon's office, would you mind?" He extended the three copies of his report, nodded his thanks and began dusting the top of the desk, gathering together a small pile of eraser crumbs.

Christie tapped twice lightly on the smoked-glass door, then entered Casey Reardon's office. He was speaking on the telephone, his feet resting on a desk drawer that had been pulled open for that purpose. He waved his hand, motioned for the report. Reardon's spacious office was warmer than the Squad Room. The sleet pounding against the two corner windows didn't pene-

1

trate the room. Christie flexed her fingers, which were stiff from cold and from too much typing.

Reardon balanced the telephone receiver between the side of his face and his shoulder. "Yeah, okay, Stoney, keep right with them. And keep in close touch." Without another word, he replaced the receiver, ran his hand roughly over his face, then through his thick, dark-red hair. "What have you got, Christie?" He looked up expectantly, then, before she could answer, he said, "My God, it's not that cold. You look like you're freezing."

"Our heat is out again, Mr. Reardon. I called the maintenance department again and they said they'd send a man up tomorrow. That's the third time they've said that and he still hasn't shown."

Reardon's amber eyes showed no sympathy. "Anything else?"

"Tom Dell is downstairs with your car."

He glanced at his watch, then picked up Ferranti's report and scanned it. "Where's your report on the Corvella Corporation?"

Christie answered sharply, the long tedious hours of note taking and typing catching up with her. "In my machine."

"It's supposed to be on my desk, not in your machine." He watched her face and anticipated the expression. Her eyes, an indefinite combination of gray and green, hardened and she started to answer but was stopped by a sudden sneeze. "For God's sake, Opara, if you're catching a cold, don't spread your germs around in here. I need your report before I leave today. See if you can hurry it up."

He watched her move across the room, admired her thin, trim figure and her attempt at dignity against an onrush of sneezing.

At four o'clock, Christie rolled the last page of her report from the typewriter and began to proofread, skipping whole paragraphs. She reached into the desk drawer and pulled out a wad of tissues in time to catch a wet sneeze.

"God bless, God bless."

Jimmy Giaconna stood uncertainly in the center of the Squad Room. Christie waved her hand in thanks. Small and wiry at seventy-six, slightly hard of hearing, Jimmy Giaconna was a well-known and well-liked character in the building. His scanty black hair was combed straight back, his tiny eyes were bright and blinking rapidly.

"Detective Ferranti here?" he asked loudly.

Ferranti, patiently awaiting Reardon's approval of his report, returned from down the hall where he had obviously scrubbed his hands clean of any traces of carbon paper. He greeted Jimmy Giaconna politely but with a slightly puzzled air.

What was immediately striking about Jimmy Giaconna's appearance, aside from the fact that he always appeared in the morning hours, was that without the little wire-legged, backless stool slung over one arm and the intricately crafted shoeshine box, he looked incomplete. What was equally unusual was that Giaconna, normally an almost rigidly courteous man, clutched at Ferranti's arm and began speaking in a loud, rapid combination of English and Italian.

Bill Ferranti, pink-cheeked and owllike behind his horn-rimmed glasses, his prematurely white hair adding to his immaculate appearance, spoke softly in English. "Jimmy, take it easy. Slow down." Carefully, he led the old man to a chair. "Now, what's wrong?"

Immediately, Jimmy leaped from the chair and his words rang out in a jumble of two languages. Ferranti put his hand on Giaconna's shoulder. It was a gentle, reassuring gesture, but surprisingly, the small shoeshine man shrugged the hand away and became more agitated.

"Jimmy, you're among friends. What's happened?"

Christie shared Ferranti's concern. The old man looked terrible. His small eyes darted about the room, his hand reached out, patted Christie's arm, then a huge sob, unexpected, folded the old man back into the chair. Christie brought Giaconna a paper cup of water which he drank, then, his eyes swimming, he lapsed into his native tongue, unable or unwilling to revert to his broken English. Ferranti listened, nodded, asked a question, slowed the old man down a bit, then listened again. He turned to interpret as Casey Reardon came into the Squad Room.

"Hey, Jimmy, what's the problem?"

3

The old man shrugged and looked at Ferranti.

"Jimmy's a little upset, Mr. Reardon," Ferranti explained. "His little granddaughter, Theresa, is missing. She was playing in front of her house a little earlier . . ."

Reardon glanced at his watch. "What time was she last seen?"

"Two-thirty, right, Jimmy?" The old man nodded.

"How old is your granddaughter, Jimmy?"

Jimmy Giaconna held up four fingers. "Four years. She has four years."

Reardon motioned for Ferranti to continue. "Theresa was playing in front of her house with a few of her playmates. Jimmy lives right around the corner, Mr. Reardon. He got home at about two-thirty and saw the children on the front stoop. At three o'clock, Jimmy's daughter looked out the window to call Theresa in, because the snow had changed to sleet, and the kids were gone."

Finally the English words burst from Jimmy. "My daughter she no just leave the kid out, Mr. Reardon. Every minute she know where the little girl is. So she no see little Theresa, right away she check with the neighbor on the phone, you know? Little Janice, her friend, come home with her sister Philomena, but Theresa no come into their house with them. So my daughter right away she put on the coat and come down and look all around. But she no see the kid. She come back upstairs and I hear all the noise in the hall. See, we all live in the same house, my two married daughters and their families and me. I ask what's the matter and we go down together and we look and we ask the neighbors and everybody." The old man spread his arms in an empty gesture. "What we going to do now, eh?"

Reardon pushed his fingers through his thick hair, closed his eyes for a moment, then nodded at Ferranti. "Detective Ferranti is going to go back to the house with you now, Jimmy. You take him to your daughter's apartment, and I'll bet you a bottle of booze that your little Theresa is home right now, crying her eyes out, and that your daughter is smacking her, hugging her and stuffing her with food all at the same time."

4

The old man smiled with relief. If a man like Mr. Reardon said it would be all right, it had to be all right.

Reardon stepped back, shook his head over Jimmy. "What the hell are you doing out on a day like this wearing just your sweater? A man your age, you might catch cold. Look at Christie here, she's coughing and sneezing and you should see the way she bundles up."

Jimmy smiled weakly, indicated Ferranti, who was bent, red-faced with exertion, as he pulled his rubber stretch boots over his shoes. "Ah, these young people, Mr. Reardon. A snowflake hits them and right away they got pneumonia. No blood in the veins. This little girl here, Mr. Reardon, ah, Christie. She look too skinny, you know? You make her work too hard, all the time I see her work, work."

"It's good for her," Reardon said briskly. "Go ahead, Jimmy, you tell little Theresa for me not to stay out in the snow so long next time, right?"

Jimmy nodded. It would be okay now. Ferranti turned and caught Reardon's signal. He would keep in touch.

Reardon reached for Christie's report, rolled it into a cylinder which he tapped absently on the surface of her desk. He stared across the room, through the window, out into the darkness of the cold, sleety afternoon. "You got a description of Jimmy's granddaughter?"

Christie nodded, held up the notes she had jotted down.

"Give the local precinct a call," he said quietly. "And stick around a while."

Tom Dell carefully placed his topcoat on a wooden hanger, brushed it lightly with his palms and hung it on the aluminum coat rack. He turned to the boy who had accompanied him into the Squad Room.

"Want to take your jacket off, John?"

He handled the threadbare, lightweight jacket with the same care he had shown his own coat. Dell rubbed his hands together, blew lightly on his fingers.

"Christie, do we have some hot coffee? This is John D'Amico, Jimmy Giaconna's grandson. Could you use some coffee, John?"

The boy shrugged and kept his head down. It was difficult to see his face. His eyes were hidden behind wire-framed eyeglasses which were rain-spotted. Christie went to Reardon's office and poured two cups of coffee from the electric percolator. She brought them back into the Squad Room and set them on a desk. Tom Dell moved easily, settled the boy in a chair, commented on the weather which had turned raw in the blackness of night.

"Is this a police station?" John D'Amico's voice had an odd, flat quality.

"No, this is the District Attorney's office, John. This is Detective Opara. She works with Mr. Reardon and me."

He was about seventeen years old. Physically. He looked around the room, then at Christie and pointed at her. "Gee, she's a detective? I didn't know there were lady detectives."

Tom sat on the edge of the desk and nodded pleasantly. "John here has been very helpful, Christie. John and me are good friends, aren't we, John?"

"Yeah. We're good friends."

For no discernible reason, Christie felt tension beginning. Not from Tom's voice or gestures or manner. Not even from his quick, sharp glance directly into her eyes. Just from something vague . . . but strong enough to tighten her stomach and her throat. She followed Dell's lead, lit a cigarette, pulled up a chair.

"You're helping Detective Dell, John? Is Theresa your little sister?"

The boy regarded her blankly.

"No, Theresa's his little cousin. Right, John?"

The boy nodded. "She got lost in the snow. She was crying because . . . I don't know why she was crying."

"That's okay, John. Drink some coffee. You look cold." Dell waited while the boy gulped the hot coffee. "It was real cold this afternoon, wasn't it?"

"Yeah. It was real cold."

Dell led the conversation, gently, easily, not insisting, letting

6

the boy respond however he wished, but irrevocably he moved closer and closer to what Christie had sensed from the moment they had walked into the Squad Room.

Yeah, John had seen little Theresa out front. Yeah, she was cold and wet. Yeah, her friends went home and left her. Yeah, she was going upstairs. But she fell on the front stoop and banged her chin.

"There was blood on her chin. And she was crying. You know how little kids cry?"

Christie's voice sounded strangely false in her own ears. "That's too bad, John. You must have felt bad to see your little cousin cry."

John D'Amico turned to face Christie. His eyes were magnified behind his glasses; they were round and empty. His mouth fell open. Dell reached over and touched his shoulder.

"Sure he felt bad. John's a good cousin. Right, John?"

His head swung around, his face pale and expressionless, toward Dell again. "Yeah. She didn't have to cry so much. I just held my handkerchief to her chin. To stop the bleeding. Because . . . because . . . you know what? Her tooth came out. It was a loose tooth and it came out, right into my handkerchief." He smiled. "I even showed it to her. That's why she was bleeding. I showed her the tooth, to make her stop crying." The boy became agitated, looked from one to the other. He had offered the tooth, why didn't his little cousin stop crying?

They didn't press him. They did it easily and by steps, Dell and Christie taking turns, offering him more coffee, moving on, waiting, stop and go. Until they had it all, and then they sat with it.

He had met his little cousin in the hallway, bleeding and crying. He had taken her into his family's apartment. His mother, a widow, was at work. His two younger sisters were at a friend's house. He just wanted to help Theresa. He held the handkerchief to her mouth. He helped her take off her wet clothing. He just wanted to. She wouldn't stop crying. She just wouldn't and then she began to, you know, pull and push at him and he didn't really

7

get mad. It was just that—she had no reason to act that way. And the crying. Gee, it made a pain inside his head. So he. Well, he just. And then, he put her in the closet in his room. Under some things. And she was very quiet and his head felt much better.

Christie took her control from Tom Dell. His expression never changed: friendly, comforting, easy. Just his light gray eyes, catching hers once or twice, seemed to have deepened. He reached for the phone on the first ring.

"Detective Dell. Yeah, Mr. Reardon." He turned his body so that his face was away from Christie and John. He spoke very softly, very rapidly. When he finished, he asked Christie if she wanted something to eat. She shook her head.

"I'm going to call up the luncheonette for some hamburgers for John and me. Okay, John?"

John D'Amico walked around the office, munching his hamburger. There was a stream of ketchup and juice along his chin and he wiped his mouth with the palm of his hand. He reached out, touched the various items on the bulletin board, asked Tom Dell questions, simple questions, and seemed pleased with Tom's answers. When the phone rang again, Dell swung around easily, kept his voice even and pleasant, but the color drained from his face.

"Right, Mr. Reardon. Yeah." And then, to himself, "Jesus."

Christie, watching him, felt nausea, heavy and insistent, almost gag her. Dell extended the receiver.

"Christie, Mr. Reardon wants to talk to you."

Reardon's voice, hard and familiar, held her steady. "Christie, do you know what's happened?"

"Yes. Yes, sir."

"Okay. I want you to come over here. Tom will give you the address. Christ, we have two mothers. You're going to have to tell one of them; take your pick. The victim's mother or the boy's mother."

Christie shook her head. "No. Uh-uh. I don't want to, Mr. Reardon."

8

There was a short pause, and then Reardon, firm and certain. "Nobody asked you if you *want* to, Detective Opara. You are *needed* over here and you have exactly five minutes to get here. Got that?"

"Yes. Yes, sir, all right."

Christie jammed her arms into her coat, buttoned it, pulled her boots on. She dug in her pocketbook, pushed aside gun, shield, makeup case, keys, and came up with some tissues. Her nose was raw from blowing and sneezing. There was a loud, hissing burst of sleet and wind against the window, but Christie felt sweat, clammy and dank, run along the side of her body. Her mouth felt dry and sticky.

"I'm going to show John some pictures of culprits we're looking for, Christie. Come on over here, John." He settled the boy at a card catalogue, then moved across the office to Christie. His hands went to her coat collar and carefully pulled the collar up over her neck and ears.

"Cold out there." Then, softly, "Take it easy, kid. You'll be okay."

She took it home with her. As hard as she tried to leave it behind, the voices, the sickened faces, the screams and cries came home with her.

Nora Opara, her eyes a brilliant blue above the royal-blue housecoat, heard Christie at the door. "Hold it a minute, Christie. I have the chain lock on." She stepped aside as a blast of cold wet air rushed into the entrance hall. "Wow, this is a great night. Good for your cold. Christie, let me look at you."

Christie kept her head down. "I'm all right. I just want to get out of these things. Nora, it's nearly two o'clock. What are you doing up?"

Nora ran a hand over Christie's forehead. Her dark eyebrows pulled together. "You're warm, Christie. You must be running about a hundred and one."

Christie shrugged. It wasn't important.

"Well," Nora said, taking her cue from Christie, "I could lie and say that I was so taken by the Late Late Show that I didn't realize the time. But actually, if you've seen one Dracula Meets the Son of the Wolfman's Daughter, you've seen them all. I'd rather be a martyr and tell the truth. My only grandson's only mother sounded pretty awful on the telephone and I figured you might need me. Or a cup of hot chocolate. Or something."

Christie hung her wet coat on the rack, kicked her feet free of her boots. "I don't think I can talk about it, okay?"

"Okay. But the hot chocolate's hot."

Christie sat in the kitchen, her fingers playing with a cigarette. "God, Nora, it was awful. Those poor women. And on top of everything else, poor old Jimmy Giaconna had a heart attack. My God, he suddenly just crumpled up. I never thought of him as an old man. He was always so chipper, so fast-moving. He just . . . they took him away in an ambulance. He looked . . . blue." Christie rubbed her arm, then, curious, pulled up the sleeve of her sweater. There was a long red welt. She fingered it absently.

"How did that happen?"

"The boy's mother. I was the one who told her. She went wild. She kept saying everyone blames John for everything just because he's a little slow. She grabbed at me and . . . she just . . . Boy, Nora, this is a rotten job. There are times when . . ."

Nora knew about "the job." She had been widowed by the job and had lost her only son, Christie's husband, to the job. Her smooth, pleasant face revealed pain when in repose, unaware.

"Mickey has a new girl friend," she said. "Your son has an absolute talent for picking real characters. You know little Vera Mason?"

Christie forced her mind to respond. "You mean that pudgy little girl?"

"Pudgy, hell. That kid is a human stomach on legs. Well, it seems that Vera is the champion spitter of the second grade. It has something to do with the way her braces are set. She can spit farther than anyone Mickey ever knew before in his whole life. Imagine, nearly seven years of searching and finally he's

10

found this treasure. We had a very pleasant dinner, my grandson and I, if you care for that kind of table conversation."

Christie stirred the hot chocolate.

"Honey, you look like the devil."

"I'm okay. This cold has got me down. And tonight was pretty awful. I'd better get to bed. Have to be in the office at nine." Christie gulped the hot chocolate, regretted it instantly. It seemed to hit the bottom of her stomach in a rush, gurgle around and surge back up her throat. She leaped to the sink, ran the water to cover her retching, then rinsed her mouth. "I'm all right, Nora, really. This has just been one bitch of a day. Poor old Jimmy. And those women. And that boy, John. It was rough."

"Christie, why don't you call in sick tomorrow? Your eyes are glassy and you have temperature."

Christie shook her head. "Reports tomorrow. God bless the endless reports. I have to get them up to date for the Homicide Squad. When I finish that, I'll take a few days off. I promise. Come on, Nora. Bedtime."

Christie took a fast hot shower, wrapped herself into a warm flannel nightgown, pulled the heavy quilt around her shoulders. She felt a surge of sickness but forced her teeth together and held it back. Then she opened her mouth and breathed in short, shallow gasps until she felt under control again. She opened her eyes wide in the darkness and followed imaginary spirals of blackness round and round into a deep, dreamless sleep.

2

Elena Vargas sat motionless, her feet curled under her, her arms folded one over the other, her hands hidden. She looked like a beautiful, tiny, dark doll, waiting patiently, helpless to move from where she had been placed. But the circle of calm detachment around her was a deliberate reality, and from within that circle she watched the men as they moved in and out of the hotel room. She missed nothing.

The detectives amused her. It was so easy to arouse the usual male reaction. She merely fastened her eyes on them, each in turn, as they approached. They fell into two categories: those who treated her with an elaborate, unnatural courtesy and those who blatantly stared at her body. All of them indicated an awareness of her sexuality.

Except the redhead. Casey Reardon.

Elena hugged her body tighter and wondered about Reardon. She watched him through the doorway to the outer room where he apparently had set up working headquarters for his squad. His hand rested lightly on the shoulder of the Negro detective, Stoner Martin. The contrast between the two men held Elena's attention. The black man was taller by several inches, narrow-hipped, carefully tailored. He had an elegance of movement and his face, in profile, very dark, even-featured, betrayed a hard pride and intelligence. He stood without commenting, almost as though he was not listening, while the redhead spoke rapidly and emphasized certain points with a quick jabbing motion of his hand. Reardon's face was almost boyish: a short nose, square chin, stubby red lashes over his eyes. His fingers raked through his thick, dark red hair. It seemed to be a mannerism. They lingered at the back of his neck where the hair was lighter and flecked with bright orange. Elena could not hear the words, but it was obvious Reardon was not happy. Things had not gone his way. Elena wondered what Reardon had expected. He turned toward her, but her stare was lost, destroyed by his preoccupation. To amuse herself, Elena examined him carefully; he was a solidly built man in his early forties, not handsome but interesting. There was a certain force surrounding him, an electric quality. Elena smiled, settled deeper into the confines of the chair.

Reardon looked into the room without seeing Elena. "Stoney, did someone call Opara yet?"

Detective Stoner Martin didn't have to check with anyone. He had notified a resentful, tired Christie Opara that her presence was required. "I called her about five minutes ago, Casey."

"She on her way or what?"

"She'll be here. You know, Christie is pretty beat up. It was a rough deal last night. And she worked a full tour today."

Reardon turned a glassy stare at Stoner. "She'll be on overtime like everyone else."

For a moment Elena thought Reardon was coming into the room, but he turned away, apparently for a telephone call. She felt mildly disappointed. She turned her gaze to the policewoman who had been assigned to stay in the room with her. The policewoman held up the heavy wooden knitting needles she had been manipulating for the last hour and displayed a tremendous mass of red mohair. She stood up, held the knitting in front of her and looked down in concentration.

"This stuff knits up fast. Look how much I've got finished already. Do you knit?"

Elena moved her head to one side and smiled. "Do I look like I spend my nights knitting?"

The policewoman rolled up the knitting and stuffed it into a tremendous leather shoulder bag. Her voice was disinterested. "Well, maybe if you spent your nights knitting you wouldn't have ended up here."

Elena laughed. "But you spend your nights knitting and here you are."

13

The policewoman shrugged, pulled at the sleeve of her navy-blue uniform, then began brushing the light coating of red fluff. "Only trouble with mohair is that it gets all over everything."

Elena stood up, stretched her small body, then held the position: head to one side, hip thrust forward, back slightly arched. The detective with the white hair stopped abruptly. He adjusted his glasses and looked ready to retreat. Elena bit her lower lip then slowly relaxed her body.

Bill Ferranti swallowed; the words stuck to the roof of his mouth. "I'm calling room service. For coffee. Or—or anything else. I mean, would you like something? Something to eat? Kathleen? Or . . . or Miss Vargas?"

He was one of the elaborately polite ones. Elena's eyes rested on his lips. "Thank you so much. I'd like some coffee."

The policewoman covered the end of a yawn and shook her head. "Not me, Bill, thanks. I've had it. I hope my relief comes soon."

Elena put the half-empty cup of coffee on the table beside her. She was tired and she was bored. But she was not worried. Enzo Giardino would have her released when he decided it was necessary. He probably had a few problems of his own; of course, nothing he couldn't handle. She didn't realize how bored she was until she heard the tough, take-charge voice in the next room, and then she felt some interest stirring. Casey Reardon, followed by Detectives Martin and Ferranti, approached her. This time, Reardon looked directly at her.

"Elena, Johnnie Brendan just died." Reardon held a paper in front of her face. "Your status has changed. You're now a material witness to a homicide and we're holding you in protective custody."

The girl shrugged. "That's my lawyer's problem, not mine." She let her eyes move slowly over him. Aware of what she was doing, Reardon acknowledged her with a slight smile, then turned abruptly to speak with the two detectives.

He likes to touch, to make physical contact, Elena noted. His hands were in constant motion, on an arm, a shoulder, through his own thick hair, at his collar, his tie. His hands looked strong, somewhat bony, rough and freckled. The two detectives were sent out on instructions which had been given so discreetly that they were still a mystery to Elena. When he turned to face her again, she saw some pale freckles across the bridge of his nose, but the hard lines across his forehead and at the corners of his squinting eyes took away the boyishness. He sat on the coffee table directly in front of her.

"Okay, Elena, to keep everything legal and aboveboard, check this out with me, right? You were informed of your rights at . . ." Reardon consulted a slip of paper in the palm of his hand, "at approximately eight P.M. this evening by Detective Stoner Martin on the premises of 812 East 55th Street. Detective Martin, in the presence of Detectives Ginsburg, Farrell and O'Hanlon, informed you that you were being taken into custody as a witness to the shooting of John Brendan, in the apartment of Enzo Giardino."

Reardon stopped speaking, ran his hand roughly over his face. This girl was literally using nothing but her eyes. They moved slowly over his face, along his lips, then back to his eyes. Not even her mouth moved. Reardon leaned forward.

"Listen, kid, if this was another time and place . . . but right now, well, you have nothing but trouble. And you are looking at the guy who can make it fall one way or the other. Giardino will be charged with homicide and he's worrying strictly about number one. He might even make bail on a manslaughter rap. In fact, I'm pretty sure he will. But we can hold you in protective custody for an indefinite period of time. So if you want to play games with me, make sure you play the right ones. Appropriate to the situation."

Elena ran her tongue over her lower lip. "I was not in the room when Johnnie Brendan was shot." She shrugged; it was a small, but eloquent gesture. "I was in the bedroom, baby, and I heard noise. A truck? A firecracker? Who knows? This town is full of loud noises. And then, bang-bang-bang," she pointed her index finger at Reardon and pumped her thumb, "your detectives are racing through the place, like gangbusters. Now, what can I tell you? I know nothing whatever. And I am very tired. And this room bores me. And these men of yours, coming in and out of here, they bore me, too." Elena leaned back, extended her legs so that her small, stockinged feet came to rest beside Reardon on the table. "Except for Detective Martin. He has a certain elegance. A quality."

Reardon said, "I'll tell him you said so. It'll make his day."

One small foot moved against Reardon's thigh. "And you, redhead. You make it all move around here, don't you?"

"You better believe it."

Again, the small shrug. "I wish I could help you. One way or another. But, you talk to Enzo Giardino. If Enzo says it was an accident, then it must have been an accident. Even Johnnie Brendan would have told you that, if he hadn't died. Me, I don't know anything. About that."

Reardon's hand rested on Elena's foot, closed and opened and closed with an easy familiarity. "Okay, Elena. Not about the shooting tonight. But other things. About Enzo Giardino, and his businesses. And who comes to see him at his apartment and what they talk about and . . ."

She pulled her feet from the table, pushed back against the chair. The words came from her in a singsong. "I have the right to an attorney; I have the right to remain silent; I have the right to refuse to answer any questions anywhere along the line." Her mouth pulled into a pout. "I don't want to talk anymore, Mr. Reardon." She studied a small fragment of red mohair which clung to her sleeve. Carefully, she lifted the fiber, leaned forward and placed the tiny, glistening piece of yarn on the lapel of Reardon's jacket. "You are smart to wear dark brown," she said. "It goes well with your hair."

Reardon brushed his jacket and smiled. "Okay, Elena. You do something to me. Now do something *for* me. More importantly, do something for yourself. It's easy enough. Just talk to me."

"I'd talk to you, baby, for a long, long time. But not with

words." The short jersey dress clung to the rounded contours of her body, barely covering her thighs. As she shifted in the chair, her hands skimmed her waist, then her hips, then rested in her lap, palms up in a questioning gesture.

Reardon's voice was hoarse. "See you later, Elena."

Christie Opara tapped lightly on the door marked 16A. The drabness of the hallway gave no indication that the rooms behind the door would be fresh and bright and furnished in excellent taste. The only staleness in the room was caused by a heavy haze of smoke: cigarette, pipe and, vaguely, the acrid fragrance of a cigar.

Bill Ferranti stood back for Christie to enter. She scanned the room, flexed numb fingers. "Where's Mr. Reardon?"

"He left about ten minutes ago, Christie. He said to tell you that he'd see you later."

"Swell."

The furniture had obviously been rearranged for working purposes. A long table had been pushed against one wall and large sheets of lined paper, filled with small figures and notations, covered the surface.

Ferranti steered Christie. "Lieutenant Andrews, this is Detective Christie Opara."

Lieutenant Andrews did not look like a policeman. He was a very tall man who did not give the impression of height until he stood up, which he did now. He was slightly overweight with an accumulation of flesh around his waistline; slightly bald; slightly nearsighted. He removed his eyeglasses, which were midway down his long nose, extended his hand, stopped, transferred his ballpoint pen to his left hand, then made a rapid, damp, limp contact with Christie's hand.

"How do you do, Detective Opara. Mr. Reardon has spoken very highly of you."

"Lieutenant Andrews is with the State Commission on Organized Crime, Christie."

17

The lieutenant carefully replaced his glasses on his nose. "If you'll excuse me," he said and hunched over the large sheets of paper.

Bill Ferranti took Christie's coat and motioned toward the door leading to the second room of the suite. "Do you know who's in there, Christie?"

"I don't even know what *I'm* doing here," Christie said irritably.

Ferranti's face was slightly flushed. His breath, as he leaned close to Christie, was minty. "Have you ever heard of Elena Vargas?"

"Elena Vargas? The name is . . . isn't she connected with what's his name? Enzo somebody? The gangster?"

Ferranti nodded. "Christie, she is really something. I mean, in the newspaper pictures I've seen, you know. But in the *flesh*." He pulled off his glasses, polished them briefly. "I beg your pardon Christie, but what I mean is, she is really a very beautiful girl."

The woolen sweater felt soggy around Christie's neck. It was too warm in the room and she was overdressed. She rubbed at her nose which was sore and tender. "Bill, I worked an eight-to-four today. Do you have any idea why I'm here? I was planning to go on sick leave for a few days."

Bill looked concerned. "Christie, I'm sorry you're not feeling well. Come to think of it, you don't look too good." There was a quick staccato of taps on the door. "That's probably Stoney. Maybe he can tell you more about all of this."

Stoner Martin placed four large, blue cloth-bound notebooks on the lieutenant's table. "This will keep us busy for a while, Lieutenant."

Andrews glanced at the books, then at Stoner Martin. He looked slightly alarmed. "But how did you get these? I mean, at this time of night?"

Stoner ran his hand lightly over the top book. "Don't worry about it, Loo. It's all legal." He turned to Christie. His dark face was alert and excited. "Well, Christie, what do you think about all this?"

"About all *what*? Why am I here, Stoney? What's going on?"

18

"The Man will be here soon, kid. You go relieve that police-woman in there before she knits them into a cocoon." Absently, he asked, "Do you knit, Christie?"

"Do I *knit?* Am I supposed to know how to knit? Does that have anything to do with . . ."

Stoner focused on her now, then slowly shook his head. "Hey, little one, you look terrible. Why are you all bundled up? You better get out of that heavy sweater or you'll suffocate. It's pretty warm in here."

"Thank you. Thank you very much." She pulled the sweater down over her narrow hips.

Stoner Martin prodded her lightly toward the second room. "You better take a couple of aspirins or something, Christie. Going to be a long night. Now don't go making your faces at me. Nothing here"—his hand swept the table filled with paperwork—"will make much sense to you at this point. Hell, it doesn't make much sense to any of us right now. Except that the figures on those sheets of paper are adding up and up and up." Deftly, he turned her back toward the open door. "Come on, little one, move, move."

"You are getting more like Casey Reardon every day."

He winked. "Why, thank you for the compliment, Christie." Then, serious, he instructed her, "Just go in and meet our prize package. Keep cool until the boss gets here."

Policewoman Kathleen Taylor and Detective Christie Opara greeted each other coldly but politely. Out of all the personnel in the New York City Police Department, on this particular night, it just had to happen that Christie would run into the only police-woman she had ever had difficulty with: years ago, some stupid forgotten incident, only the hostility remaining.

"Well, Detective Opara. Long time no see. They got you doing baby-sit jobs?"

"How are you Kathleen? Still knitting?"

"Passes the time." As she collected her various possessions—a ball of fluffy yarn, a box of writing paper, several magazines—and jammed them into her huge leather satchel, the policewoman

19

said, "This is Elena Vargas. Elena, you're coming up in the world. This is Detective Opara. First-grade detective, now how about that? That's really class." The policewoman breathed heavily as she changed from house slippers to flat shoes and rubber boots. "Well, so long Elena. See you around, Christie. I mean, if they have you doing this kind of job, for the *D.A.'s Squad*, we'll probably run into each other."

"You never know," Christie answered shortly. She looked around the room. It was a bed–sitting room, expensively furnished but without definition. She walked to the window, pushed aside the heavy gold drapes, watched the traffic sixteen floors below, turned back into the room. Elena Vargas faced Christie and made no effort to disguise her curiosity.

They regarded each other in silence, in that particular way of two women meeting for the first time, but without normal social restraints. Elena took careful, interested measure of the girl before her. About her own age, maybe a little younger, slim in a wiry way that approached thinness. Her body was hidden under a heavy blue turtleneck sweater but it was apparent that she was small-breasted and narrow-hipped. The plaid skirt was short enough to reveal long, slender legs which were covered by blue tights and fur-lined boots to the knees. Elena studied the wide-open, all-American-girl face: fair skin, eyes blue and sharp, reflecting the color of the sweater. The straight nose was reddened and the detective suddenly turned away and sneezed.

Christie crumpled the tissue and stuffed it back into her pocketbook. She had heard of Elena Vargas: call girl and sometime mistress of a notorious gang lord. In various newspaper pictures, throughout the past few years, Elena had seemed older, larger, fuller. But here was a girl of about twenty-six or twenty-seven, petite, almost fragile. There was no telltale hardness in the face studying hers. It was a dark, creamy brown with high cheekbones and smooth taut skin. The brows were black and followed a high natural arch. Her eyes, curiously slanted, seemed Oriental and were so dark, the pupils could not be distinguished. Her lashes were too thick and dark to be real but they fitted her face

20

perfectly. Her lips glistened with beige lipstick and were turned upward into an odd, mocking smile.

Bill Ferranti tapped lightly on the open door. "I sent down for some tea, Christie. Might help your cold." He kept his face down as he arranged containers on the marble table before the sofa. "I didn't know if you wanted more coffee, Miss Vargas, but if you do . . ." His hand indicated the container before her. "And some Danish. If you want."

Elena reached for a piece of Danish, nibbled a corner, her eyes on the detective. "You are so kind, Detective Ferranti."

Ferranti swallowed a mouthful of scalding coffee. "Wow, this stuff is hot," he said miserably.

"This room is hot," Christie said. "Can't we open some windows?" She reached for the window and pulled. Bill came alongside of her and Christie stepped back. She felt a deep stirring anger. His hands fumbled, his face was dark red and that girl sat there, smiling. He yanked the window open about twelve inches, backed away as a cold blast of air hit him at chest level. "I better put it down a bit. Is this all right?" He was speaking to Elena, but she merely smiled.

Christie told him it was fine.

"Well, I'll take my coffee into the other room. Lots of work to do."

Christie breathed in the cold wet air and felt the draft along the back of her neck as she leaned over the table and opened the container of tea. The cover was wedged tightly, Christie pulled too hard and spilled a small puddle of tea on the table. The tea was lukewarm and tasted of cardboard.

"How long have you been here?" she asked Elena.

"Since this afternoon." She waited, but it had been a vague question, asked without interest. There was a loud, familiar voice in the outer room. Christie jammed the cover on the container of tea and started across the room.

"I'll be right back."

When Christie entered the room, Casey Reardon waved one hand at her, continued his telephone conversation, pushed his hat

21

forward over his eyebrows, peered out from beneath the brim. He gestured impatiently for a piece of paper. Lieutenant Andrews, closest to him, tore a piece of paper from his notebook. Reardon snatched at it, scribbled some words.

"Yeah," he mumbled into the telephone, "right, right." He folded the scrap of paper into a small wad and dropped it into his jacket pocket. His eyes, now on Christie, caught her expression, seemed to freeze for an instant, then he blinked, taken completely into the telephone conversation. "Okay, call me when you have more information. I don't know, check with the office. I'll give them a number when I leave here. I'll be bouncing, just keep trying. Right." He put the receiver into place, whistled thoughtfully for a moment, then turned and regarded Christie. "You got a cold or something, Opara? You look like hell."

She started to answer him, but Reardon turned her toward the room where Elena sat, waiting. "Later, later."

The wind howled through the open window. Reardon crossed the room rapidly. "Are you two trying to catch pneumonia? My God, why is this open? It's about ten degrees out there." He shut the window and turned toward them, his voice friendly. "Well how are you two girls getting along?" He picked up a container of coffee. "This belong to anybody?"

"It is mine, Mr. Reardon, but please, be my guest. Really, your detectives are too good to me."

"Those are their instructions. Anything you need, you just let them know."

Christie dug into her pocketbook for a cigarette. Elena leaned back into the chair and watched them. Reardon moved to Christie's side, held a lit match for her. There was some interesting tension coming from the girl; she didn't raise her cigarette to the flame immediately. Her stare was cold and hard and angry but the redhead merely smiled and that made the girl pull too hard on the cigarette. She coughed and smoke came from her nose.

"Bad for you," Reardon said quietly and turned back to Elena. "I'm glad to see that you're relaxing, Elena. This is going to be home for a while."

22

"You've shown me your legal papers. This isn't too bad a place. I've been in worse. Of course, I've been in better too."

The conversation was casual, almost bantering. Elena handled it with one small portion of her brain so that the rest of her was free to watch Christie Opara. The girl was obviously angry; she stared past Reardon, barely nodded in response to his direct comments on the bitterness of the night, the comfort of the hotel. Reardon made a few efforts to draw the detective into the conversation but she sat, lips tight, silent. Reardon stood up abruptly and gestured to Christie.

"Elena, will you excuse Detective Opara and me for a few minutes. We'll be back in a little while. Come on, Christie, let's go."

Christie followed him into the hallway, started to speak, but his back was to her and he jabbed the button for the elevator, then turned. "Relax, okay? We'll have a drink downstairs. You wanted out of the room, right? Okay, you're out. Now just wait until we get downstairs."

Christie swallowed over the sore spot deep in her throat. She began to feel defensive and that made no sense at all. She had had two terrible days of hysterical, heartbroken women, had prepared reports about a strangled child and a retarded boy; she had put in an eight-hour day and had been all set to nurse her cold. Her head pounded with details she needed to be free of, her face was hot with fever, she felt cold and exhausted and in need of just a little sympathy. And Casey Reardon hummed beside her in the elevator, his face hard and alert, District Attorney expression set and ready.

The cocktail lounge was quiet and dim, the waiter soft-voiced and unobtrusive. Reardon ordered Scotch for both of them without consulting her. He studied the room and hummed until the drinks arrived.

"Go ahead, drink some. Good for you. You look terrible. Or did I tell you that before?"

"Yes. You told me that before. But it's nice to hear it again."

He pushed the glass toward her. "Come on, take a sip."

23

Christie took a short swallow, then put the glass down. Absently, Reardon reached across the table, touched her hand. "No blood. My God, your hands are like ice."

"Mr. Reardon, I'd like to know . . ."

Abruptly, he released her hand. "Okay, let's go. You first or me first?" He held up his hand. "But before you begin, let me save you the trouble. You're mad as hell, right? You worked an eight-to-four and it was rough the last few days. Okay. It was a hell of a deal. And you went home after your tour and got all settled down with your cold and the phone rang and you were told to come down here." He stopped speaking and leaned back. His eyes moved restlessly around the room. "This is a hell of a nice place, isn't it? A real class hotel."

"Mr. Reardon, if you would let me . . ."

His eyes moved back to her. "I thought we said *me* first. You going to let me finish?"

Christie picked up the Scotch and gulped a mouthful. It was sharp and medicinal. She clenched her teeth to keep from coughing.

"Take it easy, Christie, that's not cream soda. Sip it." He leaned forward slightly, his eyes narrowed. "You *really* sick?"

It was not concern; it was annoyance. Apparently, he wanted her on this particular case. Christie raised her face slightly, her eyes steady on his. He looked a little blurred. "I have a cold. That's all."

"Okay. Then let me finish what I started, right? I can understand you're feeling a little put out at being called back to work." His tone was reasonable and understanding. "We've all been working a hell of a lot of hours. But I would expect you to be a little curious at this point. No, 'curious' isn't the right word. I would expect you to be a little *interested* in what's going on."

"Mr. Reardon . . ."

"No, just wait a minute." The change was complete; he moved from her position to his own and his words now were sharp and crisp and accusatory. "Without knowing anything about this case and what is involved and what problems we have, without wait-

24

ing to find out what it's all about, you've been glaring and sulking and as mad as hell. Boy, Detective Opara, a few rough days and a head cold really are more than you can handle, right? The hell with an investigation that just might lead to . . ." Reardon put his hand over his forehead. "Christie, here I've been going on and on and not giving you a chance to say something. Listen, you must think I have one hell of a nerve making all kinds of assumptions on your behalf." He studied her face earnestly. "Listen, you talk for yourself. Go ahead. I'm really anxious to know why you're so sore."

Christie felt a long stream of cold sweat along the side of her body. The woolen sweater was clammy. He had already covered everything: stated her complaints and then dismissed them. He left her with nothing to say, yet waited insistently for her to speak.

"Well, yes, I do have a cold, and feel, you know. I was in bed when Stoney called me with no explanation, just to get to this . . . this Class A hotel and I figured it was probably something . . . very important. And then I'm assigned to a baby-sit job with . . . with a . . . an Elena Vargas and actually I'm just relieving a uniformed policewoman on a routine baby-sit job and anybody from the Woman's Bureau could . . ."

His face hardened. Her words registered in his light amber eyes. They were like clear stones. His mouth tightened and he continued to stare at her.

"Well, you want me to be honest, don't you?"

He nodded. "By all means, Detective Opara. I want you to be honest."

She faltered. Her hands moved over the table, reached for the glass, but he pushed it away from her. "Anything else you want to say, Christie?"

"Well," she said uncertainly, "I still don't know what it's all about, do I?"

"No. You don't. Do you?" The question was cold and accusing.

"Well, what is it all about?"

Reardon slammed his palm on the table. "Well, hurray for

25

Christie. She *finally* got around to asking question number one. After all the dirty looks and face-making and complaining, she finally came up with the one legitimate question. I didn't think you were going to make it. Hell, you were perfectly right to sit around thinking, 'that bastard Reardon, assigning me to baby-sit a whore.'"

In the heavy silence, Christie clinked the ice around in her glass. *She* had started out angry; she had every right to be angry. But Casey Reardon could take things and rearrange them and make it all come out a different way. And the worst part was, she couldn't find the flaws in his argument. She took a deep breath.

"All right, Mr. Reardon. Can we start again? Are you going to brief me or not?"

"Are you working on this case or not?"

"Are you giving me a choice or not?" The words had come impulsively, unplanned, in a cold harsh tone, but they made her feel better, finally able to meet him head-on.

Reardon's face relaxed, his mouth turned upward slightly. "That's my girl. Fresh. At all times, fresh. Let's put it this way. I'll give you a rundown and then give you a choice. You take it on or not. *You* choose. Fair enough?"

Christie felt wary; he was playing with her. She watched his face, but it revealed nothing. What she sought was in his voice, in the pacing of his words. "Of course, giving you a choice might, just *might*, seem to be somewhere in the category of a 'special favor.' But then, again, I guess since you *are* the only *woman* in the Squad, you might feel that once in a while, you should be entitled to special privileges. Like accepting or refusing an assignment."

He was needling her; she knew it, yet could not resist the angry reply. "I have never asked for any kind of special consideration, Mr. Reardon. It seems to me I've never been given any. I'm a first-grade detective; all of my assignments have been on that basis, as far as I know. Being the only woman in the Squad hasn't entitled me to any special privileges that *I* know of."

She reminded him of someone a very long time ago: the neigh-

26

borhood tomboy of his youth who played every game with the boys, matching them point for point, demanding that they give her no special leeway. Yet, they had all been careful not to hurt her and doubly careful not to let her know of their caution. It was true that Christie Opara carried her full share of the Squad's work and at times had been placed in real jeopardy. It was also true that his concern for her was very different from the normal concern and consideration he felt toward the other squad members.

He could mention to her that the very fact they were sitting here was a special consideration; he would hardly need to take an unhappy Pat O'Hanlon or Marty Ginsburg or Stoner Martin or any of the others for a quiet drink and explanation. Actually, he had no business sitting across the table from her now. Except . . . that she was Christie. . . .

He reverted to a neutral, official tone. "All right, if we're all squared away, I'll give you a rundown of what's involved. Elena Vargas might be the key to something very, very important. Yesterday morning, Stoney got a call from an informant. To the effect that there was some kind of trouble stirring at Enzo Giardino's. Relative to a long-time feud with Johnnie Brendan. Some of Enzo's men busted up some of Brendan's bookie joints, roughed up some of his men. That kind of stuff." Reardon waved his hand over the details. "None of that is really important. The informant had something of much greater interest, something I've been looking for, for a long time. According to the informant, the gambling activities, loan sharking, union goons, strong-arm stuff, all that is more or less a front for the real backbone of Enzo Giardino's operations. According to Stoney's man, and this gibes with other information I've received recently, Giardino is one of the prime sources in the country for the narcotics market." He caught Christie's expression, remembered something. "Listen, Christie, this is not the usual 'grab-a-couple-of-pounds-and-keep-the-market-tight' thing. This is big."

She had her own personal wound, deep inside of her that had made her turn down an offer from the Narcotics Squad; it was the one area of police work she had avoided. She was genuinely surprised by Reardon's next words.

"Christie, this is the big one. The worldwide narcotics syndicate. This could put everyone in this entire area out of business, from the top sources right to the little punks on the rooftops."

So Reardon knew about the little punks on the rooftops: the anonymous young boys who had changed her whole life. Reardon knew everything about everybody. She nodded, listening.

"My information is that the syndicate is run by five top men in five countries. Each top man has well-established interests in a wide range of well-known, legitimate businesses. They receive shipments of goods from all over the world. Included in these legitimate shipments, periodically, are millions of dollars' worth of uncut heroin. Only the top man in each country knows the exact distribution plan which spreads the stuff throughout the market. It is a very intricate, almost foolproof system. Without the exact plan, we could only catch a very minor amount of narcotics and most of it would reach the market." He paused for a moment, then added, "My information is that Enzo Giardino is the man in this country."

"And Elena Vargas is his girl?"

"And Elena Vargas is his girl. We staked out Giardino's place yesterday, a routine stake out to begin to get a picture of what his setup is. And goddamn it, that stupid bastard, Johnnie Brendan, with his penny-ante bookie crap showed up. There was a shot and Stoney and Marty Ginsburg had to step in. Brendan was on the floor with a bullet in his shoulder. Giardino is a lousy shot. We booked him for felonious assault and possession of a weapon and booked Elena as a material witness, but nothing is going to hold too long."

"Is Brendan pressing a complaint?"

Reardon shook his head. "Brendan is no longer with us. He dropped dead of a heart attack in the hospital. How about that? At least if Giardino had shot him dead . . . what the hell. We're trying for a homicide charge, but his battery of lawyers will find a way to get out of it. Giardino will be out on bail within the next twenty-four hours. We're holding Elena in protective custody, but there's something a little funny there."

"What do you mean?"

"Well, we've heard—from sources—that Elena is someone very *special* to Enzo Giardino. But he isn't making the slightest effort to get her released. And she seems perfectly content to stay put. Our informant said that Giardino keeps a ledger. *A ledger.*" Reardon intoned the words as though he were speaking of the Holy Grail. "In this alleged ledger is a rundown not only of the top-level people, but of all points of subsequent distribution. We tore Giardino's place apart last night." Reardon closed his eyes and rubbed them briskly. "Christ, we ripped walls, mattresses, just like in the movies. This morning, we opened up about five safe-deposit boxes in Giardino's name and a couple in Elena's name. And that, by the way, wasn't exactly legal, since our court order didn't extend to outside his apartment. You see how completely I trust you Detective Opara?"

"How did you manage to do that?"

Casey Reardon smiled. "I don't trust you quite that far. At any rate, of course, we didn't find 'the ledger.' Now, as in any big enterprise, sooner or later, competition rears its head. That's only traditional, right? We've received word that there are some elements of the drug traffic who are not too happy with the current setup. They would like to share Giardino's virtual monopoly, but in order to do that, they'd have to find out his operational plan. Apparently, *only* Giardino has that information." Reardon lit a cigarette, studied the match thoughtfully, then extinguished it. "But possibly, Elena Vargas knows where the information is, too. Which might explain why there hasn't been any great attempt to get her released from protective custody. We might be doing Giardino a favor by holding her."

"Well, what about your informant. If he knew all that, he must know more."

Reardon swallowed the remaining Scotch, then stared at the empty glass. "My informant is now deceased. At about five minutes after midnight, last night, he was found slumped over the wheel of his 1969 white Buick convertible in the flatlands of Brooklyn. Just below his left ear were two small bullet holes. So much for my informant, the bastard."

Christie's face registered her immediate reaction to Reardon's last remark. "Don't waste any sympathy on him. He was a punk, name of Funzi Bennanti. Operated a crane at one of Giardino's scrap metal and iron works in Brooklyn. He used to hang around with one of Giardino's employees, an old guy who used to handle Giardino's wheel in the good old days of knocking off joints. One night, the old guy got between Giardino and some acid that definitely wasn't intended for the old man. So, Enzo gave him a soft job, let him sit around the junkyard and draw pay. Funzi was picked up as a receiver some time back, buying and selling stolen TVs off the piers on the west side. He had three heavy ones on the sheet and he'd have sold his mother to keep from going up for life as an habitual. So, we played him along. He's thrown us a few tidbits. About a week ago, he called Stoney and told him he'd latched on to something really big."

"From the old man?"

Reardon nodded. "From the old man. He got loaded one night and started bragging about the old days. The old guy is a lush, has one eye, one ear and apparently, every now and then, Giardino treats the old guy to a drink or two, for old time's sake. Apparently, some loose talk penetrated the soggy old brain and Funzi egged him on enough to get the two things the old man heard: one, that Giardino is top man in the narcotics trade; two, that Giardino keeps a ledger with all the vital information."

Christie frowned. "You mean that just on the basis of what that old man told that . . . Funzi . . ."

"No, not just on the information the old man blurted out." His mouth pulled down and he shook his head. "You don't have to know *everything* about this damn case, Detective Opara. I don't know why the hell I'm going into such detail anyway. Your main concern will be Elena." He stopped for a moment and his voice changed. "She's quite a little girl, our Elena. What did you think of her?"

Christie shrugged without answering but Reardon didn't seem to notice. "Yeah, she's quite a little girl. What you would call 'all female.' She works at it. Every minute, without even trying."

"That's very interesting," Christie said shortly. "But then, I guess that's her . . . her profession, isn't it?"

Casey Reardon looked blank, then laughed. "Honey, you sound just like a woman."

"Well, in case you haven't noticed, that's what I am. Besides being a detective, I mean."

"Don't go getting touchy, Detective Opara, you know what I mean." She really was annoyed, but he refused to acknowledge it. Hell, he had spent too much damn time as it was worrying about her moods. "Now, what your job will be is to try to get next to Elena, you know, 'chummy.' Find a way to get through to her. We've got to get something on Elena, something strong enough to make her willing to cooperate."

Incredulously, Christie asked, "You mean, just like that I'm supposed to find out some deep dark secret or something? You have to be kidding."

"I'm not kidding. That's why you're in this case, Christie. We've been working on Giardino, off and on, for nearly a year. We've got backgrounds on him, his various legal and illegal operations. We've also come up with two observations about Elena Vargas: one, that she is more than just Giardino's mistress, and two, that Giardino, for some reason, has placed complete trust in Elena. Now that would give rise to speculation; Giardino is not what you'd call a 'trusting' type. Which indicates that he has something strong on Elena, so strong that he has no doubt she'll keep quiet. You're wearing your dopey expression, Opara. Yeah, I know it's vague right now, but you're about Elena's age, you're trained as an investigator. And you can be sympathetic, right?"

"Sympathetic?" Christie shook her head. "I'm not at all sure what I'm supposed to be sympathetic about. From what I've seen of her, Elena Vargas doesn't need . . . sympathy."

Reardon's eyes went past her. "Elena sure doesn't look like she needs anything. She's got it all."

"Why don't *you* offer her sympathy?" The words were out before she could stop them, before she realized the impact of her sharp tone.

"Exactly what's your problem, Detective Opara?"

Christie shrugged, stared at her hands. She didn't *really* know why being assigned to Elena Vargas bothered her, or why she was tired of hearing everyone point out to her how sensational Elena Vargas was. She felt a weary, directionless depression, deeper than her physical exhaustion and tinged with recognizable self-pity: her nose was red, her eyes burned, her sweater was too bulky, she . . .

"Listen, you want to go on sick leave?" She looked up, drawn by the anger in Reardon's voice. "Hell, if you're not feeling well, go on home, we'll manage." He glanced at his watch, impatient to get going; his eyes moved restlessly around the room.

Christie felt defensive again and resentful of the feeling. "You've assigned me to Elena. All right, I'll do the best I can."

He studied her carefully, turned something over in his mind before he spoke. "All right. But you handle it *carefully*, you got that? She's bright and sharp as hell. And she's very likely to get under your skin, the way you are tonight."

He set it up as a battle and Christie felt a surge of combativeness. If Elena was sharp, so was she. If Elena was professional at her job, Christie Opara was a first-grade detective, and that took a degree of professionalism very few police officers could achieve.

She reached for a cigarette, but Reardon picked her pack up and put it into his jacket pocket.

"May I have my cigarettes, please?"

Reardon shook his head slowly. "No," he said quietly. "Chew on your nails. It's less self-destructive."

Lieutenant Andrews opened the door at her first knock and peered at her over his eyeglasses. "Oh, Detective Opara, would you mind signing the time card I've prepared in your name?"

"The time card?" Christie glanced at Ferranti, who gestured vaguely. "What time card?"

32

Andrews carefully ran his fingers through a group of cards and extracted one. On it, neatly typed, last name first and first name last, was her name. "I always keep index cards on the people assigned to me. It's a much more accurate system than time sheets. I put you on duty at 7:30, since that's when you arrived."

"I wasn't aware of the fact that I'm working for you, Lieutenant."

"Oh, well. Not exactly. But the members of your squad will be performing chores as part of my investigation. We keep careful records as to time expended during any particular phase of any particular investigation." He pointed to the card Christie held. "You see, all the information is fed into a computer eventually so that we have a better idea of how our time is spent. Really, there is nothing *personal* involved."

Christie realized she was behaving childishly. The mild-mannered man, peeking over his glasses, wasn't being as offensive as her reaction. She knew that. Knew it was stupid of her. But she shook her head and handed the card back to him unsigned. "Take it up with Mr. Reardon in the morning, all right, Lieutenant? I'm not used to signing 'time cards' for computers or anything else."

Bill Ferranti followed her into Elena's room. The girl was watching television and seemed absorbed in a loud musical number.

"Christie, he's really a very nice man," Bill said quietly.

She felt irritated and didn't want to be pacified. At least, not by Ferranti. "What is he doing out there, anyway? Preparing the Dead Sea Scrolls for the Great Computer in the Sky?"

Ferranti carefully checked that Elena could not hear the conversation. "Bank accounts, statements, invoices, bills of lading." He ticked them off quietly. "All kinds of records from Giardino's 'industries.'" Then he winked. "Andrews doesn't know it, but about half of those records were 'borrowed.'"

Christie smiled grimly. "He'd turn us all in if he knew that. But first of course, he'd make little index cards on each of us."

"He's a bit of a nuisance, Christie, but is very knowledgeable.

He just has his little hangups, like index cards. He must have about a thousand of them. I better get back in there. Take it easy."

Christie sat on the sofa and pulled her boots off. Her feet were damp and her toes felt cold. Elena, her face impassive, slid her eyes from the television set to Christie.

"Would you mind if I turned the sound down a little? I want to make a phone call?"

Elena shrugged. It didn't matter.

Lieutenant Andrews' voice spoke pleasantly into her ear. "May I help you?"

Christie wondered, as she waited for the hotel operator to get her home number, if Andrews kept a card on telephone calls and would present her with a bill. She tapped her fingers impatiently and counted three rings. On the fourth ring, Mickey's voice, breathless and excited, broke her nasty mood.

"Hi, Mom?"

"Hi. How'd you know it was me? You a detective or something?"

"You said you'd call. It was really good, Mom, and I didn't forget any of my lines and you know what happened? Vera's braces slipped right in the middle of a song and she spit all over Susie Jacobs and Susie got mad right on stage when she was supposed to be singing about the elves and stuff and she just stopped singing and Freddie sounded very loud and then Vera started spitting all over everyone making like it was an accident but it wasn't!"

Christie felt the clear laughter of her son penetrate, lift away some of her own weariness. She listened as he told her all about the school play and how funny it was and how the devoted audience of parents and grandparents and brothers and sisters laughed at everything and how the teacher, Mrs. Clare, said it was the best show she'd seen that year. And everything.

"Gee, Mickey, I wish I could have been there." It broke the lightening effect of her son's words: the old guilt surged through her. She was away from home too much, away from her son too much.

34

Mickey brushed it off. "That's okay, Mom. But boy, it was really funny. Nora laughed like crazy, didn't you, Grandma?"

"I'm glad it was fun, Mickey. You'll have to act it all out for me tomorrow, okay?"

She heard Mickey call his grandmother, then Nora's voice, carried by the child's enthusiasm, was bright and cheerful. "Hi, Christie. It was a masterpiece of confusion, the kids all looked great and the teacher looked like she considered herself lucky to have survived. They really were cute, though."

She talked with Nora for a few minutes, tried to latch on, to be part of it, to make up for having missed another part of her son's life. Nora caught some of her mood. "Christie, you okay? Do you have any medication with you for your cold? Will you be stuck all night?"

"Yes, to all your questions. Nora?"

There was a brief, expectant silence. Christie turned, saw Elena, hesitated. "Nothing, Nora. See you later. Kiss my little Barrymore for me, okay?"

Then, thud. She was back in the hotel room.

Elena made no attempt to hide her curiosity. "You have a child? A son?"

"Yes."

"How old is he?"

"Almost seven."

"Who takes care of him, when you're working, I mean?"

Christie dug in her pocketbook, then remembered that Reardon had taken her cigarettes. Absently, she answered, "His grandmother. My mother-in-law."

Christie walked to the window, her back to Elena. She looked down into the dark street, squinted her eyes so that the street light and bright neon restaurant signs and automobile headlights all compressed into formless slashes of sharp glare. She watched the traffic light on Park Avenue, red facing the avenue, green facing the street. The cars, gunning impatiently back and forth, shot long streaks of gray slush beneath their wheels. Red all around, then darkened for a moment, then green, and waiting cars shot forward. Toward what? Where was everyone going? Christie was lost for one small moment, out there on the light-flooded street, waiting for a signal. To go. To move. Somewhere.

The nausea came on her suddenly and unexpectedly; flooded her with a feeling of light-gray cold insistence and medicinal clarity. The damn Scotch and the damn cigarettes and the damn cold. She clenched her fingers into the palms of her hands and bit down hard on her back teeth. She swayed for a moment, turned toward the window and breathed in short, shallow breaths of the cold air that escaped from the window frame. She felt a little shaky and gray and dabbed at the cold sweat across her upper lip and forehead.

"Are you all right?" Elena's voice was soft, just edged with concern.

Christie turned slowly. "I'm all right. I was just a little dizzy for a minute."

"I have some Anacin if you'd like."

Christie sat on the couch, stretched her feet out to the cocktail table. It had passed; she felt her body settle down. "No thank you."

"Do you get dizzy often?"

She was annoyed by the girl's bright stare and by her questions; she shook her head without answering.

"You look very pale. I thought perhaps you were going to be sick."

"I'm not going to be sick." And then, irritably, "Look, forget it, all right?"

Elena hesitated for a moment. "I was wondering about you. You don't look like a policewoman. I was wondering how you came to be a policewoman."

Christie spoke too quickly, her voice cold and hard to meet some implied accusation. "I was wondering about you, too. I was wondering how you came to be a prostitute."

If the words had any effect on the girl, nothing registered on her face. She drew deeper into the corners of the chair, ran her small palms over the expensive fabric, studied her fingers for a moment. "Detective Opara," she said carefully, "I imagine you were selected for a particular reason, to be here with me. That other one, that policewoman who was here with me all day and into the night, she was very different from you. Shall we be honest with each other? What is it you want?"

Christie held her hands tightly together. "All right. Let's be honest. Although, I don't know how honest you are."

"Nor I how honest you are."

"That's true. Okay." Christie took a sharp breath and spoke rapidly so that nothing would stop her words, no sense of caution, no sense of letting things get away from her. She wanted to cut directly to the heart of what this was all about: it was where they would eventually end up anyway. "I want to know where Enzo Giardino's ledger is. The ledger that spells out the various routes of distribution for narcotics that enter this country under supposedly legitimate conditions."

Elena's fingers tightened on the arms of the chair and there was a surprised smile on her lips. Her eyes were not smiling. "Well. You *are* very honest. So far. More so than any of the others. You come right to it, don't you? Very well, I will be very honest too. I don't know and if I did know, I would not tell you. Nor anyone. Because the ledger," she said, not denying its existence, "*if* I had it, or *if* I knew where it was, would be my insurance, wouldn't it? I mean, if I had it or knew where it was and gave you that information, what would my life be worth?"

Along with a sense of relief at having put all pretense aside, Christie felt a sense of release. "Exactly what is your life worth right now?"

"It is my life. To me, it is everything. It is all I have."

"What kind of life is it, Elena?" Christie felt a reckless curiosity. The girl gazed past her. "It is my life; it is what I have."

"But it really isn't your own life, is it? I mean, any man with the price can buy his way into your life, can't he?" Reardon had told her to be very careful. Caution. Be sympathetic. But Christie didn't feel like being careful and sympathetic; she felt like throwing a few darts of her own.

37

With just a trace of pride, Elena said, "The price is *very high*."

"But enough men have the price, don't they?" Christie felt the contempt in her voice, made no effort to conceal her feelings. She was aware of what she was doing, that it was wrong, unprofessional, and for some reason, personal. Yet, strangely, for some vague, indefinable reason, Elena seemed completely at ease. Her eyes, glittering and proud, her voice, low and strong, showed no disadvantage.

"I give nothing that is not fully paid for. And once given and paid for, I have no debt, I owe nothing of myself to anyone. *Not to any man.* There is *no* man, not one anywhere, who can make me suffer for one little minute of my life." Elena smiled, stretched, leaned forward. "That Casey Reardon, he is a very attractive man. A very exciting man." Her voice was brittle and mocking. "Is he *your* man?"

"That's just about what *you'd* think, isn't it?" It came out like an insult and they held it between them for a brief moment so that it could be felt full measure for what it was, so that the lines could be firmly drawn and established. Yet, the silence turned back into Christie and she felt accused.

Elena smiled. "Why not? He's very strong and dominant. He has what you would call . . . charisma?" She leaned back and regarded Christie with amusement. "Tell me, aren't you aware that it shows?"

"What shows?"

Elena's small hand sketched a vague form before her. "When there is something between a man and a woman, it shows. It fills up the spaces between them. It reaches from one to the other. Haven't you even been to bed with him?"

"Casey Reardon is a married man." Her answer seemed shallow and schoolgirlish, even to Christie. She spoke rapidly, to change the direction of the conversation. Elena had touched an area she didn't want to think about. Reardon. Damn Reardon. "How about you, Elena? With how many men does it . . . does it show? Or can't you keep count?"

"None. With none. That is a very different thing. The sex act, performed out of lust"—she dismissed it with a wave of her small

38

brown hand—"that is nothing. A commodity, bought and delivered. There are no lasting connections."

"What about with Giardino?" It was asked out of curiosity; Christie was genuinely curious now about this girl, who viewed life so differently than she did.

"A habit with him. For which he provides me with many things."

"Like customers?"

Elena shook her head. "No, Enzo is not a pimp. He does not send me men. But on the other hand, he does not mind if I care to turn a dollar for myself. There are men. There are *always* men, and as you said before, many men with the price. So?"

"Just like that?" Christie turned her hand up, imitating Elena's casual gesture.

Elena Vargas moved her hands and body gracefully as she spoke. "Oh, just like that, or just like this, or just like whatever a particular man wants it to be just like." She leaned back, her dark eyes on Christie. "Have you seen my apartment? It is very elegant. It is what they expect, luxurious surroundings. It is part of what they pay for: the illusion of luxury. Lavender, everything in the bedroom is lavender," she said quietly, her eyes half closed as though she were visualizing the scene she described. "The carpets, the sheets, the blankets, the furniture, the wallpaper, the drapes. All lavender. All very expensive." Her hand moved quickly and dismissed her room. She studied Christie for a moment, a small frown between her dark brows. "You seemed surprised when I said something showed, between you and Reardon. Weren't you aware of it? Didn't you know it was obvious?"

Christie felt herself tense up again. "You're the one who's obvious," she said shortly.

For the first time, Elena sounded defensive. "I am what I am. I owe no excuses. *Not to anyone.*"

There was a touch of passion in her tone; Christie felt aware of a small vulnerable glimpse into Elena and with that awareness, a better sense of control over her own words.

"Don't you owe anything even to Elena? Not even to the face that looks back at you from the mirror?"

39

Elena drew back, pulled her feet under her. She dropped her head for a moment, but when she looked up, her expression was serene. "I will tell you something which I don't think you'll understand. But I will tell you anyway." She lit a cigarette, reached for a small ashtray which she held in the palm of her hand. She blew the first lungful of smoke straight at the ceiling, then lowered her head. "When I am in bed with a man—any man—and I am required to do whatever it is he has paid for—one part of me is there. Just one part. This part." The hand holding the cigarette skimmed the contours of her body. Smoke trailed upward in spirals as her hand moved slowly. "That's all. Just this." Her shoulder moved in a slight, derisive shrug. "The rest of me, *the part of me that is Elena*, is never present. *I* am not present. I am far away, removed. There is no *real* part of me present. My voice says words, my lips react, my body moves, my arms, my legs, but *Elena* is not there."

Her voice had become as intimate and as revealing as her words. Christie sat, longing for a cigarette but unwilling to ask for one. She ran her thumb across her lower lip and considered the girl. If Elena had built a fiction around herself, then there had to be something at the center which needed protection.

"I thought you and I had agreed to be honest with each other." Christie noted the rapid blinking of the thick black lashes. "That little story, is that what you tell yourself? Is that how you make everything okay? You're not twins, Elena. You've got one mind in one body, like everyone else, and the mind is with the body no matter how many little stories you choose to tell yourself."

"Not the *mind*," Elena said, as though this was the point she must clarify, this is what she must explain. "Not the mind—" her hand waved the cigarette impatiently. "That is blank, empty. But another part, something else." She bit her lip quickly, stopped speaking abruptly.

Christie felt the cold clarity of pursuit. She could feel the edge to her words and see the impact on Elena. "What part, then, Elena? Oh, wait a minute. Are we talking about the 'soul'? *Your immortal soul?*"

40

Elena stood up, looked around the room, crushed the cigarette into the ashtray. "Soul? I have no soul. I am talking about the . . . " She hesitated, seemed to need to answer Christie's quietly mocking questions. "I am talking about the *essence of Elena*." It was as though she spoke of a third person, not present in the room. Somehow, as she spoke, she managed to confront Christie, not with an explanation but with a boast. "The part of Elena that will never be revealed to any man in the way that the essence of Christie Opara is apparent when that Mr. Casey Reardon is in the same room with you!"

Christie felt a sudden wave of panic and confusion. The incredible conversation had turned back into her and she felt accused again. Along with the accusation, she felt an equally incredible need to deny what Elena had said and to justify herself. That there was no feeling between Reardon and her. Their relationship had been strictly professional; some slight flirtation at times, playful bantering, certain set reactions between them. But not deep enough for anything to show. Not really. Christie closed her eyes for a moment, closed out Elena and the room. She studied the soft grayness behind her eyelids, slowed herself down. When she spoke, her eyes steady, her voice careful and deliberate, she regretted every word, yet felt compelled to make a statement. And to whom? To this girl, this, this prostitute who had no right to say that something showed between Reardon and her.

"Casey Reardon is the Supervising Assistant District Attorney and the commanding officer of my squad. I work on his staff. Period. Anything else you seem to have 'sensed' or think you know, is wrong. You're not quite as smart as you seem to think you are, Elena."

"Oh, I am very smart," Elena said quietly. "A very smart girl."

"Sure. That's why you're here. Because you're such a very smart girl."

Elena would take no offense. She had started this game and set the rules and found the advantage; it helped pass the time and was amusing and she wasn't willing for it to end. She moved about the room casually. She was relaxed and felt a pleasant

41

sense of power. The young detective was quite pale, her eyes seemed lighter than they had before. Elena dropped into a chair, her small legs dangled over the arm. "What does your husband do when you work nights, Detective Opara?" Elena noted with satisfaction that Christie's whole body had stiffened. She smiled. If they were going to keep her cooped up in a hotel room, they would do better to send men in to talk with her. This girl that Reardon seemed to have such confidence in was a fool after all.

"Does he stay at home with his mother and your little boy? Or maybe," she said softly, "maybe he gets lonesome. I know so many men who get lonesome. Maybe he is with some girl, eh?" Elena's pattern of speech changed: she had fallen into a cadence, not quite an accent, but there was something unmistakably Latin not only in her speech but in the small, meaningful, easy gestures. "Maybe he's with some girl like me who understands that a man gets lonesome." She paused, then relentlessly pursued, noting the effect on Christie. "Or isn't your husband like that? Isn't he *that kind of man?*" Her lips pulled into a mocking smile. "Only, you know what, baby? Outside of queers, there is only one kind of man: *that kind of man.*"

Christie felt hatred pound through her: hard, complete, total, for this taunting dark girl with her sharp, bright intelligent face and her insistent words and smug certainty. Deep, deep, it gathered inside of Christie and worked along her chest and throat and she hunched forward. Her voice was low and fierce, a terrible whisper that unexpectedly engaged Elena Vargas totally.

"Listen, you. Listen. You want to know about my husband? I'll tell you about him. He's dead. He—is—dead. And do you want to know how he died? Would it amuse you to know how Mike Opara died?"

A tremor, cold and shuddering, ran down Elena's back, between her shoulder blades. She pulled her arms across her small soft body. The game had gone too far but she could not stop it. It was out of her control.

"He was a detective. And he was on a roof. And there were some boys. Just kids. Boys, sixteen years old. And they were shooting it up. You know what that is, don't you Elena?"

42

Christie jabbed her index finger into the vein of her own arm, her eyes burning at Elena. "Sure, you know what that is. Well, there were these three little boys, only they were junkies and junkies don't have any age, they are just junkies. But Mike, my husband, he saw three skinny kids running and leaping from one roof to another. Across a space of five feet. His partner was on the other roof, waiting, because they knew this was what those boys would do. Two of them leaped and landed right in the arms of Mike's partner. The third boy," the words stopped for a moment and Christie, unable to destroy that third boy, moved her face slightly and the words, relentless, continued, "the third boy leaped but he didn't quite make it. He jumped short and caught on to the railing of a fire escape across the alley. Mike saw him hanging there, screaming. Pleading to be saved." Christie's voice went soft as a chant; word followed on word, as though she was powerless to stop speaking. "It was five stories down; sixty feet straight down into an alley of garbage and rats. Mike jumped and landed on the fire escape and he reached down and pulled that boy up and got him on the fire escape and tried to open a window into the apartment. The boy whirled around and caught Mike off balance and shoved him through the stairway opening." Christie's face was expressionless, a blank mask. "And my husband fell, sixty feet, straight down, crashing into the sides of fire escapes and into the garbage. And the boy, he wasn't quite sixteen. Just a poor deprived boy with no home and no one to look after him." Christie blinked rapidly, her eyes came back into the room, saw the dark-eyed girl watching her intently. Her voice became a sharp, deliberate parody of Elena's. "He was just a sonofabitch of a *Puerto Rican* kid who didn't mean any harm. He got scared of the big man on the roof, he thought the big man wanted to throw him off the fire escape. He didn't know the big man was a cop. He thought maybe he was a bad man who wanted to hurt him or something." Christie shrugged, her voice became vicious, strange to her own ears. "He didn't mean to push da beeg man down into the alley, see, he just so scare, he didn't mean to harm no *policía*."

Christie caught her breath, then added softly, the voice her own now, "But he *did* push the big man off the fire escape. *And my husband died in that garbage.*" She reached for the package of cigarettes on the table, felt her hand tremble as she held a match and inhaled. The artificial coldness of menthol hit the back of her throat and she exhaled slowly and raised her face. "So you see, I know where my husband is when I work nights. He's where he's been for the last six years. He is in his grave."

Elena's face changed; the color went from a rich, warm brown to a sickening yellow haze; it started around her mouth and worked upward along her cheeks and forehead. Beneath the smooth, perfectly applied makeup, the terrible color showed. Her mouth opened slightly and she moved her jaw, but no sound came.

Christie stood up abruptly. She ground the cigarette into the nearest ashtray, looked around, spotted her boots, damp and bent against a chair. Without thought, she reached for them, sat on the edge of the chair, bent over, jammed her feet into the boots. She stood up again and her voice was a harsh, controlled whisper.

"*Oh, I know you, Elena*. You're a part of it. The mistress of one of the men who make narcotics available to the little boys on the roofs all over this city. You're not a junkie, you're worse, much worse. They are what they are. I've accepted that a long time ago. They can't help themselves, they're sick. But *you*," Christie was filled with contempt and loathing, "you live on the money and the filth and the death. You sleep with whoever has the price and the price, from the kind of scum who pay you, almost inevitably comes from narcotics. And you think it doesn't matter where the money comes from, it's just money and it puts the clothes on your fancy little back and it pays the rent on your luxury apartment. But the money you find on your dresser—or whatever the procedure is—comes from the pockets of the little boys on the roofs." She exhaled sharply, tried to clear her lungs of the mentholated nausea. "You'd like to think you're free of all that filth, that you've built a nice little protective screen around yourself. The 'essence of Elena' is not involved." Christie's mouth twisted into an un-

44

pleasant smile and she saw the small, quick, gasping intake of breath, the uncontrolled twitching of Elena's mouth. "Well, let me tell you this: *the essence of Elena is a whore!*"

The girl shook her head from side to side, denied the words. Her voice was a long, drawn-out moan. "No. No, listen to me, Christie Opara, listen to me . . . "

Christie reached for her pocketbook, her back to Elena. "No, I don't want to listen to you." She turned suddenly. The face watching her was strangely contorted. "You know what, Elena? I don't want to be in the same room with you, the same city with you, the same world with you. I don't want to listen to you and do you know why?" Her eyes were level with Elena's; her voice was as clear and as inflexible as steel. "Because there is nothing— *nothing*—you can tell me about yourself. I know you, Elena. *I know you.*"

Christie crossed the room toward the door but Elena darted ahead of her and blocked her way. She held Christie with a terrible, painful, naked burning of her eyes. Her mouth, which had been so strong, so smug, so certain, trembled visibly. Her hands, moving restlessly, tried to hold on to something, reached compulsively for Christie's arm, but Christie wrenched free of the touch with loathing, as though the girl's hand contaminated her.

"Don't you judge me," Elena said. "No one can judge me."

Christie started to turn away, but the voice, ragged and insistent as death, seemed to have paralyzed her. Elena leaned forward, her eyes burnt out and empty, her face the color of dust. "You don't know me. You don't know me. *You don't know anything.*"

For the first time that night, Christie looked at, *saw* Elena Vargas; saw through the mask of expensive makeup and languid certainty and mocking superiority. The terrible, exposed nakedness of Elena's face made her turn and run from the room because she had seen too much, did not want to know.

45

3

$\top$he twelve-hour cold capsule had only been working for an hour. Christie felt clearheaded but slightly glassy eyed. She held the oblong brass doorknob leading to the District Attorney's Special Investigations Squad for a moment, took a deep breath, then opened the door. If she had expected any particular reaction to her arrival, the men present were all too involved in their work to notice her.

Marty Ginsburg was hunched over the old Underwood, pounding his index fingers over the keyboard. The speed of his typing was remarkable, and he kept pace with the words dictated by a tired Bill Ferranti.

Detective Pat O'Hanlon, tall, pale, soft-voiced, was whispering into the telephone, one hand cupped over the receiver, the other hand sketching furious scrawls on the green desk blotter. His head bobbed up and down. "Yeah, good, I got it, I got it. I'll be down there in about an hour." Then, his voice went slightly higher, in an attempt at charm. "Listen, pal, old buddy, it would save me an awful lot of time and leg work if you'd get me a photostat." His mouth turned down. "Ah, come on, your boss doesn't have to know, what the hell."

Stoner Martin sat bolt upright in his chair, his eyes half closed in concentration as he rapidly touch-typed at the Royal. His partner, Detective Arthur Treadwell, absently rubbed at the collection of dark brown freckles which stood out against the tanness of his face. He shifted uncomfortably in the small chair and tried to adjust his ample body. Treadwell nodded at Christie, then told Stoner Martin, "Christie's here. Want to tell Mr. Reardon?"

Stoner Martin raised his fingers from the keyboard and flexed them. "Take five, Art." He shook his head. "Christie, Christie." He gestured toward the chair which Treadwell had vacated. "Better sit down."

Christie glanced toward Reardon's office. "Is he in? I didn't see Tom Dell around."

"Is he ever in. Wait right here. I'll tell him you've arrived so he can turn off his stopwatch."

"I thought I was early. It's only a quarter to nine."

"We've all been here since eight." He disappeared down the corridor and returned almost immediately. "He has been informed. Now is the 'Christie-is-sweating-it-out' period. Well, do you want Uncle Stoney to advise you?"

"How about Uncle Stoney going in for me?"

The dark face was sad. "Now that I cannot do. In fact, if I could, I don't think I would. Ask for my money, a pint of my blood—it's yours. But there are some sacrifices a friend just cannot make."

Pat O'Hanlon came over to them. "Coffee, tea or arsenic? I'm going around the corner."

Christie sighed. "Arsenic. In a container of tea with a drop of milk." She dug into her pocketbook, but Stoner handed Pat a dollar. "On me. That much I can do for you." He leaned back in his chair. "Okay. Want to talk?"

Christie lit a cigarette. "Well, I guess you know how I loused up last night?" Stoner nodded. "Well, it was . . . a bad night. I mean, I know I was wrong to leave an assignment but . . . I didn't feel well."

"An excuse, but not a reason." His voice was unmistakably Reardon's.

Christie turned quickly toward Reardon's office, but the sound was Pat O'Hanlon leaving the Squad Room. She stubbed out the cigarette. "Okay. What do I do now?"

"Well, like when a man catches you with *your* hand in *his* cash register, and he is holding on to your wrist and you are holding on to his money, baby, don't try to tell the man a story. You look at the man and you take a long deep breath and you say 'guilty-

47

without-an-explanation.' Unless of course there is an explanation, and if there is, it better be pretty damn good."

She shook her head. "Nothing. Not really. Nothing I could tell him."

"Christie, I'm sure you know there's a lot riding on this case for Mr. Reardon." He stopped abruptly; her face was puzzled. Stoner Martin didn't often let something slip. He had the feeling that he just did. He spoke quickly. "Now, Detective Opara, you are going to go into that office and throw yourself on the renowned mercy of Mr. Casey Reardon. . . ."

She ignored his banter and interrupted. "What did you mean? What's *riding* on this?"

He shrugged. "Couple million dollars worth of narcotics is pretty special, no?"

"That isn't what you meant. What else?"

Stoner's black eyes moved over her face carefully. He tapped his fingers on the keys of the typewriter. "Nothing else. Can you read Art's notes to me? He goes too slow and breaks the tempo of my very rapid typing."

Christie read the cramped handwriting, stopped now and then to rephrase the information into a sentence, but she stored one fact away, deep inside her brain, for future reference. There was something in all of this that Reardon hadn't told her. She looked up gratefully when O'Hanlon put the container of tea on the desk.

"One with arsenic," he said pleasantly.

"Boy, do I need this."

Christie pried the plastic cover from the container, put the dripping teabag on the cover and leaned forward. Steam rose from the container and she carefully took a sip. Casey Reardon's voice unexpectedly cut through the room, blasting from the intercom on Stoney's desk.

"Tell Detective Opara to come into my office."

Christie sucked the tip of her tongue. It felt scalded from the one quick contact with the tea. "His timing is perfect," she whispered to Stoney.

Stoney winked. "Stay down for the count, kid."

48

She tapped lightly on the door, but Reardon didn't look up when she entered his office. He dug some papers from beneath the general debris on his desk, scanned them, initialed them and tossed them into the out-basket. He looked up, seemed surprised that she was standing before his desk.

"Sit down." He gestured at a chair. "Okay, you got something to say to me?" Reardon watched her with such total concentration that Christie began to feel transparent. Her lips parted but he ignored his own question. "Because I have something to say to you." His hand moved roughly over his face, a familiar, impatient gesture. "I received a telephone call last night. At about one A.M. At my home. Lieutenant Andrews was calling. He was supposed to have gone off duty at midnight but he had to stay on duty because of the particular situation in which he found himself."

Each word was a careful, calmly delivered accusation; District Attorney to defendant. "I was told that you walked out on your assignment at about nine P.M. Is that accurate?"

She nodded. "Yes, sir."

"Well, Lieutenant Andrews, knowing full well that it is essential that a woman police officer be present when a female is in custody, particularly under the circumstances surrounding the particular female in question, realized there was a serious gap in proper procedure caused by your abrupt departure. It took some emergency arranging, but a policewoman did arrive within an hour. The policewoman found herself in a rather uncomfortable situation. There was our subject, Elena Vargas." He interrupted himself. "I take it you remember Elena Vargas?"

His eyes measured the effect of his words. He missed nothing, not the paleness, the unexpected twitch of her lips, the soft, stifled cough, the fingers tightly interlaced in her lap.

"Yes, I've heard of her."

"Yeah, I thought you might remember Elena. Well, little Elena, who had been so well behaved and relaxed, had a change of heart. She began acting like the little bitch she no doubt is and she put on quite a performance. Would you care to hear about the tantrum the policewoman walked into?"

49

Christie shook her head and studied her fingers. "No. Not really."

"No, not really," he echoed softly. "I don't blame you. I didn't care to hear about it either. At any rate, nothing would satisfy little Miss Vargas but that she call me. She only wanted to speak to Mr. Reardon." His smile was tight and unpleasant. "Now, on any other occasion, that would be very flattering. But at one A.M. this morning, it wasn't too flattering. I imagine our Lieutenant Andrews must have done a lot of soul searching before he made that phone call. Wouldn't you think so?"

Christie thought of the tall, conscientious lieutenant carefully flicking through his index cards perhaps for some clue as to how to handle Elena Vargas. Carefully, she monotoned, "Yes, I guess he gave it a lot of thought."

"Wonderful. So far we seem to be in complete agreement." He switched to a hard, cutting voice and his pace picked up. "Now here is where I think we're not going to agree, Detective Opara. Would you care to hear the substance of Elena's middle-of-the-night telephone conversation?" Christie shook her head. "No, I didn't think you would, but I think you *should.* Elena Vargas said, quote: 'Maybe you think I'm a fool, Mr. Reardon, and if you do, you are very much mistaken. You can't hold me forever, you know it and I know it. If you want the *ledger*,'" his eyes burned into Christie and his hands flattened on the surface of his desk, "'the *ledger*,' the girl said, 'ask Enzo Giardino about it.' She said, 'You have no bargaining power, Mr. Reardon, and your little girl friend is not quite as good as you seem to think.'" His silence lasted for nearly ten seconds before he added, "Unquote."

He moved his fingers to the edge of the desk, studied them for a moment. His eyes, motionless beneath the short thick red lashes, were translucent and more red than amber. "That was what Elena Vargas had to say at one o'clock this morning." His voice shifted to the present moment. "Now here's what I have to say. It seems to me that I adequately explained the importance of your assignment with this Vargas girl. And I recall, very distinctly, cautioning you to play it very carefully. Now, in all fairness"—the puzzled, concerned near kindness only partially disguised his best sarcasm—"I want to ask you something. Did you understand what I told you last night? I mean, did *anything* I say confuse you, or what?" He accepted the quick shake of her head. "You see, I stayed awake for several hours trying to figure out what the hell went wrong. Since Detective Opara is a first-grade detective, I thought, maybe she felt the assignment *was* beneath her professional competency." He stood up, jammed his hands into his trouser pockets. In the silence, the clicking of coins between his fingers sounded loudly metallic. He walked around the desk, leaned against it and looked straight down at her. His voice was cutting-edge steel. "Is that what the problem was, Christie? Even after all I told you, did you decide that it was just a baby-sit job?"

"No," she answered quickly, raising her face. "No, it wasn't that. . . ."

"Fine, that eliminates my first thought. Now, my second thought is a little harder to dispose of. My second thought, Detective Opara, really has me concerned. My second thought was that for some reason you *deliberately* loused up this assignment."

Her mobile face registered her complete surprise. *"Deliberately?* But why . . . why would I?" She stopped speaking. It raced through her; not answers, but questions. Why would he think that? What reason would she have? What more was there to all of this?

"Yeah, why would you?"

Because he was wrong, at least in this, Christie could meet him now, had some ground on which to stand. She narrowed her eyes. "Mr. Reardon, I messed it up last night. Okay. Guilty. Without an explanation. Guilty of . . . of unprofessional behavior or . . . or incompetence or of personal dislike or whatever."

She saw the hard face relax. Somehow, she had just cleared herself of something. He nodded abruptly. "Okay, go ahead. What happened?"

The impact of some hidden accusation propelled her. "You want an excuse? No excuse, okay? Elena Vargas and I just . . . we just didn't like each other. We . . . we needled each other. It got out of hand." She moved her hands vaguely and choked

51

back the words she could not say: that we touched on areas that should not have been reached. Her sigh was weary and resigned. "I was not behaving in a proper, professional manner last night."

Reardon watched her thoughtfully. His anger continued but it seemed different now, almost forced. "Well, I can understand how offensive it must have been for you to have to spend the night with a girl like that. Of course you'd feel antagonistic. Any woman would." He sat on the desk now, his hands on either side of him. "Except that you're not just any goddamn woman. You're a first-grade detective and that was your assignment."

He slid off the desk, brushed against her crossed legs as he turned and searched through a stack of paper, picked up a single sheet. He held it in front of him for a moment, then handed it to her. "Here, Detective Opara. Read this."

Christie scanned the paper, then looked up at him.

"Did you read it already? You read pretty fast. But actually it's a pretty short memo. Short, direct and with no detailed explanation. You realize that dropping a first-grade detective to third grade is entirely up to the Squad Commander? That memo will take effect the minute it arrives at the office of the Chief of Detectives."

"You mean . . . just like that?" She snapped her fingers. "Just like that, you're dumping me to third grade?"

Reardon's mouth fell open. His laugh was a short hard sound of surprise. "Opara, you really kill me. I mean, you have more goddamn guts. You walk out on a vital assignment and have the nerve to sit there, absolutely stunned at the thought that I'd *really* do such a thing. You're lucky I don't send you all the way back into uniform. How long has it been since you worked a midnight-to-eight-A.M. guarding a bunch of female winos and boosters?"

Christie leaned forward and carefully placed the memo on Reardon's desk. She swallowed dryly, moved her hand across her forehead. The sleeve of her dark-green sweater brushed her eyes. "Mr. Reardon, I'd like to ask you something."

Curiosity held his anger back. "Go ahead, Christie. What?"

"Are you going to send that memo through?"

There was a silence between them. Reardon reached for the memo, held it by one corner. "Tell me why I shouldn't?"

She raised her face. She blinked rapidly and her eyes were shining. "Because I've earned my first grade rating. A couple of times over. And . . . and I think if you'd give me a chance, I can still do the job you assigned me to last night . . ."

Reardon rose and walked slowly to the window in the corner of the office. He stood silently for a minute, then turned. "I'm going to ask you two questions, Christie. Give me two straight answers, right?"

She nodded, tense and ready.

"Have you discussed *anything* relative to this investigation with *anyone* outside of this Squad?"

Everything about her changed; the paleness receded, color flooded her face. Her eyes hardened with anger; all of her uncertainty and defensiveness disappeared. Reardon was oddly touched by the transformation, by the fact that she could not control or hide her indignation, by the fact that she almost passionately attacked his question.

"I have *never* discussed *any* assignment with *anybody* outside of this Squad. Or *inside* of this Squad either unless they happened to be working on the same case. And if you don't know that by now, Mr. Reardon, then I'm not even going to answer your other question!"

Reardon held up his hand. "Okay, okay, Christie. Second question." He kept his voice serious and official, but his eyes moved slowly over her. "When you got dressed this morning, did you deliberately pick out that outfit?"

"Huh?"

Reardon rubbed the back of his neck. "Forget it. Or think about it later if you want to." Briskly, he said, "All right, now I assume you've given some thought to the situation since last night and that you came here prepared to continue your assignment, right?"

"Yes, of course, but . . ."

"But not back in the hotel room."

She had to relinquish what advantage he had given her by his confusing questions and turn her attention back to Elena Vargas. "No, not back in the hotel room. But, I know this will sound crazy, under the circumstances, Mr. Reardon. But in a way, Elena and I *did* communicate last night. In a way."

Reardon's red brows shot up. "I'd like that explained. Hell, that really requires clarification."

"Well, you might say we communicated negatively, but in a way I did learn something about her. That, in retrospect, she *is* vulnerable in some areas. That she isn't really what she seemed to be. I'd like to do a background on her and see what I come up with."

"All right, but you'll have to move fast. Put in a little overtime, right? Make up for some skipped hours. Check with Sam Farrell, he's been working on another angle, but he might have something of value. Marty Ginsburg can give you a hand for a day or so, but that's all." She was jotting notes down as he spoke, but the pen was poised, her face trancelike. "Hey, Opara, are you with me or what?"

She blinked rapidly. "I'm sorry. I was just remembering Elena Vargas. The way she looked before I left last night. I think that if I can find the right information . . . that she will be very vulnerable. That she will cooperate completely." The words seemed to surprise her and amuse Reardon.

"What the hell is this, some of that 'feminine mystique'?"

"I don't know. I just thought of how she looked last night."

"All right, Detective Opara, you get going. And keep in touch with the office. Well, now what?"

She stood uncertainly, her eyes went to the memo. Reardon opened his top drawer and slid the paper into it. "For the time being," he said sharply. "Anything else on your mind?"

"Well. What you said before. Asked before. About when I got dressed this morning. . . ."

Casey Reardon's eyes moved over the green skirt and sweater, down, then up until he met her eyes directly. Softly but firmly, he said, "Goodbye, Detective Opara."

4

Christie Opara ignored the dark, suspicious eyes that watched her enter the tenement. She glanced at the scrap of paper. Top floor. Always, no matter what, it was the top floor. Any police officer, in any country in the world, on any assignment, always knew that the person being sought would be found on the top floor.

She climbed the long, tin-edged flights of steps, her eyes squinting in the brown darkness. The acrid odors cut through her nose and lungs in a potent mixture of human body odors and rancid cooking fumes. She walked carefully on the center of the stairs, being sure that no part of her clothing made contact with the wall; one quick glimpse revealed furious scurryings of unidentified insects. The four long flights of stairs made her gasp for oxygen. There were four doors on the top landing; none were numbered or lettered. The number on the scrap of paper she held was "12." Christie glanced around, tapped her knuckles on the nearest door. It opened immediately, a dark inch that did not reveal the face of the speaker.

"Sí?" The hoarse whisper asked, "Sí? What you want?"

Christie strained to see the face but only a slash of unidentifiable clothing showed. "Gonzalez?" she asked.

The door slammed shut and there was a heavy sliding of chain and a twisting of locks. Christie waited for a moment, then moved to the next door. She felt as she had felt from the moment she had entered the building: that she was being watched by hidden pairs of eyes, but there were no openings or peepholes on any of the doors. She turned, tapped randomly on the next door and waited. There was a jumble of sounds, voices, feet moving. There were children's voices, loud and high pitched, then a woman's voice, irritably silencing them. The door was flung open abruptly and several small dark faces stared up at her. Then, a woman, not much larger than the children, appeared among them, pulling them back into the room so that she could stand in the doorway. She started to close the door, but Christie moved forward, casually but deliberately, and placed her shoulder against the opened door.

"Mrs. Gonzalez?"

The woman nodded, her eyes intent on Christie. Christie raised the detective shield, that was cupped in her left palm. The woman's eyes slid quickly to the shine of gold, then back to Christie.

"I'm Detective Opara of the District Attorney's Squad. I'd like to talk to you about Elena."

The woman moved her head from side to side. "No, I don't know any Elena. Wrong house." As she spoke, she plucked small grubby hands from her skirt, pushed children away from her, automatically, without looking at them.

"Aren't you Elena Vargas's sister?"

The woman's face betrayed nothing. "I have no sister," she said slowly, without passion. "She is dead. My sister Elena died a long time ago."

Christie's shoulder resisted the pressure of the door. She moved over the threshold and sensed the woman's resignation. Elena Vargas's sister stepped back, moved her hand toward the room wearily.

Christie glanced at the children. They ducked their heads shyly but their eyes stayed on her as she sat on the chair next to the table.

"I will get you coffee," Elena's sister said. She moved toward the narrow stove set between two tattered upholstered chairs. She kept her face down, her eyes on the scarred coffee pot.

Christie felt the room: it was cold and dark and crowded with odd pieces of furniture and children. Consuela Vargas de Gonzalez and her dark-eyed brood dwelt within a riot of color: each ornament of religious adoration decorating the chipped walls, each slash of plastic curtain and flower, each angular slab of varied patterned linoleum placed over God-knew-what corruption of floor, each panel of brightly painted wall encompassed them blatantly within the confines of their small tenement rooms. The ugly garish colors leaped from all directions; the children wore shiny slippery iridescent clothing which did not keep them warm but seemed somehow to dominate and defeat them.

It was a room containing parts of a kitchen: stove, table, aluminum-framed, plastic-covered chairs, small dripping sink; parts of a living room: broken, heavy upholstered chairs; parts of a bedroom: two cots, one against the other, stale-smelling, grayed with use. And a television set: twenty-one-inch, brightly flickering, sound turned down, picture radiating, providing most of the light in the room. The children were more interested in their visitor.

Consuela, a small woman, burgeoned with a late pregnancy. She stood, surrounded by her tired, old-faced little children, and plucked warily at a thread which had once held a button midway down her worn maternity smock. Her sallow face was lost amid the ugly flowers winding down both her breasts. There was no trace of bloom on her cheeks. Her features, small and delicate, were totally lost in her surroundings. Christie tried to see Elena somewhere in the dark eyes, but a tired, beaten, bitter and totally unfamiliar woman placed a cup of coffee on the table before her.

"Maybe you won't like my coffee," she said.

Christie sipped at it, swallowed hard. "It's fine, thank you very much."

Consuela took a huge swallow from her own cup, then gave it to a pair of small hands, which snatched at it. She issued some instructions in Spanish and the children drank from the cup, one after the other.

"I put a lot of sugar in it," she explained. "They are greedy for the sugar."

Christie could not tell if there were five children or six of them or more or less. They stood clustered around their mother in that shy yet calculating way of small slum children: how might this strange visitor affect them? She smiled tentatively, and as her eyes made contact, first with one small child and then another, dark heads ducked down quickly then, irresistibly, bobbed up again to study the pale and soft-spoken intruder.

Consuela stood up and they moved against her like magnets. She pushed them from her with a languid, automatic motion of her hips, nothing more than an adjusting of her weight from one leg to the other. The smallest child—not clearly identifiable as to sex, just a small, tousle-headed child of indeterminable age, thumb shoved into a mouth ringed with some grayish, powdery substance—fell to the floor. Its head cracked against the cold linoleum. Instinctively, Christie leaned forward, but the child, without relinquishing the thumb, pulled back and picked itself up silently. The large eyes never left Christie's face.

Christie realized she would have to speak before this small and curious audience. "Mrs. Gonzalez, Elena lived with you for about a year. I understand that she had also lived with a family named Fenley before she came to live with you." Christie consulted her notebook, then slipped it back into her pocketbook. "I'm just beginning to piece together Elena's background. It is very important for me to do this. Can you tell me about the year that Elena lived with you?"

The woman's small dark hands plucked at the thread on her smock. She did not ask Christie why, or by what right, or for what reason she was being questioned. Never once did she assert that this was her home, her domain. She merely sighed and began to speak.

"Elena left the Fenleys for no good reason." Suddenly, she slapped at a head that poked against her body for a better view of Christie. The slap was hard and flat but there was no outcry. "She did not like to work, that girl. Always, Elena thought she was something she was not. The sisters at the home, they meant well, but they let Elena think she was better than the others, God forgive them."

Consuela's eyes came alive, glowed darkly with remembered malices. "Yes, she was quick to learn, my youngest sister. She was the youngest of us all, so she learned the English the fastest, the best. The sisters, they made a pet of her." The voice was stronger now, harsh. "There were seven of us when we were put into that orphanage. Elena was only two years old so they made a baby of her." She shrugged away a sticky hand that reached for her face. "They placed her with the Fenley people when she was sixteen. They were a nice family, they lived nice. But Elena was too good for that life. She said they wanted her to be a servant, a maid." Her expression was no longer blank; it was animated and cruel. "So, she came to live here, with us." Her hands spread to encompass the room. "There were not so many kids then, but even so, my husband did not make so much money. And Elena was young and healthy. At that age, at seventeen, I had Paco, my first son." She glanced around, then shook her head. "He's not here now."

Shrill voices chanted, "Paco's got a girl friend. Huh, Maria! Paco loves Maria." A quick slap shut the mouth of the more vocal of the chanters. The others squinted meanly at the crying child who kicked out at his tormentors. A sharp command from Consuela hushed them all.

"I told Elena I would get her a job where I worked. At the dress shop. She knew how to sew. We were taught by the sisters. Oh, but not Elena." Her voice went lower, tasted the words. "Not that one. Not at a 'factory,' she said. 'I'm better than that,' she said. Huh. All the time, she sat with her little pad, writing those shorthand words. Crazy little wriggles all over the papers, listening to the radio and writing down what the announcers said. My husband, he told her, 'You want to stay here, you get a job.' She said she tried, but everywhere she go, they look at her 'funny.' " Consuela's lips pulled back in a bitter, remembering smile. "They look at her funny all right. 'Elena,' I told her, 'you're not going to sit in any office with white girls and play at being white!' "

Suddenly aware of the blond paleness of the policewoman, Consuela bit her lip, turned her head, shoved a child from her knee. She shrieked some words in Spanish and the children scampered away but returned, silently, one by one. "You want some more coffee?" she asked Christie.

59

"No. No thank you, Mrs. Gonzalez. This was some seven or eight years ago?"

The woman tried to keep her voice light. "Sí. Yes, eight, maybe nine years, I'm not so sure. It's different now, you know? They got all these equal employment things. But it was different then, you know?"

Christie nodded. "What did Elena do then?"

Consuela leaned her elbows on the metal surface of the table. "Well, she came to work with me in the shop. But she was not happy there. She did not eat her lunch with the rest of us. No, not Elena. She would go into the office at lunch time and show off."

"What do you mean, show off?"

"Type, on the secretary's typewriter. To show the boss she could do the office work, you know. I told her, the other women they told her, stop playing, Elena. Do your own job, earn your pay and be thankful. And I looked out for her, too. All the time, the stockboys, the salesmen, the cutters, they watched her. She was very . . . you know." Her hands sketched curves in the air. "And with her face, all sweet innocence, they watched her, the men."

A hard glint came from the dark eyes. A small, joyless smile pulled her lips down. "My young and pure little sister. I told her to stay out of that office. The boss was a young man and he could see her body, the way she moved around. And the boss' wife could see, too. She worked in the office, the boss' wife, and she told Elena to stay out. But the boss, he started to let Elena do some letters and bills for him, when the secretary was out sick. Then, Elena started to go into that office like she had a right to. She said she wanted to get some good experience, so that she could look for a 'nice' office job and say she had real office experience. It would be different then, she said. I told her it would be the same." The small, clenched hand hit the table. "But no. Elena fooled herself. Something wonderful would happen. She would work in some beautiful shining building on Fifth Avenue." She made an ugly grunting sound and closed her lips firmly.

60

Christie thought of Elena, a young Elena, filled with hope for something wonderful. She forced herself to look at Consuela, to speak quietly. "And what happened then?"

"Well, it had to end bad. I told her it would, but Elena never listened. The boss' wife caught her."

"Caught her? What do you mean, 'caught her'?"

"Well, Elena had saved up her money and bought an old type-writer. She used to sit, all night, bang-bang-bang, clicking at those keys." Her fingers beat an angry sound on the table. "She drives my husband crazy, but she said she would become so fast, so good, she would get a good job and give us lots of money. But she needed paper and those . . . those typewriter ribbons. And the boss' wife . . . Holy Mother . . . I knew it would end badly. The boss, he went on a business trip and his wife caught Elena taking paper and ribbons from the office supply. She said Elena took money, too, from the . . . what do you call it? The petty cash. She had Elena arrested."

Christie remembered; Sam Farrell had shown her a yellow sheet on Elena. One arrest for petit larceny; she remembered also seeing the word "dismissed" on the sheet.

Christie thought of all the white collar crime, all the employees marching home with pockets loaded with paper clips, staples, rubber bands, pencils; with manila envelopes stuffed with carbon paper, stationery, envelopes. But Elena Vargas had been arrested.

"They put her in jail," Consuela continued. The children, around their mother again, listened. Their eyes were large and beautifully dark and shining. Their complexions ranged from nearly fair to deep brown, the color of their mother. "I was so ashamed." Her hand covered her forehead for a moment. "I didn't want to see her, not in a place like that. But I went. I was her older sister, after all."

"But the charge was dropped, wasn't it?" Christie asked.

Consuela shrugged, weary now. "The boss, he came back and made his wife drop the charges. He said that he gave Elena per-mission to take the typewriter ribbons and paper. And he said that *he* took the petty cash money before he left on his business trip. But who knows?" She made a sharp clicking sound with her tongue. "Eh, I wonder what Elena gave *him* for these favors?"

The air around Christie was heavy and stale and thick with the small unwashed bodies. The faces of the children seemed cruel and mocking, old and wise and knowing as their black eyes slid from their mother to Christie to gauge the effect of this information on their visitor.

"Where did Elena go then?"

"Oh, not here. Not back here." She shook her head over the obvious statement. "The court, they sent her to that doctor. I don't remember his name. Somewhere on Long Island. She worked for him for a while. I don't know for how long." She absently reached out and moved her fingers through a curly thick black head of hair; the child so favored pressed against her hand, enjoying the unexpected caress.

"I had my own troubles. But I have never been arrested. I am what I am. We had the same upbringing, Elena and me. But Elena would not be what she was. She was 'better.' So now, her face looks out from the newspapers for everyone to see what she is: a whore, a prostitute, a *puta.*" She made a gurgling sound, deep in her throat, then a dry, empty, hawking sound. "I spit at her name. She is dead for me. She is dead for my children."

It was with great effort that Christie forced herself to stand, to quietly speak some words, to reach out and stroke a thickly matted head of childish hair by way of farewell. The face of Consuela Vargas de Gonzalez reverted to the weary expressionless stare that had first confronted her. She offered no word to send along to her youngest sister.

Christie's feet thudded on the hollow tin-edged stairs. The progression of staircases seemed to be growing longer and longer, without end, bottomless. Finally, she yanked at the narrow door leading to the street. She whispered an unheard excuse to the startled old men who had been leaning against the door and fell into the hallway.

Christie moved rapidly along the narrow sidewalk, squinted against the thin glare of winter sunlight, twisted her body to avoid crashing into garbage cans and young women with shapeless bodies whose hands were pulled behind them by small children. She hurried on as though pursued, as though she dare not stop for fear she would be caught and held and trapped within the confines of that narrow living street of human bodies and sounds and odors and despairs. She slowed her pace finally, breathlessly, and struggled to regain control. She forced herself to stop and to turn and to look back and face the street where Elena Vargas had lived. She faced it and absorbed it and breathed it into her body, into the pores of her skin, and she held it all inside of her.

5

Mrs. Adrienne Fenley was a beautiful woman. Her high cheekbones were as flushed as a school-girl's. Her huge luminous gray eyes dominated the small, finely structured face. The corners of her mouth turned upward, and when she smiled, the small crinkles alongside of her eyes were surface deep, suggesting pleasantness, not age. Her hair, caught up and away from her face by a pink bow, was a subtle shade of golden beige. As she moved about the huge room, lights played upon her soft jersey jumpsuit which was also a subtle, almost indefinable color: the same tone as her hair.

Her voice was a particular kind of voice, a low, elegant, assured growl. "My God, I was expecting an amazon. Let me look at you." She placed her long fingers on Christie's shoulders, turned her toward the light which streamed evenly from the ceiling.

"Mrs. Fenley, I can see that you are very busy and I don't want to take up too much of your time, but if . . ."

"No, wait a moment." Mrs. Fenley's hand moved to Christie's chin. The fingers were long and cold as she tipped Christie's face upward. "You beautiful, beautiful child," she explained. There was a totally natural pleasure in her words. "Have you ever modeled?"

Christie felt heat along her cheeks and forehead and moved her face away from the cold touch. "No. Why . . . no, of course not. Er, Mrs. Fenley, if it's inconvenient for you to talk with me just now . . ."

Mrs. Fenley whirled around, her arms thrust out. It was a theatrical gesture, encompassing the room, yet she made it seem a natural movement. "All this, isn't it a disaster area? It's always like this before a ball. My God, the work that goes into these things. Sometimes I think it would be easier to just write a check. But, you see, it *is* expected of us." She shrugged and sighed, confident of Christie's sympathetic understanding.

Thrown carelessly over velvet couches and chairs was an assortment of dresses and other items of clothing: feathery things, bright, metallic shining fabrics, sheer misty yards of chiffon that seemed to have no form but floated over each other in graceful folds.

There was too much to see in one slow glance. The room could be better appreciated in a series of color photographs, studied a section at a time. The ceilings were unbelievably high; the huge fireplace was the first Christie had ever seen in an apartment; the paintings were placed in such a way that they did not call attention to themselves but were available for quiet appreciation. Everything in the room was right, emitted a confidence, provided a setting.

"Do take your coat off, for heaven's sake, my dear."

Christie wished she could hide her coat and her Irish knit sweater and tweed skirt. She held her coat uncertainly, reluctant to place it next to any of the garments tossed about the room. From nowhere, a small, unobtrusive girl in a pale-green maid's uniform appeared and took the damp coat from her. The thin sunshine had receded and cold rain was hitting the city again.

Mrs. Fenley gathered some dresses together to make room on the sofa: it was crushed brown velvet. "Do sit down, my dear. Out of all of these, I have to choose four. Four! God." She held a fringed garment before her, made a face. "Look at this little disaster." She lowered her voice and a smile glowed from her eyes. "Enrico would die if he heard me say that."

Christie sat on the edge of the couch, aware of her wet boots. Her leather shoulder bag emitted a damp, sour smell. She slid it to the floor, next to her feet. "Mrs. Fenley, as I told you on the telephone, I'd like to talk to you about Elena. Elena Vargas."

65

"Yes, yes, of course." The profile was perfect, as though drawn in one quick steady certain line. "Do you hear that? I mean, have you *ever* heard such a shrieky voice?"

The voice was high and petulant with a rush of words that couldn't be clearly understood. Mrs. Fenley waved her hand by way of excuse and crossed toward the doorway, as the owner of the voice plunged into the room.

"What, exactly, if you don't mind, Addie, does this mean? I would like to know, sweetie, I would really like to know, if we are going to have a delightful little circus tent here Saturday night or if we are going to have an absolute *shithouse?*"

Mrs. Fenley shrugged tolerantly at Christie and moved toward the young man. "Baby, don't let it get you down. You are getting too emotional about the whole thing, Dobbie."

He was a chunky young man with a head full of light-brown curls and his stubby fingers, covered with rings, patted the curls along his forehead and smoothed his long sideburns. Christie sat, fascinated, a spectator at a performance. Dobbie was exquisite. His eyes danced about the room, along the walls, the ceiling, the floor, past Christie. He wore a shiny pirate shirt of deep purple. His rather wide hips were accentuated by low-slung, striped pants which belled over his ankle-high boots. His fingers dug at his belt.

"And this damn thing is *killing* me, Addie. Take it off me. This was all your idea. Take it off me. Take it off me, *now!*"

Mrs. Fenley smiled, sighed and moved her fingers expertly along the intricate belt. It was a series of rectangular compartments linked together by bits of leather. She turned to Christie. "It's for his own good. It's done wonders for my waistline; exercises you all day long without any effort. But he is unbearable, really he is." She spoke in a fondly exasperated tone and the young man pulled his mouth down. "An hour a day at least wouldn't kill you, darling, and it would take a few of those extra inches off."

Dobbie dropped to the floor and rubbed his waist. "Now we'll discuss my weight, shall we, dear?" His long lashes moved up and down, then his eyes rested on Christie. "Addie, who is this? No.

66

Wait." He rolled forward to his knees, inched toward Christie. He peered up and studied her. "Don't move. Don't you *dare* to move."

Or you'll what? Christie thought, but she sat perfectly still. She felt herself taken in: by Mrs. Fenley and her good-natured sighs; by the boisterous, petulant young man; by the room, warm and large and elegant and airy; by the completely isolated, unconnected-to-reality commotion all around her.

Dobbie dug furiously through a pile of clothing, clutched at a green silk dress. "Here," he said, turning to Christie. "This one. Come here, stand up. Oh, for God's sake, stand up. Nobody listens to anything I say."

Christie stood up. Mrs. Fenley smiled. Dobbie held the dress against Christie. "Look at her eyes, Addie. I knew it, I knew it, they're turning green." He spun around. "This dress and your emerald, Addie. I want her in the entrance hall, in emerald. In an emerald booth." He turned again to Christie and his voice went higher. "Who is she? Why haven't I seen her before?"

Christie felt herself become an object: a part of the room, a subject for discussion. For some peculiar reason it was not an altogether unpleasant experience.

"Darling, if you will just settle down for a moment." Then, to Christie, "Dobbie gets very emotional when he's been working hard. And believe me, this boy has been working like a trooper for days now. She isn't a model, Dobbie. Unfortunately. You will simply not believe this. She is a policewoman. Or should I say a detective? Is there a distinction, my dear? You must forgive my ignorance."

It was clearly an area foreign to Mrs. Fenley. There is a distinction, Christie thought, but miserably she admitted to herself, it is a distinction of very little value here. Mrs. Fenley didn't wait for Christie's clarification. Her attention went back to Dobbie who expressed his awe, his delight, his curiosity, his disbelief.

The feeling of unreality began to crack; Christie felt her uncertainty give way. There was a slight hard edge which she tried to keep from her voice. "Mrs. Fenley, I can see you're very busy and I have a few things to do too." She glanced at Dobbie.. "Can we speak here?"

Dobbie was on the floor again, his arms wrapped around his knees, his head hunched forward. "Oh, talk here, Addie. I want to hear, please. I need some distraction from this goddamn stupid circus ball of yours."

Christie sucked the inside of her cheeks between her back teeth. One quick movement of her booted foot and Dobbie would roll across the thick carpet right into the fireplace.

"About Elena Vargas, you said?" Mrs. Fenley motioned to the maid who carefully carried a large silver tray. She smiled her excuse to Christie; the last interruption, the smile promised. The maid was young, dark, unpretty. The hostess was gracious, assured the unsteady girl that the arrangement of cups and saucers and pots and cakes and plates was fine, and that she might leave.

"Not a word of English," Mrs. Fenley said in her deep amused voice. "From Colombia or the Dominican Republic or some such God-forsaken place."

"Ugly as sin," Dobbie said. "She unnerves me. All that silence. Something sinister about it."

"Don't be unkind, dear. And just one sugar cube, if you insist on not wearing that belt. I bought it for him at Abercrombie's," she told Christie. Her eyes moved to Dobbie. "Self-restraint, Dobbie. Have you ever heard of it?" The charcoal eyes slid toward Christie; there was a slight hardening, barely discernible. "Look at her bone structure. My God, the hipbones actually stick out, even when you're sitting. Madame Krousisky would lose her mind over you."

Her thin flatness was envied by this rich and beautiful woman; her natural slenderness was apparently greatly esteemed. Somehow, Mrs. Fenley's beauty seemed slightly diminished now, slightly manufactured. Her slenderness was revealed as not natural to her; the fine bone structure of her face was the result of semistarvation. Only the very rich had this particular look, and beneath the carefully applied beauty Christie sensed an ugly desperation.

"Elena Vargas?" Christie prodded, determined now to get on with the interview.

"My dear, there have been so many. But yes, of course. Elena was from that home upstate. God, it was a long time ago. She was quite young. Let me see . . ."

"She was placed with you about nine years ago. She lived here with you for one year. As a companion to your young daughters, I believe?"

"Yes. Yes, of course. A dark girl. Beautiful. Very beautiful." She glanced at Dobbie. "There was a face you would have appreciated. But, what exactly, Detective . . . is that correct? . . . Detective Opara, am I supposed to tell you?"

Tell me about Elena. Silently, words flooded Christie. Tell me about Elena Vargas and how she survived her year with you.

"Well, as I understand it," Christie said professionally, all traces of the awed young interloper gone now, "Elena came to you directly from the Good Shepherd Protectorate upstate. She had finished high school at sixteen and was to attend evening classes at Rochelle Business College here in Manhattan while living with you. I've checked at the college and their records show that Elena started the course but dropped out after less than two months. According to their records, she was an extremely bright girl and was taking a course in bilingual stenography. I was wondering if you could give me some further information, as to why she . . ."

Mrs. Fenley's attention had strayed from Christie. She looked past her and her smile was automatic but lacked pleasure. "Here's someone who might be helpful. Kelly, darling, do come into the room and see if you can assist."

The girl was tall and lanky. Her hair hung in two long ropes of shining gold, half hiding her face. Her body was covered with what appeared to be blankets, that reached almost to the floor. Her bare toes, as they moved across the carpet, were dirty. Long fingers played restlessly with the hair, pulling it across her face.

"This is my daughter Kelly."

"By her first marriage," the girl said. Her voice was harsh and ragged.

"Don't be bitchy," Dobbie said as he wiped a crumb from the corner of his mouth, then licked at his finger.

"You just wish you *could* be," Kelly informed him. There was a surprising lack of emotion; the words, though rancorous, fell flat.

"Kelly, darling," Mrs. Fenley said, as though she had heard nothing, "do you remember Elena Vargas? It was some time back. Let me see, you couldn't have been more than eight or nine years old."

The girl stood, her hands working inside the blankets. "I was eight or nine years old. You were divorcing Harrison. It was after you met Arthur." For the first time, she spoke directly to Christie. "Arthur is Fenley. The current and all-time champ. Timewise that is."

"Don't be rude, dear. This young lady is a detective. She is inquiring about Elena Vargas. Although, to be perfectly honest," the quick smile, the innocent ignorance, "I really don't know why, do I?"

"A routine matter," Christie said.

"She's a call girl now, isn't she?" The girl shoved small wire-framed eyeglasses along her nose. "I've read about her. In the *Daily News*. That's the grooviest paper, isn't it? All those great pictures about dead people and stuff. How many does she take on in a night?"

"Don't be so vulgar, Kelly," her mother told her.

"It's her *style*, Addie. God, I've told you a million times, let the girl have her style." Dobbie's eyes shone.

Kelly looked down at the decorator. "You're a little shithead, Dobbie, do you know that?"

Christie kept her eyes on her match, inhaled tobacco, blew out smoke. She carefully ignored the tension and spoke quietly to the girl. "Kelly, do you remember anything about Elena Vargas?"

The blanket rose, shuddered, then fell over the girl's shoulders. "She was scared to death. All the time. Of everything. Of us."

Mrs. Fenley's voice was still pleasant, but firm. "That's a terrible thing to say, Kelly. I'm sure we treated her kindly."

"Sure. We treated her kindly." The girl collapsed on the floor in a heap of blankets. "Shove your fat ass over, Dobbie. You take up too much space."

Christie waited until they arranged themselves. "You were a little girl when Elena was. here, Kelly. Do you *really* remember her?"

"Yeah. I really remember her. I remember *everything*. Don't I, Mama?" The voice was mean, cut off by a quick unhappy laugh and followed by a sigh. "Yeah. I remember Elena. She was real nice. She was supposed to go to school at night. I heard you talking about it just now and then I remembered. I listen at doorways. And I listen in on telephone conversations. And I listen outside of bedroom doors. It's a gas sometimes."

Dobbie blinked rapidly. "Kelly, you are becoming an all-time bore."

"It's my style, *sweetie*." It was a perfect imitation of her mother's voice. She hunched forward. "I'll tell you about Elena. She had no one. No one. That's a crummy feeling, you know? And here she was, in all of this." Her hand moved a few inches, then withdrew. "She had a nice room. I used to go to her room. To get away from my sister. My sister is a member of the Junior League. Couldn't that like knock you out? I mean, the *Junior League*." The long gold hair covered the face completely as she leaned forward. The glasses glinted now and then from behind heavy strands of hair. "Elena was a real person. I mean, she was *real*, know what I mean? Like, she *cried* at night. From the heart. *Real tears*. Like . . . like *despair*."

Mrs. Fenley's face was taut; the smoothness was masklike. She poured tea into her half-empty cup. For the first time there was impatience in her voice. "Get on with it, Kelly. Detective Opara hasn't all day, and frankly, I've given more time to this entire matter than I can spare."

The girl covered her head with the blanket, then let it partially fall. She peered over the rim of her glasses at Christie. "She cried because she wanted something out of life. You know what she wanted? She wanted to go to a lousy, yukky secretarial college. She even had a scholarship from that orphanage she lived in.

71

Isn't that groovy, she was a real orphan. That's what it was about Elena, she was *real*."

"Why did she drop out of the secretarial college, Kelly?"

The blanket shrugged. "No way. No way for Elena. She had to miss too many nights. You remember, don't you, Addie? No? Addie wouldn't remember. 'Elena, dear, you won't mind staying home with the girls tonight, will you? We are in such a state; cook's sister died and the maid is pregnant and the agency just sends us this endless stream of little colored girls . . . I beg your pardon, my dear, but you know what I mean, and they are just not reliable and I am so relieved that you're here in my time of crises,' and yak-a-ta-yak-yak-yak."

"Kelly, you are making all of this up. You know you are." The growl was no longer charming; it was angry.

"Maybe I am. Maybe I'm not. What's the difference? You get the picture, don't you, lady cop?"

Christie wondered if the girl was on something; there was a sallowness to what little complexion showed and her voice was flat, her cadence a little singsong.

"Well, Kelly, it's no big tragedy if Elena had to miss school now and then. It's no reason for her to have dropped out completely. Especially if she had her heart set on a secretarial career," Christie said, waiting.

"No. That wasn't the reason." Kelly's face emerged, turned toward her mother. "Was it, Mama?"

Mrs. Fenley sipped at her tea, carefully put the fragile cup on the fragile saucer. "I will be perfectly frank with you, Detective Opara. It sounds dreadful, I know, but I haven't much recollection of this Elena Vargas. I . . . traveled for much of the year that the girl lived here. As my daughter so . . . generously informed you, I was having certain marital difficulties at the time. My recollection of Elena is quite dim."

Kelly rolled her shoulders against Dobbie. She held a long lank strand of hair to one side and her glasses glinted. "Cutie, you too can become a dim memory. Forgotten. You ever think of that, doll-baby?"

Dobbie pulled back, brushed his body where the blanket had made contact with him. It was of some fluffy material and he became very concerned that no trace of it remain on his purple shirt.

"You know what Mama told her?" Kelly swung her head toward Christie. "Mama told Elena that she had it made here. That she was foolish to stay at that secretarial school. I mean, Elena *was* practically black, right, Mama? Even though her features were practically Caucasian. Is that the right word? Yeah, Caucasian. That's a nasty-sounding word, isn't it?" The girl's long hand combed the hair over her face, then parted it down the center, like a curtain, as she turned toward her mother. "Oh, I forgot. You don't really remember Elena, do you Mama? Well, *I* do. She was beautiful." Again, toward Christie. "But Mama told her that it was just nonsense, this going to secretarial school, when she had it made right here, living with us. And taking care of us. And she was *practically* one of the family and she could watch all the nice parties and all the pretty . . . no, all the *beautiful* people right here. And in Palm Beach and in Newport and even in—now get this—even in sunny Spain from whence her ancestors had probably come long, long ago, even though Elena came from Puerto Rico and believe me, the Spaniards in the part of Spain where Mama hangs out would take one look at Elena and say, 'This way to the kitchen.'"

Kelly ran out of words and dropped her head against her knees. She pulled the blanket over her head, then, not looking up, she asked, "Don't you really remember Elena, Mama? Not even now?"

Beneath the magically smooth, transparent makeup, Mrs. Fenley had gone chalk white. "I must apologize for my daughter's incredibly bad manners, Detective Opara. She seems to be going through a particularly hostile stage just now. I would advise you to discount practically everything she has said. It is sheer fantasy."

Dobbie waved his hand before his face. "That cigarette smoke is killing me."

Christie crushed the cigarette into a small rounded dish that appeared to be an ashtray. Kelly watched her, then laughed.

"Beautiful," she said. "That is beautiful. It's a nut dish."

"Really, Kelly, your manners . . ."

"Yeah, it's a nut dish," Kelly said. "But *she* would sit there and let you grind your butt into that gen-u-ine Modigliani over there before she'd tell you that you had boffed. That, my dear, is considered good manners. And good manners, my dear, will see you through any and all situations. Including, my dear, the nuclear holocaust to come." The girl stood up, arranged her blankets. "When we have succeeded in blowing up our world into little pieces, lady cop, if by some real crazy fluke, the likes of you and me have survived, we shall see that the other survivors, the ones *really* meant to be survivors, will have good manners and enough compassion to organize charity balls in order to provide some little bits of food and clothing for us 'poor unfortunates.' They will carefully succeed in re-creating the splendid society in which we find ourselves at the present time. In the meantime, I shall just stay inside my blankets, where it's safe and there aren't any circuses and like that." She yanked at the blankets, pulled one hoodlike over her head, but the blanket dropped clear to her shoulders. For the first time, the young face emerged. Kelly was a pretty girl with thin, hollow cheeks and dark intent eyes. "Hey, lady cop. When you see her, Elena, tell her Kelly said . . . 'peace.' " The burst of laughter was genuine, young, honestly delighted. "Oh, wow. Tell her 'peace' or 'piece,' however it means the most to her. Oh, boy."

Christie didn't watch the girl as, huddled inside of her blanket, she left the room. The laugh seemed to turn deeper, dangerously close to a sob. Christie stood up, caught her shoulder bag by the leather straps. "Mrs. Fenley, I'm sorry I've taken so much of your time. I realize how terribly busy you are." Christie's arm swept the room. She realized it was the same gesture that Mrs. Fenley had used earlier.

The large gray eyes were vacant for an instant. The long thick lashes, too lush to be real, too subtle to be false, moved twice slowly, then twice rapidly. In an easy, graceful motion, the lithe body rose, the cold hand was offered. "My dear, I must apologize

74

for all this disarray, but we are absolutely frantic. Our ball is tomorrow night and there are about six zillion things we have to do. Oh, Dobbie, for heaven sakes dear, do get up and try at least to *look* animated. By tomorrow night, my little magic worker here will have transformed that great hall into the jolliest circus you've ever seen. The workmen should have been here by now. Dobbie, don't you think you should give them another call?" The gray eyes searched Christie's face, then roved over her body. "You would look marvelous in the green, my dear, if you could possibly . . ."

"No, thank you anyway, Mrs. Fenley. I'm going to be very busy."

"Of course, of course. Marie will get your coat for you. It was so lovely to meet you. And good luck in . . . in your work."

Whatever that is, Christie added silently. The maid appeared in the hallway without a word and carefully held Christie's coat for her. Dobbie's screeching voice rose from the living room, apparently anguished by some delay on the part of the workmen. It was an anguish, however, that could be easily corrected. Christie adjusted the toggles of her coat, reached for the doorknob and pulled open the door to the small, private hallway.

She heard a long, low hissing sound somewhere over her head. She looked up and Kelly, hunched on the steps of the duplex apartment, her face pressed between spindles, stared down at her. She pushed the blankets off her arm and poked her hand out into the air. Her fingers formed a V-sign.

"Hey cop," she said in a low and mournful voice. "Peace even unto the cops."

The girl's face was young and sad and pained. Christie held her right hand up high, returned the salute. "Peace unto all of us, Kelly."

75

6

Marty Ginsburg reached for the switch which controlled the heater. "Christie, I better turn this up. You look like you're frozen solid." He gestured with his thumb toward the back of his station wagon. "We got some quilts somewhere in the back. Why don't you climb over and find yourself one?"

Christie shuddered against the cold for a moment, then nodded. "Right. And please, Marty, watch the road. I'll find the quilt myself."

Marty was a confident driver. He was accustomed to driving a wagonload of boys of all ages, sizes, shapes and temperaments who had one thing in common: the level of noise issuing from healthy young throats. The father of five young sons, Marty was unnerved by silence and Christie Opara had been particularly quiet for the last ten miles. About the only noise from her was the chattering of her teeth.

"Hey, Christie, while you're there, dig around a little, huh. One of the kids usually leaves something to eat back there: pretzels, gumdrops, whatever."

Christie was at the very back of the station wagon. Marty's entire face confronted her. "Marty, at sixty miles an hour on the Thruway, will you please face the way we're going?"

Her body was stiff with cold as she climbed over the seats and wrapped the crocheted quilt around her legs and thighs. Her fingers were rigid inside her fur-lined leather gloves, but she struggled to unwrap a hard candy for Marty. If she handed it to him, he'd probably release the steering wheel and use both hands to get at the candy.

"Don't you want one? You know Christie, you ought to eat some candy. The sugar will warm you up. You know why you're so cold?"

"I think maybe the fact that it's about twelve degrees has something to do with it."

"Naw. Listen, kid, are your hands and feet cold? I mean, like all the time?"

"All of me is frozen. Marty, I can hear you. You don't have to turn to me."

Marty nodded. He focused on a Volkswagen and was determined to overtake it. He wanted a look at who could be taking off on a ski trip on a Wednesday morning. As he spoke, he increased his speed.

"Now this is a very little-known medical fact which my cousin Sidney, the doctor, told me. See, my wife always has cold hands and feet. And a cold nose. It can get very creepy, especially on a hot summer night, you know? Well, I told Sidney about it and Sidney knows things that sometimes I think he makes it up but this time he was right. You know what he told me?"

"No. What did your cousin Sidney tell you?"

"You ready for this? Well, see you smoke too much. My wife smokes too much and that was the first thing Sidney asked. Did Estelle smoke too much? And right away, Sidney told me that every time a person smokes a cigarette, all the Vitamin C in that person's body gets used up. I mean, I don't know the technicalities of *how* it gets used up, but it does. So, Sidney gave Estelle these vitamin capsules, Vitamin C and riboflavins, and she took like eighteen times the amount a human being needs every day. But, now get this. Also, Sidney said Estelle had to eat an orange every single day."

"What's so unusual about eating an orange every single day?"

"Ah, that's the catch, see." Marty's foot pressed harder on the accelerator. "A whole, entire orange. Not just the orangey part, but the whole entire thing. Skin and all."

Christie glanced at the speedometer. It was edging toward seventy. "Skin and all?"

77

"Yeah. Like Estelle had to learn how to just keep eating. 'Eat the garbage part too,' Sidney told her. It took a little getting used to, but Estelle's a pretty game kid. She even got to like the skin. Kind of. She started a little at a time and worked her way up to the whole thing."

"Did it work? Did it help her cold hands and feet? And nose?"

"That's the crazy part." Marty turned to her, his face puzzled. "The darnedest thing. After about two weeks, Estelle's hands and feet and nose were just like anybody else's. But she had to give the whole thing up."

"Why?"

"Because everything that was cold warmed up, but her face started to turn yellow."

Christie pulled the quilt around her against a sudden chill. She started to reach for a cigarette but changed her mind. "Marty, are you putting me on?"

"No, really. Honest to God." Marty pulled out of the lane and paced the Volkswagen. "Look at those skis." He leaned across Christie and tried to see the driver of the small car. "I knew it," he said triumphantly. "The guy has a beard." He accelerated, passed the small car and pulled back into the right lane. "You know, I think maybe my whole life would be different if I could grow a beard. Like, instead of driving upstate on an assignment, I could load up the wagon with the kids and skis and sleds and stuff and spend a couple of days in Vermont skiing. Right in the middle of the week. Those guys know how to live."

"What guys?" There were times when it was difficult to follow Marty's rambling conversation.

Marty gestured behind him. "Those guys. With the beards. I tried to grow a beard one summer. It turned out seedy. Like, it just never grew more than two days' worth. In two weeks, it looked like I just needed a shave. And what is even worse is that if I shave early in the morning, by nighttime, I look just the same as if I haven't shaved in a week." Marty slid his hand over his cheek. "Oh, well, what the hell. Christie, unwrap me one of those butterscotch candies, okay?"

Beyond the banks of traffic-stained gray ice mounds on either side of the Thruway, the snow rose high and white shadowed by skeletal black trees and dark thick pines. The sky was painfully blue, totally cloudless, and the sun hit the wet road in sharp glints. Christie pushed her green sunglasses to the top of her head and narrowed her eyes. The houses were clustered together in tight little areas, almost as though for protection against the vast uninhabited pine forests. No black smoke spoiled the air. Now and again, puffs of white, steamy and rapidly dissipated, floated from brick chimneys, and Christie visualized fireplaces and yellow warmth. Now and again, a single, isolated house, set high on the face of a mountain, held her attention, and though she nodded and commented briefly as Marty rambled on, she wondered what kind of people lived in such far-off houses.

The Good Shepherd Protectorate was three miles off the Thruway. Marty slowed the station wagon and carefully took the right turn under the archway which marked the boundary of the orphanage. The narrow road, which had been cleared, ran between vast fields of untouched white snow. The main building was gray and Gothic and ugly. A group of children stopped working on a variety of snow sculptures and watched them curiously. Some of the children waved, others turned back to their work with concentrated effort. Their voices were sharp and clear in the cold, windless air.

Marty pulled the heavy door open and his voice was unnaturally low. "Hey, Christie, you do the talking, okay?"

Christie was surprised that Marty was somewhat subdued by the high-ceilinged entrance and the silence that encompassed them. Or possibly by the huge crucifix placed high against the whitewashed wall and dominating the area. She nodded, then rang the small bell inside the door frame. The sound of the bell was soft and melodious in the vastness of the room.

A young nun, red-cheeked and smiling, appeared from behind a door to their left. "I'll be with you in a moment. I'm on the telephone."

Marty grabbed Christie's arm. "Hey, how come she's dressed

like that? I thought, you know, nuns wear long black robes and things."

"I guess her order has adopted modern dress," Christie told him.

The young nun came out of the office and offered her hand. "Hi, I'm Sister Veronica Matthew. You must be the detectives from New York." She was taller than Christie and her handshake was firm. Her dress was light gray, knee length; a band of crisp white, almost like a headband but attached to a short gray veil, was placed on her thick auburn curls. "Mother Superior will be with you in about two minutes. I buzzed her that you were here. Why don't you sit down over here"—she led them to a long dark wooden bench. "It's out of the draft."

A buzzer sounded and the nun grinned. "She has radar. Right down the hall, please."

There was something almost boisterous about Sister Veronica Matthew. Her radiant good health was apparent from her clear eyes, her full red cheeks, her long, easy strides. It seemed she spoke softly with great effort, and when she tapped on the door of the Mother Superior's office, her first knock was loud and hard. She grimaced at Christie, pulled her mouth down comically, shrugged her shoulders and tapped twice more, lightly. She pulled the door open but didn't come into the room with them.

"Reverend Mother, this is Detective Opara and Detective Ginsburg."

The woman sitting behind the massive mahogany desk was dressed in traditional black garb. She rose and the layers of black material moved as though blown by billows of wind. "Thank you, Sister. Please don't"—the door slammed behind the departing nun —"slam the door," she added softly.

The Mother Superior was apparently a very busy woman. Her desk was piled with an assortment of file folders, correspondence, notebooks and textbooks. She indicated the chairs before her desk.

"She takes my breath away—all that youth and vitality. Now then, Detective Opara, which one are you?"

Christie smiled. "I am, Reverend Mother."

"Then that means you're Detective Ginsburg." Marty nodded.

All that showed of the woman were two small thin restless white hands and an oval face. The face was long and narrow, marked by dark brows over light eyes which narrowed in concentration as she studied them briefly, each in turn. Her voice was crisp and precise and she spoke very rapidly.

"Now, then. Let me see if I have this straight. You want to know what I can tell you about Elena Vargas? Well, what do you want to know?"

Marty's eyes slid irresistibly over the woman's head, drawn by a crucifix identical to the one in the hallway. It was placed midway between the floor and the high ceiling and the Christ figure had a particularly realistic face.

"Detective Ginsburg," she said crisply, "does that crucifix puzzle you? If it's going to distract you, let's get it cleared up right now."

Marty blinked, glanced toward Christie, but he did not receive any signals from her. He was in foreign territory and wasn't sure of his ground.

"Well, as a matter of fact, Holy Mother," he said uncertainly, "I was wondering if all these crucifixes are strictly necessary."

The warm laugh was entirely unexpected. "You've elevated me to a station beyond my most immodest aspirations, Detective Ginsburg. Call me Reverend Mother, or Sister, if you're more comfortable with that. As for the prevalence of crucifixes, well, it is a question some of us have been examining recently." She paused for a moment, then her voice filled with the warmth her laughter had suggested. "As a matter of fact, last spring I took a course in Comparative Religious Symbolism at Union Theological Seminary given by Rabbi Alvin Winsimer and we discovered a great many interesting . . ."

"Al Winsimer? You got to be kidding!" Marty's voice rose to its normal dimension. His aura of uneasiness disappeared completely.

"Do you know him?"

"Sister, I mean, Reverend Mother, Al Winsimer and me, well you might almost say we grew up together. As a matter of fact,

81

well, when he was researching for his doctorate, well, he let me read some of his material. You see, like as a hobby, I do some studying of early Hebrew literature. Not religious literature, strictly, but I was interested in seeing how much of Hebrew literature could be classified as 'folklore' and how much as part of a more really religious tradition."

It was a side of Marty Ginsburg which Christie had never seen before. He carried on his share of the brief discussion with vigor and intelligence and a certain passion. He even realized when it was time to end the conversation and get on with their job.

"Now, then. Let's hear from you, Detective Opara. Elena Vargas . . . what do you want to know?" As she spoke, the woman reached for a file folder, opened it and rested her hand on a collection of papers. "It's all here, her records, her background, her school grades. All down in black and white. What will all this tell you about Elena?"

She was sharp and direct and that made it easier for Christie to discard the usual routine preliminaries. "Reverend Mother, I am trying to find out what *kind* of girl Elena was. I realize that she was here a long time ago and that you've had hundreds of children through the Good Shepherd before and after Elena, but I thought you might possibly remember something about her."

The white hands closed the folder and rested flatly on its surface. "Hundreds and hundreds, but only one Elena. I'll tell you a little secret. We all say that we are impartial, that one child is as valuable and as precious to us as any other child. And of course, that is true. But we are human, and if it is a fault to have a special feeling for one particular child, then so be it." One hand turned, palm up, an acceptance of guilt. "Elena Vargas came to us when she was two years old, the youngest of seven children. She spoke no English and very little Spanish because apparently no one had found it necessary to bother teaching her. She was undersized, undernourished, underdeveloped for her age." The Mother Superior's hand moved through the air. "As most of them are. But Elena. There was a light burning in that child—a glow. A *need*, out of the ordinary. She was reading by the time she was four years old. Self-taught, mind you. The books were available to her, and while we did not particularly encourage her, neither did we discourage her at that tender age. Sometimes things like that—some special ability—evens out, the child catches up with herself chronologically when formal schooling begins. But Elena was years ahead, as though she could not hold back the excitement of a world unfolding before her. We kept her close to her own age group in school but gave her extra work, to keep her mind alert, to let her continue her self-exploration. She was a beautiful child, modest, not aware of her own intellectual capacity. She was more concerned by all the things there were to know than by what she was learning."

"A little girl like that," Marty ventured, "couldn't she have been placed up for adoption?"

The Mother Superior held up her fingers. "Two things were against her." She bent her index finger. "One, her mother was alive when the children were placed with us. She died about four or five years later. For whatever reason, maybe hope that some day she could provide a home for them, she wouldn't discuss relinquishing any of her children for adoption. As for the second reason"—the middle finger bent—"the second reason was all-encompassing, Detective Ginsburg. Elena Vargas was a beautiful, brilliant child of Puerto Rican birth and the color of her skin was the color of God's own pure earth. There are not many adoptive parents on the lookout for a bright, delicately featured child with dark skin." She moved her hand to indicate Christie. "Now, Detective Opara, at age two or four, with hair about two shades lighter than it is now, and green . . . or are they gray . . . eyes. Well, we would have had lists to choose from."

The dark face, the bright slanted eyes appeared before Christie. She blinked rapidly, dismissed the image. "Reverend Mother, from what I've gathered, Elena was placed with the Fenley family when she finished high school."

"From what *I* gather, you know what happened to Elena at the Fenleys', more or less." The thin white face leaned forward, light eyes intent on Christie. "You have a very expressive face. Is that good for a detective? It would be disastrous for a nun."

Christie felt her face grow warm. "It's not too good for a detective, either," she admitted softly. "I was at the Fenleys' yesterday."

"And you wonder why in the world Elena was placed there." There was no apology offered, just a straightforward explanation of fact. "Elena was sixteen years old and finished with all high school requirements. She had never been in the outside world. She had lived in this"—she indicated not just the vast room, but the entire, enclosed world of the protectorate—"this highly unrealistic little universe for all of her growing years. She wanted to continue her education, of course, and of course I wanted her to. She had so much to offer. But there are realities to face. In order for Elena to attend college, she needed a complete scholarship. Not just for her tuition, but for her living expenses. She was offered several partial scholarships but they were just not enough." The Mother Superior's face went hard, just for one moment of memory. "I went to the Bishop. I brought Elena's records." She touched the folder lightly. "But there were too many other children. Too many other absolute necessities. Someone from the Bishop's office was in touch with me within a few days of my visit. They had come up with the Fenleys and evening business college." The tone of her voice never changed. It was brisk, businesslike, matter-of-fact. "And from your expression, Detective Opara, you know what Elena's life was like at the Fenleys'. She stayed for nearly a year. And then she came back to me."

Christie hadn't known that. "What happened when she came back here? I thought she went directly to her sister's."

"She came here one lovely summer day and made the announcement I had been expecting. 'Reverend Mother,' she said, 'I want to become a novice.'"

Marty's voice was loud. "Elena wanted to become a nun?"

"No, Detective Ginsburg, of course not. Not really. Elena suffered her first contacts with that world outside. She had had her first inkling of what she had to overcome. There was her first contact with a boy, who found her attractive, but not 'presentable.' It was at a dance. She couldn't handle it. No, she did not want to become a nun, she wanted to hide behind the veil." The nun moved her head slowly from side to side. "I explained to

84

Elena what she really knew herself: that she had no vocation. That in order to serve God through a religious order, she had to know, to be certain within herself that it was a life she would be embracing joyously, completely. That the religious life was undertaken after other choices had been tried, examined, discarded; that the vows had to be undertaken as an inevitable decision, not in a panic and through a need to hide."

"What was Elena's reaction, Reverend Mother?" Christie asked.

The small hands clenched together tightly, rose to rest on the broad forehead. Then, the Mother Superior dropped her hands to the desk and looked directly at Christie. "Elena told me that I was just like all the others. That I rejected her because she was dark-skinned." The pain was discernible not in her voice or eyes, but in the set of her lips.

"Er . . . Reverend Mother, maybe it's out of line, but I'd like to ask you something. Maybe out of curiosity," Marty ventured.

"Do I think now that I was wrong? That I should have encouraged her?"

Marty's heavy shoulders moved. "Well, something like that. I mean, I guess you know what Elena is . . . now."

The crisp voice had an edge of annoyance. "That Elena has become a prostitute. Oh, Detective Ginsburg, don't be delicate with me. Do you know the backgrounds of the children who are in my care? They are the remnants of a society that hasn't worked. They are the products of rape, ignorance, lust, violence, atrocities almost beyond belief. Yes, I could have encouraged Elena, but it would have been opposed to everything I believed. Elena was equipped far beyond any girl we have ever had before or since. She had an inner glow, an awareness and an ability."

"But she didn't have enough to make it, did she?" Christie was surprised both at her own sharpness and that her question was recognized as an accusation.

"Detective Opara, there are three hundred and twenty-two children here at this moment. I cannot estimate how many children have come and gone since Elena left us. If I were to cry for each of them, if I were to *allow* myself to weep, I would have drowned in my flood of tears a very long time ago and what little good I am able to accomplish for any of them would not have been achieved."

"I'm sorry, Reverend Mother."

"Oh, Detective Opara, don't apologize. But I am glad that you recognize the fact that there were no tears for Elena. It is a pretty significant fact, isn't it?"

Christie nodded. In the brief silence, there seemed nothing more to say. Then, something occurred to her. "When was the last time you saw Elena? Did she ever come back to you, after she went to live with her sister?"

For the first time, the nun seemed evasive. Her eyes fastened on the folder. Beneath the black robes, her shoulders moved slightly. "That will be something for you to discuss with Elena."

"You mean, she did come back?"

"You're prodding now, Detective Opara. Touching on an area of confidence I cannot reveal."

Christie felt a surge of excitement. There *was* something else of value here. "Reverend Mother, you may be holding back something that could be very important to me."

"Ask Elena," the nun answered firmly. "I'm not trying to be mysterious, young lady. I just feel I've gone as far as I've a right to go. Now, is there anything else?" It was clear that the meeting was at an end.

The Mother Superior led them through the entrance hallway. She was very short, her forehead just about level with Christie's chin. Sitting, speaking, she had seemed a larger woman. Her eyes moved about the room, she waved to several small girls who walked quietly, whispering and giggling, along the wide staircase.

Her handshake was quick and firm. "Detective Opara, I hope you've learned something worthwhile about Elena. I rather think we might speak again."

"Yes, possibly," Christie answered.

She held Marty's hand and her eyes took on a deeper color. "Detective Ginsburg, I want to compliment you on your appearance."

"Huh?"

"Well, since you grew up with Rabbi 'Al' Winsimer, I must assume you are approximately the same age as he. For a man in your early seventies, I think you are in marvelous condition."

Her face was amused. Marty swallowed, glanced at Christie, whose face registered shock. "Well, Reverend Mother," Marty said, "I'm real surprised to learn that Al is in his seventies already. You know, I always told him that the religious life was too much for him. He wouldn't listen, though. So, you see, I was right after all. I'm still only thirty-four and poor old Rabbi Winsimer. In his seventies . . ."

The Mother Superior squeezed his hand tightly, then pushed him away. "Detective Ginsburg," she said, "I always did admire a man with *chutzpah.*"

7

Detective Sam Farrell carefully cradled his bandaged left hand in the palm of his right hand. The nearly severed index finger throbbed with the slightest motion and he tried to concentrate on dictating his report, but Christie typed faster than he could phrase.

"Hey, Christie, let's knock off for a minute, okay? Man, I never even knew before that I had an index finger on my left hand, and now it's like my whole body is my left index finger, know what I mean?"

"Are you taking anything for the pain, Sam?" she asked sympathetically.

"Well, yeah. But I took my wife's allergy pills this morning by mistake, so I thought I better not take the pain pills." He shrugged his wide shoulders. "The combination, you never know."

Sam Farrell was a man who should not have helped his neighbor repair a broken snowplow. If, in the entire piece of machinery, there had been only one movable part, that movable part would have somehow taken the measure of Sam Farrell and found something to attack. Sam's left index finger was being held in place not only by stitches but by virtue of the fact that the owner of the broken snowplow was a physician who had acted quickly. He should have known better than to solicit Sam's help in the first place.

Stoner Martin, bent over a series of charts which covered the long gray table across the front of the Squad Room, carefully printed words and numbers with a steady hand. The black india ink gave him a certain satisfaction in his meticulous work. He straightened up immediately when he heard Sam approach.

"Hey, Stoney, how's it going?"

"Sam, stay away. Come on, move about y-a-y more steps back, buddy."

Farrell's innocent round blue eyes registered no offense. He could still see the clear printing. "Giardino Industries. Man, are all those"—his right hand relinquished the wounded left hand for a quick sweep of the table—"all those other charts, part of Giardino Industries, too?"

"You better believe it. Hey, Christie. Come over here and see what we're dealing with."

Christie drained the lukewarm remnants of a container of bitter tea. "Stoney, it's pushing five o'clock. If you don't mind, I'd like to wind up Sam's report and take off."

Stoner Martin massaged the back of his neck. "This kind of work can sure leave you kinked up." He went to Christie's desk, reached for her cigarette, and drew a light for his own. "I guess I forgot to mention it to you, kid."

"Mention what? Oh, no. Don't tell me. I'm not finished when I finish this report. I'm going to be assigned with the rest of you to the Great Cataloguer from the Secret Service. Go ahead. Mention it. Tell me."

"The Man said you should stick around until he gets back. Which will be, exactly, when he gets back. Dig?"

A sudden sneeze caught Christie by surprise. She felt assaulted by unanticipated chills, exhaustion, clogged sinuses. "Oh, boy. My cold capsule just died a sudden death. Stoney, are these things really safe?"

She handed him the box of medication and he carefully read the small print. "Christie, you're getting to be a regular pill-popper. What you ought to do is, you ought to go home, take a very hot bath, then rub yourself fore and aft with mentholated salve, flannel up to your chin and down to your toes, sandwich yourself between about five blankets and sweat the cold out for about twenty-four hours. In the meantime, however," his long brown fingers pushed one of the capsules from the cellophane-covered hole on the cardboard, "here, take one of these with several gulps of water. The effects of these things tend to run down, though, the longer you take them."

Sam Farrell moved from the water cooler and stepped back for Christie. Absently, he wiped his dripping chin with his bandaged hand and winced. "Hey, Stoney, I wonder if those cold capsules could keep a cold going indefinitely. Like, say Christie takes one now, you know, so the cold symptoms stay hidden for the next twelve hours. Then they appear again, so she takes another pill. Like, sooner or later, doesn't the cold have to appear and run its own course?"

"That's a very nice thought, Sam," Christie said. "Thanks very much. Stoney, what are all these companies? And why all the charts?"

Stoner Martin kept between his work and Sam Farrell. There were ten large white oaktag charts, neatly lined and lettered, partially filled with figures. "It's very impressive, isn't it? You might say this is a study in optimism. Hopefully, these charts will be used before a Grand Jury, if this investigation goes the way we want it to. This is a picture of Giardino Industries, but only a partial picture. It doesn't show where the original capital came from: these are all legitimate businesses."

Christie frowned. "But if they're all legitimate, then what's the point?"

"The point is that Enzo Giardino, through his various companies, is doing business with the city, state and federal government. Most of these organizations," Stoner's hand swept over the charts, "are in one way or another involved in subcontracting through governmental agencies. Here, for instance." "Here" indicated the first chart to his left. "Giardino Scrap Metal and Iron Corporation. A three-million-dollar-a-year organization. All the little blue stars indicate dealings with the city; all the red stars, dealings with the state. Now, this chart, "Three Boro Waste Disposal"—a private garbage collection agency which subcontracts during times of sanitation emergency in the city. Otherwise services restaurants, small industrial plants, right down to ye local street merchants. Now, over here," Stoner moved, carefully avoiding brushing the still-wet lettering, "the Chemical Disposal Corporation of Corona; this one, Sewer Pipe Specialties, strictly city contracts. Here's another very lucrative business, Metal Sign Corporation of Staten Island, handled over two million dollars' worth of business with the Metropolitan Transit Authority alone. Now, this particular company, Refreshments, Incorporated, provides most of the candy and gum machines in public locations throughout the city. And this little sister company, Fresh 'n' Nice, provides all the goodies that fill all those machines. And this company, Sure-Service, supposedly sees to it that all the machines are in working order."

Christie stared at the charts; bright dabs of color throughout each chart were explained by color codes at the bottom of each chart. "But, what's it all actually add up to Stoney? These are legitimate, right? We've done Dun and Bradstreets on most of them. What does this actually give you?"

"They are legitimate, yes. All genuine, certified companies and corporations. They are all owned or controlled by Enzo Giardino, as well as about thirty or thirty-five other organizations throughout the country. But the catch is, kid, that our Enzo Giardino came to this country with his proverbial shirt on his immigrant back and the first three business enterprises he was involved with failed. But within a period of the last fifteen years—coinciding with the growth of the narcotics industry—Enzo Giardino found the hard cash to invest in all these different businesses. The point is that syndicate money has put away any and all competition in all of these particular areas. You can't compete with untaxed cash if you're an honest businessman."

"So syndicate money established a virtual monopoly in all of these various enterprises?"

"That's the girl, Christie. And it is all but impossible at this point to trace the capital back to its original source. By now, Giardino is strictly legitimate in all of these businesses. But what we'll hope to bring before a Grand Jury—and baby, we've got a lot of hard legwork ahead of us—is that these companies were establish by illegally gotten funds, which gives an illegal edge

91

to them during bidding for governmental contracts. At least, we can hope to get Giardino's companies disqualified from future bids."

"What about import–export companies? Mr. Reardon said something about that, but I'm not sure what."

Stoner Martin shrugged. "That area is almost too dense to wade through. It would be a matter of the most complicated research: trying to trace Giardino's legitimate investments on the stock market. Actually, we're not handling any of that; the IRS people are pretty skilled at that kind of paper work. All they can hope to do would be to prove that Giardino, somewhere along the line, left a serious gap in his declared and actual income. Then, they could bag him on income tax violation. I'd much rather *we* get him on the narcotics. All of these companies were founded on the drug trade. Prove it, the Man says." He shook his head. "Anyway, my charts are nice and neat. I could have been a good sign printer. Step back, Sam, you make me very nervous."

Sam sorted his various scraps of paper into some reasonable sequence. He stared at a mysterious india ink stain which had somehow appeared on his bandaged finger.

"I don't think you should let Stoney see that," Christie whispered.

She typed steadily, stopped only to rephrase and reword as she went along. Sam Farrell had spent most of his day on Long Island, investigating various branches of Giardino's suburban subsidiaries. Christie rolled the last paper from her machine, carefully indicated where Sam was to sign his name.

"Oh, Christie, I got some information for you about Elena Vargas."

Since Farrell had been working on the Island, Casey Reardon had told him to have a look at the Quiet Haven Rest Home in Great Neck, Long Island, where Elena Vargas had lived and worked for eight months.

"This was when she was seventeen," Sam said, consulting some small, cramped notes. "Yeah, here it is. Miss Tinsley, the social worker attached to Youth Division of Criminal Court, found the job for Elena. See, Elena was made a ward of the court after she got locked up on that hokey theft charge, something about stealing office supplies?" His voice rose, then he nodded at Christie's reply.

"Yes, I know about that from the yellow sheet and from her sister. That was a bit of a raw deal."

"Yeah. Well, anyway, she worked as a secretary. I checked the employment records out there. She had regular working hours, you know, nine to five, averaged about sixty-five bucks a week, plus room and board. She worked directly for this Dr. Henderson, but he was an old geezer even then. Seems he croaked about two years ago."

"Was there anyone there who remembered Elena?"

Sam dug through his papers and shook his head. "Naw, Christie, it's the kind of place gets a big turnover." Finally, he found the paper he wanted and handed it to Christie. "Here. I stopped off at the Probation Department, Christie. Figured I'd save you the trouble." He leaned over and placed his finger under his handwriting. "Here, see the kid came of age when she'd been at this Quiet Haven place about seven months and then she wasn't a ward of the court anymore. That's just about when she left, and the court didn't have jurisdiction over her anymore."

Christie nodded appreciatively. Sam Farrell had saved her a good deal of legwork. "Sam, what kind of place is it—Quiet Haven?"

"Nice place. You know, class. Lots of lawn facing on Manhasset Bay. Must be real pretty in the spring. Lots of quiet old folks sitting around. Not much for a young girl. I guess that's why she left. . . . "

"I guess. I still don't know how she met up with Enzo Giardino, though."

Farrell grinned. "Maybe he had his old mother in Quiet Haven. Who knows?"

Christie asked thoughtfully, "Can you think of any reason I should do a rundown on Quiet Haven?"

Another detective might have been offended that his evaluation

93

hadn't been fully accepted at face value. Farrell cradled his sore hand gently. "Nothing visible, Christie. Looks like what it says it is."

"Good enough. I'll drop your report on Reardon's desk. And thanks, Sam."

"Thanks for the typing job, Christie. Boy, I think I'll get going now and take some of the pain pills. This thing feels like it's getting bigger and bigger by the minute."

Reardon's office was warm and quiet. Christie placed the report on top of a folder in the center of the desk, then placed the desk pen directly over it so that Reardon wouldn't miss it. She wasn't even tempted to scan the collection of papers, folders and reports which covered the desk. She had enough on her mind. As she walked the short distance through the connecting corridor between Reardon's office and the Squad Room, Christie said, to no one in particular, "Boy, Reardon's office is the warmest in the winter and the coolest in the summer. There ought to be a law . . ."

Casey Reardon straightened up, his finger still lingering on a line of numbers that Stoney had indicated to him. "There is a law, honey," he said. "It's very simple: the boss gets the best."

Christie smiled weakly. "Good law. If you're the boss."

"You better believe it. Go on in my office and wait for me. And try to absorb some of the warmth because we're going out into the cold, cold night."

8

Soft music seemed to hum from the walls of the lobby; it was carefully modulated and unobtrusive. Christie wondered if anyone ever used the expensive furniture which was arranged into room settings, each separate and apart from the others. The whole wide area looked like a furniture store, but a very discreet furniture store where the customers didn't look at the price tag before arriving at a decision. Reardon finished his conversation with the doorman, who turned away, laughing and shaking his head over Reardon's last remark.

"Okay, straight ahead, Christie," he instructed her. He touched the tip of his finger to the recessed square elevator signal, and the door slid open immediately.

The music followed them out of the elevator and down the carpeted corridor to Apartment 901. Reardon pointed to the small engraved brass nameplate set into the door. In delicate script, it bore the name "Elena Vargas."

Reardon was familiar with the apartment. As he pocketed the latchkey, he reached to his left and pressed a silent switch which flooded the entrance hall with soft light. "Give me your coat, Christie, it's pretty warm in here." He tossed her coat and his over the intricately carved wooden railing that separated the entrance from the sunken living room. "Well, what do you think of this place?"

It was large, lavish and as totally impersonal as the lobby. There was no trace of an individual, no trace of Elena anywhere apparent. "I don't think I could afford it," she said.

"Six hundred and fifty bucks a month," Reardon told her. "Not on your salary you couldn't afford it. Wait a minute." He dug in

95

his jacket pocket, extracted a slip of paper. "Here's the list of clothing our little witness has requested. If there's anything that looks a little too . . . inappropriate, just forget it. I'll get a suitcase out of the hall closet." He walked to the bar which was built into one wall of the hallway. "Want something for your cold?"

Christie shook her head. "No thanks."

The bedroom was dark and Christie slid her hand along the wall searching for a light switch. Her fingers hit a collection of switches: light filled the room in quick, sharp flickers, gashing across the walls. Sound came at her from overhead, hard, staccato drumbeats and low whining electronic screams. Christie jiggled switches up and down; each switch produced an immediate, unexpected effect of light or sound. With the palm of her hand, Christie quickly pushed all of the switches to the down position. She leaned into the living room and called, "I . . . er . . . seem to be having a problem, Mr. Reardon. With the lights."

"Try the switch to the right of the door, inside the room."

"Oh. Okay."

The room was as clearly and naturally lit as if by afternoon sunlight. The bed was the first thing that caught Christie's attention. It was larger than any she had ever seen and it was covered by a thick, lush lavender-velvet spread. As Elena had said, everything was lavender: springy shag carpeting, drapes, large dresser, even the mirror, floor-to-ceiling set into a panel facing the bed, was lavender tinged and it reflected not only the bed but something Christie could not identify. She frowned into the mirror, then turned. Wallpaper lined the room, interrupted only by doors or draped windows. It was, in keeping with the rest of the room, soft lavender, tones of lavender flowing according to the intensity of shadow and light as caught by the camera. Larger than life, hundreds of nude lavender Elenas, in all conceivable and some inconceivable poses, watched Christie Opara.

A tense, curled Elena waited near the floor; an exuberant, almost innocently naked Elena, the back of one hand flung over her eyes, head tossed back, leaned against the hip of an Elena in studied repose. Some of the figures were complete statements, others were fragmentary portions of a rounded female body, puzzling because they bore no connection to any other part of any particular body. Yet, unquestionably, everything on every wall—roundly, lushly, lewdly, joyously, obscenely, eyes opened wide or closed, face blatant and taunting or unawares and turned away, body offered or teasingly concealed by some other abstract section of body—everything surrounding Christie was Elena Vargas.

"Well, what do you think of Elena's lair?"

Christie turned, startled. She hadn't heard Reardon enter the room. "Well. It's . . . different." She realized that her hands were moving in empty gestures, indicating the walls, the bed, the whole room.

"Sit down," Reardon said. He pulled a chair from the dressing table. "Here, sit down. I'll show you some of these gadgets."

Christie sat tensely on the edge of the chair. The room went dark.

"Now," Reardon's voice was soft in the darkness, "let's say a little soothing of frayed nerves is called for." Music, gentle and quietly melodious, swept across the room in easy waves. "Then, we can pick up the tempo. Maybe a little Latin." A beat took form, built in intensity. The blackness softened, was no longer black; there was no actual light apparent but rather a lightness. Christie could see Casey Reardon clearly outlined, his hand poised over the switches. "Now," he said, "let's say our particular problem is with a guy who needs to be bombarded with sensation."

A scream flashed across the room with a burst of light, then was gone. Each shock of sound seemed to be carried within a beam of light and each beam of light disclosed, in rapid succession, one blinding flash of Elena, or some part of Elena's body. The flashes changed from yellow to red to green to violent purple and hit the walls and ceiling and bed in such perfect synchronization with the sound that the light seemed to be shrieking. The

97

noise and light stopped abruptly; soft music welled up; it was dark again, then the light, natural daylight, filled the room.

Reardon ran his fingertips over several other switches. "The rest of these I won't demonstrate. I'll let you speculate. This whole panel can be preset to run in any given cycle for any particular period of time. Well, what do you think about all this, Christie?"

Christie clenched her fingers tightly. She shrugged. "Well, I've never, you know, never seen anything like this. I guess, well, if the men who come here want . . . entertainment . . . I guess this is the kind of thing." She stood up abruptly. "I don't know, this whole place is pretty . . . unsettling."

Reardon pressed his fingers into his eyes for a moment then blinked. He put the suitcase on the dressing table and jerked his thumb toward a closet. "Get the things Elena wanted."

"Right." She slid the closet door open and was confronted by eighteen feet of shelves and hanging garment bags. She turned in confusion. "I don't know what I did with the list you gave me. From Elena. The list of clothes and things."

Reardon leaned against the dressing table and his eyes flicked from Christie to the bed. "Go over to the bed."

"Huh?"

"The list is on the bed."

"Oh. Right."

Christie felt the tension along her throat, in the dryness of her mouth and in her hands which were cold in spite of the warmth of the room. Elena Vargas intruded not only from the walls and from the very air of the room but from within her own brain. The empty spaces between Reardon and herself were not empty and they both seemed to know it now.

She grasped several dresses without consulting the slip of paper, folded them and reached for the suitcase. "Excuse me," she said without looking at Reardon. He moved slightly. "Mr. Reardon, do you have to stand there like that? I mean, this will take a few minutes and . . . "

"What's the matter, Christie?"

She started to answer but stopped, slowed herself down, raised her face to his. "You know what's the matter."

Reardon nodded slightly. "Yes. *I* know what's the matter. I want to know if you do, too."

"This . . . this room," she turned, moved her hands. "And those, those lights and switches and noises and . . . this room and everything."

"And what else, Christie?" He persisted, gently but insistent. Christie took a deep breath. "And you. And me."

Reardon moved toward her, his physical presence the only reality in a room of fantasy. He pulled her to him, his solidity warm and certain. Christie's hands felt the fabric of his shirt on his chest, then slid, naturally, easily, inside his open jacket until she felt the solid muscles of his back and shoulders. She felt the scrape of his chin along her mouth and she rubbed his face against hers. She closed her eyes tightly, let all sensation come to her through him, as he pressed his mouth on hers and moved against her steadily. The resistance her body offered was not really resistance but increased the pressure of Reardon against her.

She felt the bed beneath her, soft and yielding, the cover warm against her back and Casey Reardon's mouth warm along her neck, her cheek, her mouth. She turned her face away, unexpectedly, and he waited.

"Say my name," she whispered, not looking at him.

His hand ran gently along the contours of her face, turning her toward him so that she looked directly into his eyes. His expression was different from any she had ever seen those hard features assume: a kindness, a patience, an understanding she had not anticipated. He sat up, his hands pressed down on her shoulders and held her as he leaned forward and kissed her again, but lightly, first on the forehead, then on the lips.

"Go ahead," he said, "ask me."

"Ask you what?"

He touched her face with the back of his hand. "If it's because of you or because of the room. That's what stopped you, right?"

She turned away, but he forced her to face him. "It's okay, Christie. But we should get one thing straight, right now. This room is one vast gimmick. It wouldn't matter to me if this was a ten-by-ten broom closet. You understand what I'm telling you?"

"Yes, but . . . "

"No buts, Christie. This room hasn't a damn thing to do with us. Come on, relax. It's the wrong place and we'll let it go at that, okay?"

She reached up, her fingers light on his face, along his lips. "All right, Mr. Reardon." She bit her lip. "All right, Casey." She had never addressed him by his first name; in this setting, on this bed, with him, with his hands still holding her, it still felt strange and she was annoyed with herself. Elena confronted her from the ceiling: the smile was mocking. "You'd think she'd get tired of seeing herself," she said shortly.

Reardon laughed and pulled her to her feet. "I doubt that she even notices all of this." His eyes moved over the walls, slowly, then he looked at Christie sharply. "Hey, what else? Come on, now, Christie. You look like you're about to strangle on something. Say it, Christie."

"All right. If . . . if *she* was here, right now, instead of me. Would . . . would you make love to her?"

He answered immediately. "Nope. Not 'make love' to her. I would *use* her. I would respond to the stimuli all around me and to the various techniques she would offer me. I would *use* her sexually and she would encourage me to satisfy myself any way I wanted. Hell, that's what this room is all about, Christie. I wouldn't *use* you. I'd *make love* to you and there is one vast difference. But not here."

Christie's voice was low and steady. "Why not here?"

He was silent for a moment. His hands went to her shoulders and tightened. "Because afterward, you would begin to wonder. You would think about this room and this bed and about Elena displayed all around the place and you would begin to brood. You'd look at me and you'd begin to turn everything over and over in your mind. And it wouldn't come out the way it was meant." She closed her eyes and nodded. "I told you once, a long time ago, Christie: I can read you. Clearly and accurately." He released her, took a step back. "When I make love to you, Christie, it won't be in the bedroom of a whore, and you won't have to wonder if it's because that whore is not around. There will be absolutely no doubt in your mind as to why. And you won't have to ask me to say your name. Now," he turned her toward the dresser, "you go and collect the things you're supposed to collect and let's get the hell out of here."

He stopped at the door, turned and faced her again. Reardon shook his head over the room, himself, the bright and pretty girl who wasn't really sure yet just how she felt. "And make it fast, Opara, or I just might forget everything I've just said."

Christie sorted the various garments indicated on the list but her mind wasn't on what she was doing. She raised her eyes and was confronted by a mocking Elena, lips drawn back in a contemptuous grin.

"Go to hell," she said softly.

9

Christie leaned back against the wooden frame chair and shivered inside her heavy toggle coat. The atmosphere of the room was composed of various shades of brown, amber and tan, all calculated to give the effect of mellow age. Directly across from the table where Reardon had led her was a three-foot-high, English-script-on-old-wood listing of the specialties of the house: hamburgers, fried onions, French fried potatoes. The rest of the items had been obscured, apparently, by time. There was no aroma of food, only a mild mingling of various kinds of smoke. Christie caught sight of Reardon; he stood, his hand on the waiter's sleeve. They looked in her direction, the waiter nodded and wrote on his order pad.

Reardon moved to the bar, stopped beside a man whose face she couldn't see. He gestured toward the table, then worked his way through the narrow aisle. His face was warm and relaxed. "I ordered something for your cold. And some hamburgers. You ever been here before?" She shook her head. "Ah, here comes my man now."

Everything about Detective Bill Dudley seemed too much: he was too tall, too broad-shouldered, too handsome, too vivid. He had a thick mass of dark-brown curls which spilled along the edge of his yellow turtleneck sweater. His sideburns were wide and led to a neat, clipped beard. His moustache was perfectly suited to his face and did not distract from his surprisingly blue eyes. Reardon introduced them, and Bill Dudley's hand, large and warm, held Christie's tightly for a moment. When he smiled, his teeth were square and very white.

"With hands this cold, Christie, you have to have a warm heart."

102

He had a way of moving his eyes, of leaning slightly forward, that indicated all of his attention was fixed on the person he addressed. "You'd better take your coat off, Christie." He helped her, placed the coat over the back of her chair. He reached two long fingers into the small pocket of his yellow-and-brown plaid vest and consulted a gold watch. "The clock up there is generally off by anywhere from five to ten minutes or one to three hours. Mine has stopped completely." He reached across the table and, with easy familiarity, turned Christie's wrist toward him. "I'll set my watch by yours, Christie."

"I'm usually ten minutes off, one way or the other."

Reardon's voice was sharp and familiar. "Ten minutes *late* usually."

Everything about Dudley would have seemed an affectation in some other man, but even the easy flirting seemed genuine. Christie glanced around the room, her eyes scanned the old-fashioned schoolroom clock, the stained-glass chandeliers, the dark wood, but inevitably she kept coming back to Bill Dudley. He was the unreal, physically perfect male animal seen in cigarette ads and Christie was aware of Reardon's close scrutiny. She felt slightly giddy.

The waiter, wiry and expressionless, put two plates in the center of the table, gave Reardon a drink and wrapped a napkin around a steaming glass which he placed in front of Christie. He leaned to Dudley and said, "Hey, Dude. Celia's at the bar. You want her over here, or what?"

"Thanks, Jack. I'll join her." When he stood, a huge shadow covered the table. "Casey, we'll give you fifteen or twenty minutes, then I'll bring her over." He touched Christie's glass carefully, then smiled. "Wrap your hands around this, Christie. It'll make the cold go away."

Reardon took a long swallow from his drink, then rotated the glass between his open palms. "You're gaping, Opara. Do you know that your mouth is open?"

"I'm just trying to breathe, Mr. Reardon. My cold has me all stuffed."

"He's a good-looking guy, Dudley the Dude."

Christie shrugged. "Really? I hadn't noticed." Then she grinned. "My God, he doesn't look real."

"He's real all right. And a hell of a good man for his job. A guy like Dudley can do it either of two ways: muscle or charm. The only problem is, sometimes he can't seem to relax the charm." He abruptly pushed a plate of food toward Christie. "Come on, get something into you." He moved his hand over his face. "You got something to say, Christie? You've got a peculiar look on your face. What the hell are you laughing at?"

It was the first time she had ever seen Reardon rattled and she enjoyed it. Her smile was deliberate. "I don't know what you're talking about, Mr. Reardon."

"The hell you don't. Will you eat that goddamn hamburger?"

The hamburger was dry and tasteless and there were no ketchup bottles on any of the tables. It would probably be considered outrageous to request anything to enhance the specialty of the house. Cautiously, she sipped the drink, which didn't seem too hot until she took a larger swallow. Tears sprang to her eyes and she felt her voice go hollow. "Wow. What is that stuff? It tastes like cleaning fluid."

"That's what it is. Hot cleaning fluid. Are you really choking, Christie?"

She kept her head down and tried to stifle the coughing. Reardon took an ice cube from his glass with a teaspoon. "Here, tiger. This won't 'make the cold go away,' it'll make the hot go away."

Christie sucked on the ice cube and studied Casey Reardon. Her eyes on his, she reached for the drink, wrinkled her nose at the taste.

"Look, if you don't want it, don't drink it."

He really was angry; it even occurred to her that he sounded offended. Carefully, Christie reached for a teaspoon and began to sip the drink from the spoon. "Hey, it's really very good, after you get over the first shock."

Casey Reardon's smile was short and wise. "You're playing games, aren't you, Christie?"

She held the spoon in her mouth for a moment, then carefully licked at it. "Who, me?"

Bill Dudley moved carefully from the bar, along the narrow aisles, turning sideways at times to avoid an elbow or a chair. His smile and greeting were returned at practically every table: this was definitely his territory. Christie couldn't see much of the girl who trailed behind him until they arrived at the table, when he stepped back politely.

"Christie, Casey, this is Celia." He moved a chair back for the girl. "Celia, baby, you're among friends." He turned his head and the waiter materialized, cleared the table. Dudley's finger circled the table, then pointed at Christie. "Another one of those, Christie?"

Christie locked her fingers around the half-filled glass and shook her head. "I'm fine, thank you."

At first, Christie thought it was some trick of the lighting, the dimness hitting Celia's blouse at an odd angle. She had never before seen anyone wear a completely see-through blouse over a completely see-through bra. Celia was a big girl who did a lot of stretching and shrugging and looking around. Her hands moved restlessly through huge masses of very dark hair. When she put her right hand on the surface of the table and tapped her fingers, Christie noticed that a strand of wirelike hair was caught around a dragon ring which covered two fingers.

The girl's makeup was vivid, applied with a heavy but professional hand. There was a streak of silver glistening over each eyelid and furry eyelashes over somewhat small eyes. Underneath all the makeup, which carefully contoured and shaped and sculpted, there might very well be no face at all: just a blank space, waiting to be decorated.

"Celia, you're going to tell us a couple of things about Elena Vargas. Remember, I spoke to you about this last night?" Bill Dudley's voice was gentle and prodding.

"Where's my Scotch? Jack's getting old, Dude, you know that? Hell, I wouldn't want to be as old as Jack." Celia verged on the

105

edge of drunkenness; her voice was thick and her lips, shining with a wet-look lipstick, quivered.

Reardon glanced at Dudley, who winked. He knew how to handle Celia. "You'll never be as old as Jack, baby. You've got too much know-how. Here we are, see Jack brought your Scotch. But you just take a little sip of it now. That's the girl. Put it down, and later on we'll drink, okay?"

He held the girl with his voice, created an intimacy that eliminated Casey and Christie and everyone else in the room. "We're trying to find out something about Elena Vargas, Celia. You knew her when she first hit the route, when she first became Enzo Giardino's girl. How did that happen?" He sounded puzzled, curious. His large hands turned palms up over the table, appealing to her. "How did those two get together?"

The rings disappeared into the hair as the fingers raked. "Oh, yeah. Elena. Well, you know, Dude. At the scrape place. I went there once. Before the pill." She leaned her arms on the table. Her breasts were large and fully revealed with each breath. "Hey, I bet a lot of people got put out of business because of the pill, huh? I mean, you would really have to be dumb to get knocked up nowadays. Or a dumb kid, huh? I don't think I even heard of anybody needing a scrape job in years." She turned to Christie. "You heard of anybody, honey?"

Celia's mouth, which had been slack, tightened. She moved the heavy lashes up and down and pulled back in her chair. "What the hell are you looking at?" she asked Christie. "Hey, Dude, who the hell is this?" She pulled her shoulders back and smiled. "You're lost in that sweater, baby. Or that sweater is lost on you. Yeah, that's it, the sweater is lost on you. You look like a little boy."

Reardon warned her, without a sound. Christie received the silent message and kept her mouth shut; let Dudley handle it.

"Hey, Celia, you sure do justice to that blouse." Her head swung away from Christie. "Nobody but you could get away with it."

"I get away with plenty, right, Dude?"

He held the Scotch to her. "Take a little sip and get on to Elena, okay? What scrape place are we talking about, Celia?"

Her eyes widened shrewdly. "*We're* not talking about: *I'm* talking about. I'm drunk, honey, but not too drunk. And I got my goddamn reasons for drinking tonight." She moved her hands vaguely and told Christie, "A man. What else? What the hell other reason is there, right?"

Christie nodded. "Right."

"Hey, Dude. I like this girl. I like her. She's okay. Whoever the hell she is. Oh, yeah. The scrape place. Out on Manhasset Sound or Bay or something like that. Rest Harbor or Rest Haven or something." She caught the sleeve of Christie's sweater. "What the hell was the name, honey?"

"Quiet Haven."

"Yeah. You been there? Never mind. We all been there. But not since the pill. Yeah, Dude, okay. Little Elena Vargas was working out there. Really straight work." She held her hands in the air and wiggled her fingers. "Typing and stuff like that, real square stuff. Straight from nowhere that girl was. A convent or something equally like that. And she never even realized, get this, because it's so goddamn funny . . . " Celia started to laugh. It was a deep gurgling sound and she bent her head down and moved it from side to side.

Dudley sat patiently and waited. "She didn't know she was working at an abortion mill?"

Celia raised her face. One of the furry eyelashes was slightly lopsided. "Hey, Dude, how did you know that? Dude knows everything. That's right, she didn't know. Well, what could you expect, growing up in a convent orphanage, she thought it was all real. You know, in those days, Enzo took good care of his girls. I mean, you know who used to go out to Rest Haven . . . Quiet Harbor . . . whatever the hell it is . . . in those days? Like, you were in class company, with all those little college girls from all those fancy schools." She reached for Christie's arm and tightened her long fingers. "You look like them. Like a fancy little college girl. Yeah. They're all flat-chested too." She looked

107

down at her own body. "Hey, Dude, nobody'd think I was a fancy little college girl, huh?"

"And you met Elena out there, at Quiet Haven?"

"Hey, Dude, I just told you that, didn't I? Did I? I don't remember. She was a nice kid and supposed to stay away from the patients, just stick to her office. But I guess she saw young girls, like her own age, and she was glad to see them after all those old croakers all over the place. And they either talked or she just figured it out for herself after a while. And she couldn't quit. I mean, that old bastard of a doctor had her but for real over a barrel."

"Why couldn't she quit, Celia?"

She turned to Casey Reardon. "Hey, redhead. Real dark red but there's light red, like orange on your chin." She reached out, ran a finger down Reardon's jawline. "I am dead drunk tonight, Red. Dude is ashamed of me. I know that."

"You're fine, Celia. If anybody has a reason tonight, you have. I told you, baby, you're among friends. Why couldn't Elena quit her job at Quiet Haven?"

Dudley was gentle; he was a big, handsome, muscular man and never once did his expression harden into impatience or annoyance. He moved her on, skirting the endless interruptions easily, constantly encouraging her.

"Oh, well, she could have just quit. I mean, yeah, quit. But Elena wanted to blow the whistle. Can you imagine that, she wanted to blow the goddamn whistle, so Enzo went and had a little talk with her. Gee, she was only a baby then. After Enzo had a talk with her, they let her quit her job."

"After she promised not to blow the whistle?"

"Well, Dude, I guess she promised. I wasn't there. Ask Elena what he said to her. How would I know. But there wasn't no rough stuff. I know that much. Enzo liked Elena." She tapped her temple with an index finger. "Hey, it comes back. Like they told Elena she could quit the job but they had some kind of a frame all set for her. Yeah. She had got the job through the court, she'd been arrested for something or other and they had a frame. So that if she blew the whistle, they'd hit her with grand larceny or something. Yeah, something like that. That's the way it was. So they let her quit."

"When did she get together with Enzo Giardino?" Christie asked.

"Later. I don't know. Later. A year maybe."

"How did Elena get into the life?" Reardon asked.

Celia made that odd gurgling sound again. Her fingers went to her hair. "You tell him, honey," she said to Christie.

"A man?"

"You bet a man." Celia stopped speaking and her mouth fell slack. Dudley got her going again.

"Come on, Celia. That's my girl. The same old story, huh? For Elena? Some no-good bum walked out on her?"

She turned to Reardon. "You know Elena?" Reardon nodded. "Elena is special, right? I mean, she has got it. And up there, in the scrape place, like living in the country, the only boys she met, well, sometimes a brother of one of those college girls. Or a grandson of one of those old-timers they had laying around waiting to die, right? Oh, was she ever ripe and ready for one of those little bastards." She moved her head from side to side and moaned. "Poor little kid. Poor baby. All those nice little white boys, you know and Elena. What the hell does color have to do with anything? You tell me, Dude, because I'll be damned if I can figure it out. You tell me."

Dudley reached across the table and held both of her hands inside his own. "You're a nice girl, Celia."

"Yeah, that's me. Miss Nice Girl. So there was Elena, knocked up with some bastard's kid and he pulls that crap on her, you know—I'm not going to be the father of any . . . oh, you know, Dude."

There were two long streams of tears cutting through the heavy makeup. Dude carefully blotted her face with his handkerchief. "Close your eyes for a minute, Celia." His fingers were surprisingly agile. He adjusted the lopsided eyelashes.

"Did Elena have an abortion?" Christie asked.

Celia shrugged. "I didn't see her until she was Enzo's girl. Like, I saw her at Rest Haven and then about a year or so later, Enzo's got her set up."

"You mean, she might have had a child?" Christie's mind was racing. If there was a child, Giardino would know about it. Reardon's foot pressed on her shoe, his eyes signaled her not to pursue it. Celia's face had pulled into a hard, ugly expression.

"What the hell would I know about a kid? You want to know, you ask Elena, not me. What am I anyway, some kind of a patsy? Hey, Dude, can I finish my drink now?"

"Save a little, baby, just sip it. Now, what about Elena and Enzo Giardino? Come on, honey, think a little. You told me last night they had a 'different' setup. That Enzo didn't send Elena out like trade."

She wiped her mouth with her hand and the hand was stained with shining lipstick. "Oh, Elena's not in trade. Not any more, not in the regular way, anyhow. You know, it's hard to turn a buck." She gestured around the room. "Take a look. You should see this place on a weekend. All the so-called nice girls. Hell, everybody's up for grabs. When I come up from the South—did you know I was from the South?" She laughed heavily. "Yeah, South Jersey, how's that. When I come here, there were good girls and bad girls. I was a bad girl. Now, hell, they all go parading around; you like the looks of a guy, so you screw and nothing more to it. You know what that leaves the pros? The sickies. And the older guys, you know, Mister Potbelly: cream-cheese-and-jelly ulcer diet and my wife don't like to screw. But we used to get the college boys, the real loaded kids who used to hold hands with the girl friend and go to bed with us. Hey, Dude, there is a change of social values going on, right under our very noses, did you know that?"

Time and again, Christie was lost in the barrage of words and emotional gasps and stops and starts. But neither Dudley nor Reardon ever lost the thread. Both hung on, waited for a pause to insert a question.

Reardon took his cue from Dudley and held his natural impatience in check. "But you said it was 'different' for Elena. That Enzo didn't send her trade. Did he keep her for himself, or what?"

Celia's hand played against Reardon's cuff for a moment. She muttered to herself, then looked up at him. "Oh, well, you know. Enzo is no great lover, right? I mean, he's busy with things, you know, things." She became vague, her fingers grasped Reardon's hand. "You got freckles on your hand, did you know that?" Her head fell forward and her fingers opened.

For the first time, Bill Dudley's face and tone changed. "Okay, Celia. Look up. Now, what was the setup with Enzo Giardino and Elena Vargas? No more games."

She glanced around quickly and her face showed fear. "Dude, nothing about Enzo Giardino. Look, you know better."

"Celia, tell me."

Celia was starkly, completely sober. The slur had gone from her voice. "You want to know about Elena. All right. She gets lots of money. The pad, her clothes, her trips to the Island, Enzo finances. She turns a trick, it's strictly on her own. Enzo doesn't take no cut. It's cash, she keeps what she gets."

"That's pretty unusual, isn't it?" Christie felt the anger emanate from the girl, but she was unprepared for the cold, harsh response.

"Look, you, whoever the hell you are. Whatever the setup is, you ask Elena. I'm not looking to end up . . ." She looked around, and the fear in her eyes was genuine.

Dudley's voice was kind and persuasive again, reassuring. "Baby, nobody's going to hurt you. Look at me, Celia. You believe me, don't you? You trust me, don't you?"

The sound was more of a sob than a laugh but she reached for Dudley's hand and pressed it to take some of the edge off her bitter tone. "Oh, yeah, Dude. Sure. Sure, I trust you."

It was Reardon who latched on to the fragment of information she had carelessly thrown out. "The trips to the island, Celia. Puerto Rico?"

"Who said anything about Puerto Rico?"

"Does Elena go often? To visit relatives down there, I guess?"

"How the hell would I know?" She shrugged. "Yeah, I guess so,

111

Red. She like commutes you might say. Look, I don't know anything about Elena or Enzo Giardino or anything about anything."

Dudley pushed his own glass toward her. "Finish my drink, Celia. It's Scotch, baby, same as you've been drinking. I've been saving it for you."

"You're a good guy, Dude. Yeah. You know about Dude?" She turned to Christie. "Dude takes care of things. He's the only cop I know who isn't a bastard. At least, not completely. Just a little bit of a bastard. Jesus, I'm loaded." She swallowed deeply and her words began to slur again. Her face looked ruined. "Hey, I didn't say anything, did I, Dude? I didn't say a goddamn thing, did I, honey?"

"Not a thing, Celia. I'm going to get you something to eat now and then I'll take you home, okay?"

Christie caught Reardon's signal. She eased her coat over her shoulders and Dudley reached to help her. His eyes moved over her carefully and his smile was warm and friendly. And automatic. And professional. "I hope we run into each other again, Christie. Some time when you're feeling better. Take care of that cold."

Celia's face was down, low over her drink and she didn't notice them leave. Christie glanced back over her shoulder and saw Dudley smiling and waving to some people at a nearby table. Reardon pushed her along with his shoulder.

"Come on, Opara, let's get the hell out of here."

10

They were silent in the elevator. The car slid to an easy stop on the sixteenth floor. Reardon held his hand against the rubber bumper and stood aside so that Christie could exit first. The corridor of the hotel had a somewhat musty odor.

She started in the wrong direction, momentarily confused. "No, this way," he told her. "Here, you carry this." He extended the suitcase containing Elena's clothes and waited until Christie pulled off her gloves and shoved them into her shoulder bag. He studied her face for a moment in the dim light. "Can you handle it, this time?"

She felt the weight of the suitcase and nodded, then stopped. They had spoken very little during the drive to the hotel. Each had been considering various bits of information which Celia had let drop into her rambling conversation. Reardon either ignored or was seemingly totally unaware of Christie's sense of panic when she realized where they were heading. And that she would have to face Elena. He treated her exactly as he would treat any other Squad member, offering neither doubt nor support. At first, Christie had felt resentment: she wasn't ready, she needed time to prepare. But now, standing outside the hotel suite, his question was a challenge and she felt herself tense up. Her mouth opened slightly and she met his steady gaze evenly.

"I can handle it *this time*," she said.

"Good. Because if you louse up this time, you are really in trouble."

Christie smiled at his hard, serious expression. "You know, Mr. Reardon, I respond much better to kindness than to threats."

113

"Don't be a wise guy."

He tapped on the door in a series of prearranged knocks. Sam Farrell's voice asked for identification, and then the door opened.

The furniture had been rearranged to what apparently the room had been originally: a pleasant sitting room. A newspaper was on the floor beside the chair where Farrell had been sitting. His cigarette had fallen from the ashtray on the table beside the chair and was burning a black mark into the leather surface. Farrell picked up the newspaper, glanced at the cigarette. "Gee, look at that." He stubbed the cigarette into the ashtray. "All quiet here, Mr. Reardon."

"How's the hand, Sam?"

Farrell considered his bandaged hand. "Not so bad, now, Mr. Reardon. The doctor gave me some new medicine. It don't throb now, only if I forget and use it or something."

"Good. How's our girl been?" He jerked his thumb toward the inner room.

"She's been real nice and quiet. She got a whole stack of magazines sent up. We got a young policewoman in there. Margie Gibson. You know her, Christie?"

"No."

Christie took her coat off and tossed it over a chair. She waited for Reardon, but he offered nothing. She felt both a sense of relief and a sense of desertion when he spoke to Farrell.

"Send the policewoman out for a coffee break. Opara is going to talk to Elena for a while. You can reach me at the office or they'll know where I am if anything comes up."

"Right, Mr. Reardon." Farrell tapped on the open door and went into the other room.

Casey Reardon stood, his hands deep inside the pockets of his coat. He watched her attempts at control, the few deep breaths, the quick wetting of her lips. She moved her chin up slightly and he admired the certain edge in her voice.

"Don't worry about a thing, Mr. Reardon."

Casey Reardon smiled tightly. "I never do."

Christie exchanged greetings with the policewoman and told her to take her time. Her eyes went directly to Elena Vargas, who was stretched full length on the beige couch. Her bright red jersey blouse and slacks vividly outlined her body. There were copies of magazines on the floor beside her and her face was hidden by the latest copy of *Vogue*. She let the magazine fall across her chest and brought her head up. Her eyes went dark and alert.

No personal feelings; strictly professional. Christie forced her voice, controlled the situation. *This time,* she had to set the tone. "Hello, Elena. How have you been?"

"Why are *you* here?"

Christie placed the suitcase on the cocktail table in front of the couch. "I brought you some clothes. Not everything on the list. Some of the things I couldn't find."

"You were at my apartment?"

"That's right."

Elena pulled herself into a sitting position. "Why you?"

Christie shrugged easily. "Why not me? It's my job."

"Where's Reardon? I want to see him."

Christie reached for a magazine, let the pages fall at random. "Mr. Reardon took off for parts unknown. He doesn't check in with me."

"I have nothing to say to you. I overestimated Reardon's intelligence. Does he really think I'd talk to you, after . . ."

Christie tossed the magazine onto the table. She felt stronger than she had anticipated. "Let's cut the nonsense, Elena, all right? I'm just doing my job. You're my assignment. There's no rule that says we have to like each other. But it would be a good idea if we were civil to each other, all right? I mean, actually, neither of us has a choice."

Elena regarded her curiously; she felt cautious and wary. "I am generally civil to people. Just leave me alone. I don't want to be bothered. What did you bring?" She leaned forward and opened the suitcase. "Ah, the blue jumpsuit. It's real silk." She tossed the garment to Christie. "Do you know genuine silk when you see it?"

115

"It's very pretty."

"Pretty?" Elena stood up, retrieved the jumpsuit from Christie and held it against her body. " 'Pretty' is hardly the word. Look in those magazines, Detective Opara. You'll find words like exotic, sensuous, mysterious, elegant. Not 'pretty.' " She pulled out some pink garments. "My lounging pajamas. Pucci. What do you lounge in, Detective Opara?"

Christie's eyes rested on the clear colors and unique designs. "Well, usually in dungarees and a turtleneck sweater. Definitely not in Pucci pajamas."

"Did you ever try on clothes like these? No, no I think not. You wouldn't go into Bergdorf's or Saks, not into the boutiques on Madison or Fifth. But wouldn't you like to?" She held up a clear, vivid blue dress. "This would look good on you. The color, anyway. It would not fit you the way it fits me. It was made to my measurements."

Christie sat on a chair and ignored Elena. She began slowly, quietly. "Kelly sends regards."

Elena frowned. "Kelly? Kelly who? I don't know any Kelly."

Christie leaned back and studied her fingernails. "She's about seventeen years old now. I guess she was about eight or nine when you knew her. Kelly . . . no, her last name wouldn't be Fehley, would it? That's her mother's married name." She looked up at Elena. "Actually, I don't know her last name. What is it?"

Elena sank slowly to the couch, the blue dress clutched against her red outfit. "Kelly Endright. You saw Kelly? But she is a child."

"No. She's not a child anymore. She's very grown up. And she sends regards. Apparently she liked you very much."

Elena's eyes were wide and unblinking; her body was rigid and her mouth opened slightly as the fact penetrated. Christie Opara had dug into her past: had asked about her, spoken about her, had found out things about her. She realized suddenly that she was holding the dress against herself, almost as though trying to hide behind it. She tossed it to the suitcase and folded her arms and smiled. "And is Mrs. Fenley as lovely as ever?"

"She's an A-number-one bitch."

116

The answer surprised Elena; more than that, it alerted her. She could afford no alliance of any kind with this detective. "I learned from Mrs. Fenley," she said. "Many things. Including the appreciation of beautiful things."

Christie carefully pulled at the corner of a broken fingernail. One after the other, she sorted bits and pieces of information. Silence hung between them but it was her silence now, completely hers to control. It was, at one and the same time, a good feeling and an ugly feeling. She dropped the shred of fingernail onto the cocktail table and, without looking up, she asked, "How many children does your sister have, six, seven?"

Elena leaned her head against the back of the couch and whispered in Spanish. Some of the words Christie had heard before, others she seemed to know instinctively.

"They are beautiful children, Elena."

The response was bitter and tore at the sincerity with which Christie had spoken. "Yes, beautiful children. And they live in a beautiful world, eh? And they will live beautiful lives, eh? Here in this beautiful city. Look, you don't want to talk to me about my sister and her children. They are nothing to me and less than nothing to you. I think you are just showing off a little bit, Detective Opara." Elena's voice settled down; she moved her hands in small, controlled gestures. "So, you've done your job and now you say to yourself: now I know Elena Vargas. Now I can question her and get what I want from her." She moved her head to one side and smiled. "So, what do you think you know?"

The question was thrown out too casually; Christie sensed an underlying tension in Elena's effort to discount whatever Christie had learned. She timed the interval before responding. She could not engage in banter. Not this time. She had to frame her questions precisely while at the same time she had to keep her voice completely neutral.

"When you worked at Quiet Haven you became involved with a man. A boy, probably. You became pregnant. He refused to marry you and didn't want you to have his child. Am I right so far?"

117

Elena was prepared; she shrugged. "But that is an old, old story. Of course, for me, at that time, it was unbelievable. I was a very little girl. So, you found out at what point I grew up. So what?"

"So what became of the child?" Christie threw the question out almost before it had formed in her brain. It was one of those instinctive questions, unanticipated and unplanned.

"Oh, you have just got to be kidding. All that hard work, looking into Elena's life, and you ask me that? It isn't possible that you didn't find out about Quiet Haven: abortion heaven for wayward rich girls. How far did you think I had to go? On-the-job-fringe-benefit, baby, free of charge."

The hardness was more than surface hardness. It was totally a part of Elena, revealed in her voice, in the set of her mouth, in the studied ease with which she moved her body about the couch. But Christie thought of the other Elena: young, inexperienced, frightened, hurt, humiliated.

"No," Christie said, believing the words as she spoke them. "No, I don't think so. You were fresh out of the Protectorate. You had spoken of taking vows. I don't think you *could* have had an abortion. Not at that point, Elena."

"Oh, are we talking about 'morality' now?" Elena's voice was bitter. "Are we talking about 'Catholic morality'?"

"It's the morality in which you were raised."

"Well, let's talk about a *purer* morality, Detective Opara. A more *realistic* morality. I had an abortion at Quiet Haven and it was an act of morality purer than anything I had ever learned at the feet of Mother Superior Catherine Therese."

Elena revealed a passion she had not shown before. Christie had touched something raw and painful and she sensed it had to be pursued. "You'll have to explain that to me," she said quietly. "I find it difficult to equate an abortion with an act of morality."

Elena's eyes gleamed with an angry light. She licked her lips, slowed herself down and regarded Christie thoughtfully. "How old was your son when your husband was killed?"

The question was totally unexpected, caught Christie by surprise, but she found a quietness within herself and answered slowly. "I didn't know I *was* pregnant until almost two months after my husband's death."

"You mean . . . you *knew* your child would have no father?"

"Yes. I knew that right from the beginning."

"And can you truly say you *wanted* to have that child, that you never regretted carrying him?"

The balance between them shifted; each girl was aware of it. Elena now had touched on something Christie still found incredibly painful: some long-forgotten torment, one brief, blind, agonizing half-admitted resentment of the living body within her. But that had been a part of her grief and not a separate entity. She decided to be completely honest. "No woman wants to bear a fatherless child, regardless of the circumstances. My pregnancy was not the way I wanted it. Yes. I resented it at first; I felt trapped and betrayed at first. But at no time, *never*, did I even vaguely consider abortion. You see," she added softly, carefully, "I loved my child's father."

"And I *thought* I loved the father of the child I was carrying. But I was unwilling to bring into this world a fatherless child. My abortion was an act of morality for that child. Of course, we cannot be equated, you and I. It is a different world for your son than it would have been for mine. You saw my sister's children. There are *nine* of them. Yes, they are beautiful, now. But, one by one, they will go out and they will become what other people will make of them: just some more *little spics*." Elena clenched her hands tightly in her lap. "Not *my* child. My act of morality, my act of protection, was for the child."

Christie absorbed all the words, let them fill her brain. She reached into her pocketbook, dug out a cigarette, lit it. Slowly, she moved her head from side to side. "No. I don't believe you, Elena. You are not who you were seven or eight years ago."

"I am who I have always been. If you think not, it is your concern, not mine."

Elena snatched a magazine from the table. She turned back a page, scanned it quickly, then held it up to Christie. "Did you

119

ever feel sable like that, Detective Opara?" Not looking at the ad, she recited the copy, "Why not the finest? When you are someone special, let the world know."

"Well, the world will just have to figure out some other way of knowing how 'special' I am. I'll see you again, Elena."

"There would be no point to it."

Christie stood up, pulled her shoulder bag into place. "Ya never know." It was an unconscious imitation of Casey Reardon. Elena caught the inflection. She stretched her small, softly curved body against the cushions of the sofa and raised her hands over her head.

"Oh, by the way, Detective Opara. There *is* one thing I wanted to tell you."

"Really? What's that?"

Elena propped her head up on one hand and smiled. "That Casey Reardon. He is very, *very* good·in bed."

Christie stood absolutely still for about five seconds, then she returned Elena's smile. "Yes," she said. "I know."

11

The brilliant sunshine on the poster sparkled on unbelievably blue and green expanses of water. Christie concentrated on the pale-beige sand, willed herself to become the warm, tanned, languidly self-indulgent girl in the bikini.

"I'm sorry this is taking so long, Detective Opara, but as you can see, I'm running a madhouse here. My partner's been sick for a week, two of the girls are out: one quit and one eloped. Just my luck, everything at the same time."

Mr. Fernaldi's tan had an oddly flat quality which seemed unrelated to fresh air and sunshine. At his desk, surrounded by glaring travel advertisements, he had a look of ill health: the look of a man badly in need of a vacation.

"Take your time, Mr. Fernaldi. I'm traveling all around the world." Christie glanced to her left and was confronted by hot, dry, pale Spain and frantically colorful Mexico-in-Fiesta. Fernaldi looked up from his small steel box of index cards.

"You got a vacation coming up? Look, by next month, I could fix you up with something in the islands." His hand, held at eye level, waggled back and forth. "You know, we could *arrange* something."

"Not until next summer. I wouldn't mind having some of that Caribbean sun right now. I think I'd even settle for some New York sun at this point."

"Don't say that," Fernaldi told her. "The sun comes out in New York in the middle of February, we lose the last of our holdouts. I'm glad, really glad, that the crummy snow is still falling. Excuse me." He reached for the telephone, answered several questions, jotted down notes.

121

In the twenty-five minutes she had spent at the World-Over Travel Agency, Fernaldi had spent approximately five minutes in conversation with her. He hopped from desk to desk, dug in drawers, dialed and spoke quickly to several people ("confirmations," he had told Christie). Though she was tired after a long day, Christie didn't really mind sitting in the comfortable, contoured plastic chair, surrounded by proof that the world was out there, waiting for her. If she could stare at the blue sky of the Bahamas long enough, Elena Vargas would become totally meaningless.

But, of course, Elena Vargas was not totally meaningless. Christie fingered the small battered leather notebook and scanned what little information she had copied during nearly seven hours of intensive research. She wondered if Casey Reardon had ever sat hunched over musty records, inhaling ages-old dust, index finger sliding down and down, over line after line of information, page following page. The estimated date of Elena's child—assuming of course that she had had a child—was extremely tentative. From literally thousands of pages of vital statistical data, Christie had come up with two possibles-but-highly-unlikelys. Both infants had been born to women named Vargas; both women had left the name of the father off the birth certificate. One woman, first name of Luisa, listed two previous births; one woman, first name of Emily, listed her age as thirty-four and no previous births.

Christie turned a few pages, then checked her watch against the note in her book: Mother Superior Catherine Therese would call her sometime after 7:00 P.M. That particular telephone conversation, earlier in the day, might have saved all the hours at the Department of Health. But the Reverend Mother, Christie had been informed, was not at the Protectorate and, as a matter of fact, was in New York City attending a conference on child health care. Yes, a soft voice informed her at the New York number, the Reverend Mother was on the premises but attending meetings. Then, a message was taken, delivered and a reply relayed. The Reverend Mother will call you at your home after 7:00 P.M., thank you.

On her last ring to the Squad office, Christie had been instructed by Stoner Martin to stop at the travel agency and get a rundown on Elena's visits to Puerto Rico. It had been determined, through an informant, that this particular agency handled all of Elena's travel arrangements.

Through an informant. Christie knew that one of the most valuable sources of information for any detective was a collection of reliable informants. Everyone in the Squad had an informant of one kind or another, whose services were offered for one reason or another. From time to time, cryptic little telephone voices had whispered in her ear, asked for Tom Dell or Stoner Martin or Pat O'Hanlon or Marty or even for Reardon himself. If the man was present, the ensuing conversation would invariably be conducted with a hand cupped over the mouthpiece of the phone or a shoulder turned protectively away. There would be a series of abrupt "yeses" or "no's" or "uh-uhs, uh-huhs," and Christie would know that an informant had just reported in. She was probably the only member of the Squad who didn't have one single informant. She wondered what mysterious half-existent person had told Stoney that of all the hundreds of travel agencies in New York City, this one particular agency handled the travels of Elena Vargas.

As Mr. Fernaldi returned to his desk with a large folder, the informant suddenly became less than mysterious. In fact, his identity became so obvious that Christie could probably have claimed him herself, sooner or later. The doorman at Elena's apartment building. Doormen were notorious gossips and they always seemed to know everything.

"Here, I finally found Miss Vargas's folder. It had been misfiled. Probably by the girl who eloped. That kid was so confused for so many months, I only hope she took off with the right guy." He opened the folder on the desk and turned it toward Christie. "Now, like I said, we generally keep folders on our clients who travel as frequently as Miss Vargas. To make sure that the level of accommodations is satisfactory, you know, travel, hotel accommodations, the whole schmear. Be my guest, you have any questions, just yell."

Christie set to work copying any information which might be pertinent. She was interested in learning how often Elena traveled, her destination, if she rented an automobile and the average length of her stay. The plastic contour chair was not as comfortable as she had first thought. It seemed to be forcing her back into an abnormal disc alignment. Her fingers began to cramp and she flexed them, then shook her hands vigorously. She squinted over her own handwriting. The notes were becoming almost stenographic. Christie began editing; it was stupid to copy everything verbatim. The facts: Elena traveled from New York to San Juan a total of nine times during the course of the past year. She alternated among three major airlines with first-class accommodations; registered at a suite in any of four of the largest, most luxurious hotels. Whenever she was in San Juan, a brand-new white Ford, automatic shift, was at her disposal through the Driver Best Company.

And where did she drive the automatic-shift, brand-new white Ford? Now, that was a question which could be answered only if . . . Christie felt new energy. Why not? Several of the men had taken out-of-town trips on investigations. Mr. Fernaldi could make all of her travel arrangements. She could travel tourist class and stay at a less-than-suite-size room. That didn't have to face the ocean. In the mornings and afternoons, she could check out Elena's various contacts and movements. And the evenings would be free . . .

"Well," Mr. Fernaldi said, "you look as though you're pleased with the information you've found."

Christie grinned. "All this cheerful sunshine coming at me from all these posters must have done something to my spirits."

Mr. Fernaldi's expression was morose. "Well, yeah, I guess. I never really look at the pictures. Too busy making arrangements for clients. Like I said before, if you decide to travel, stop by. We'll work something out."

"I just might. Things might turn out that way after all."

Christie felt her shoulder bag slide down to the crook of her arm, but she kept her hands curled inside the pockets of her coat. Somewhere along the way she had lost her fur-lined gloves and her fingers felt frozen. She kept her head down against the slashing wet assault of sleet and rain and occasional feathery wafts of snow. It was not quite cold enough for a real snowstorm but there was an undercurrent of frigid air, low to the ground, so that the sidewalks were slippery. It was four blocks to the subway, but Christie ignored the cold and the wet bleakness and thought of Puerto Rico and beaches and the very real possibility. She had convinced herself completely. If she was very careful, logical and persuasive, she could convince Casey Reardon. After all, it was a legitimate part of the investigation: of *her* aspect of the investigation and she should be the one to follow . . .

Christie's eyes were on the sidewalk and though she anticipated the curb at the end of the block, she didn't anticipate the automobile. And actually, the automobile was blocking the crosswalk so that as she hit against it, her hands, pulled from her pockets instinctively, made contact with the rear door. She had an odd, fleeting impression that the car had been idling there, rather than having stopped abruptly after failing to beat the changing traffic light. As she pushed herself away from the car, she felt the man beside her right shoulder, felt his presence before she actually saw him. She could not have said from what direction he had come: he had just materialized.

As he moved, Christie thought he was trying to help her or to see if she had been injured. He was a small man, his face level with her own, and though he made no physical contact with her, he seemed to encompass her. In the wet reflected street light, Christie could make out a hard, totally expressionless face with small monkey eyes which stared at her intently. He had a fighter's flat nose and his jaw moved as his teeth cracked a wad of chewing gum. His long hair, flecked with spots of sleet and snow, was combed into a careful, stiff wave which added a little to his height, but not much. He reached for the rear door, and suddenly wary, Christie stepped back. As he opened the door, a light flooded the interior of the car.

"Mr. Giardino wants to talk to you," the man told her in a harsh rasp.

"Mr. Giardino?"

"Yeah. He's in the car. He wants to talk to you." He moved his head toward the car but his eyes stayed on her face.

Christie's mouth went dry. She looked into the car at the man in the back seat of the long black Mercedes. He leaned toward her, nodded, indicated a place beside him. All she could see was a bulk of dark coat and a gray homburg. She turned and realized that she was hemmed in by Giardino's man and the open door of the car.

"For a few minutes, you might like to come in out of the rain." The voice from the car was soft and inflected with a slight accent. "Tonio, take a walk for yourself. You scare the lady."

Without a word, without the slightest facial adjustment, the small man turned and walked rapidly down Third Avenue.

"Come on, come in out of the rain." It was a coaxing voice, the patient voice that encourages a reluctant child to do what's best. He leaned closer to the open door and Christie could see a face beneath the hat. "If you want, I will get out, but it seems foolish to stand and talk in all that bad weather." Enzo Giardino's voice filled with perplexed wonder. "You know, it never even occurred to me that Detective Christie Opara would be afraid to talk to me."

It was a shock: the stating of her name. It was as though something terribly personal had been violated and there were implications she could not even begin to consider at the moment.

"I'm not afraid of you," Christie said. It was true. She was not afraid of the physical presence of the man in the automobile. There was nothing sinister about his invitation or his expressed willingness to get out of the automobile. The streets were cold and wet and empty. Tonio was nowhere in sight. Christie turned, as though checking her location. Quickly, her numb fingers found her revolver inside her pocketbook and closed around it. She withdrew her hand from the pocketbook and slipped it into her coat pocket. She was not afraid of Enzo Giardino but she felt less afraid with her revolver resting against her hand.

126

Enzo Giardino carefully lifted his hat from his head and placed it on the seat between them. The light behind his head cast dark shadows on his face. "Well, so I have convinced you to come in out of the rain. It's a bad night to be in New York, eh?"

She had heard his name spoken a hundred times; had encountered his name in newspapers and in official reports; had seen his photograph, seen him in television newsclips, but he translated as a total stranger. His face was thin and long and his nose blade-like. There were deep black half circles under his eyes which extended down his flat, almost concave cheeks. His lips were thin and colorless and pulled back into a stiff smile which revealed surprisingly white and square teeth. His gray hair, streaked through with black, was thick and carefully groomed: a point of vanity. Mixed with the odor of leather emanating from the soft upholstery was a tangy, spicy cologne. Enzo Giardino was a meticulously groomed, late-middle-aged man, who expressed concern for her in a fatherly voice.

"You shouldn't be out on the cold streets on a night like this. You should be where it's warm. How many hours a day they got you working—ten? twelve?"

Christie shrugged. It was the kind of gesture with which she responded to older people who sympathetically told her she should eat more, she was too thin, she should take vitamins, she should dress warmly, she shouldn't work so hard, she should . . .

She should not be taken off guard so easily.

"What is it you wanted to talk to me about, Mr. Giardino?"

"Ah. Yes. I have something that I want you to give to Elena." He reached forward; his hand went into a small pocket that was set into the back of the front seat. It was an envelope. Giardino tapped the envelope against his knee for a moment. "You're a nice-looking kid, Opara," he said appraisingly. "How the hell did a nice-looking kid like you get mixed up in such a dirty job?"

"You have other jobs for girls that aren't so dirty, right, Mr. Giardino?"

There was a small rumble of appreciation, not quite a laugh. "You got guts, too. I like that. Tell me something." He leaned

127

toward her, his voice went low: a whispered confidence. "Just between the two of us. You're not even a little scared, sitting here with me?"

Christie shook her head from side to side. "Mr. Giardino, I have my fingers wrapped around my .38 Detective Special and it's pointed straight at you. Why should I be scared?"

The laugh was real this time, short and hard. "Hey, kid, you really think you fooled me? I know you got the gun into your pocket before you got into the car. But that's good, that's good. Shows you're using the brains. But why would I want to hurt you, huh? I got a job for you. Here, you give these pictures to Elena." He withdrew several color photos from the envelope. Christie glanced at them but couldn't make out the figures.

"Elena and the kid," Giardino explained. "They just come back from the Kodak people. I thought she might like to have them. Take them, you look at them later, when you're not so tense. Or when the light it's a little better, huh, little detective." He held the pictures at arm's length, muttered something about his eyes, about getting old, needing glasses. Then, "They're not too good of Elena, but the boy looks real nice. He's getting to be a big boy, Raphael."

"Raphael?"

Giardino's voice changed; everything about him seemed to change. A cold hard certainty stiffened him. He had been playing with her. "The kid," he said. "*Elena's kid.* You spent all day trying to find his birth certificate. You wasted your time. He wasn't born in New York. She had him on the Island. They run home to cousins, the little spic girls, when they're in trouble. You're a detective, you don't know that?" The thin lips pulled back contemptuously; his words taunted her. "How many times did she go to see her little bastard this year? Huh? Nine times, ten times down to the Island? You find out at least *that* much today? You tell me."

Christie felt the full impact now; it all hit her. *She* had been watched, checked on, reported on. Some vague, vast, faceless "they" had done to her what she had done to so many others. But that had been her job. And checking on her had been "their" job.

Her mind raced: at the Bureau of Vital Statistics, clerks, officials, city employees, helping her with the endless dusty volumes, making phone calls. To Giardino. At the travel bureau. Fernaldi and his whispering telephone calls. This car had been waiting for her, at exactly this location. Where it was known she would be. Enzo Giardino had been waiting for her.

Though he said nothing threatening, not even vaguely suggestive of threat, Christie felt vulnerable. She drew her breath in sharply, audibly, in response to the tap on the window at the driver's side. Tonio peered at her.

Giardino's voice was warm again, friendly. "Ah, Tonio has a sense of timing." He gestured at the door. "Come on, Tonio, get in, get in. We'll give you a lift to the subway," he told Christie. "But only if you want. The Independent is a couple of blocks down. Why should you go out into that rain again?"

Christie put the envelope of pictures into her left coat pocket. "What do you want me to say to Elena?"

"And I thought you were a smart kid, Opara. I say *nothing*. That way, you can't repeat nothing. Just give her the pictures of her kid. It's a friendly gesture. You don't want a lift? Well, suit yourself."

Cautiously, Christie moved backward against the car door. A blast of cold wet air filled the car and Giardino reached for his hat. He leaned toward her and looked up at Christie who stood, oblivious to the rain.

"By the way, that's a good-looking kid *you* got, too. A little younger than Raphael, eh?"

12

Mickey Opara cradled the large gray tiger cat against his chest. There was a deep rumbling sound along the animal's throat.

"Hey, Mom, is this dumb cat purring or growling at me?" The boy lifted the animal to his face, then quickly dropped him to the floor. "Sweet William stinks. Boy, Sweet William do you stink. Don't you think he stinks, Mom?"

Christie watched the boy closely. Had they followed him? Had anyone spoken to him? There was no way she could broach the subject. She reached out absently and touched his thick dark hair.

"Don't say 'stinks,' Mickey. It's an ugly word."

"What's a better one, Mom? One that means the same thing, but isn't ugly?"

Christie carried on the conversation with one small part of her consciousness. She was glad Nora had gone to the theater. Nora would have spotted something wrong.

Christie regarded the fat, short-legged cat carefully. "Well, you could say Sweet William is malodorous. Means the same thing, but it's a big word and might make him feel important."

"Malodorous." Mickey tried the word, then grinned. "Sweet William, you are malodorous." He flung himself on the floor, his face inches from the cat's. "And that means you *stink*!" His hand went under the cat's jaw, raised his face. Sweet William kept his eyes locked tight. "Hey, Mom, did you see his newest wound? See, the cut down his nose, it goes all the way into his cheek. Nora and me pulled a claw out of it, just about here." His finger dabbed at the gash. "We put some of the vet's medicine on it and Grandma said to do it once more before I go to bed."

Christie sat down beside her son and rubbed her hand into the heavy fur. The deep rumble this time was definitely purring. "Why do you suppose he gets into so many fights?"

"Well, maybe because it makes him feel good. Or maybe because, well, maybe sometimes he gets mad at something that somebody else does to him." Mickey propped his head on his hands. His eyes were so round and clearly blue that Christie wanted to reach out, hold him, protect him. But she closed off one part of herself and listened to her son. His smooth forehead was touched with a childish frown. "Like, sometimes I get mad at something someone does to me."

Mickey twisted his body, rolled into a cross-legged sitting position beside his mother. His hand thumped the cat.

"Did you get mad at somebody recently?"

The small hand moved rapidly, ruffling the fur. "Well, yeah."

"Did you have a fight with somebody recently? Like today?"

The small face looked up; there was color rising along his cheeks. "Hey, Mom, how did you know that?"

"Because I am a Master-Mind-Detective who knows all things, right?" She pushed his hair from his forehead. "Well, suppose you tell me all about it anyway."

The words came in a torrent of indignant phrases and accusations. The small body reenacted a scene of childish combat. Mickey had been betrayed by a best friend. Something about his turn on the sled. A push. Angry words. A tussle in rain-wet snow.

"And then, I took a handful of wet slush and shoved it right down Timmy's neck."

Christie thought that under the circumstances it was a reasonable action. The boys were evenly matched, pound for pound. For a moment, she had forgotten who Timmy Taylor was.

"Well, what did Timmy do then?"

Mickey's sigh was deep and perplexed. "Well, he didn't *do* anything. He said something." He sank to his knees beside Christie. "Something like . . . about he wasn't going to 'respond to my hostilities.' He always says something like that when he's losing a fight. Mom, what does that mean, anyway?"

131

Timmy Taylor was the second of three sons of two practicing psychologists and he had picked up their jargon, at times applying it properly.

Christie regarded the earnest face and gave her full attention to her son. "Well, Mickey, what do you think it meant?"

"I think it meant that Timmy didn't want to fight anymore."

She smiled and nodded. "That's what I think, too." Christie moved suddenly, a quick, darting grab that caught Mickey off balance. She nearly pinned his shoulders flat, but he rolled suddenly and she let herself go limp and the small, strong hands pushed against her.

"I give up. I yield to your hostilities."

Mickey rolled on his back, flung a hand over his head and gave a loud, happy yell. When he heard the phone ring, he grimaced at his mother. "Oh-oh. That's probably Timmy's mother calling about . . . you know. The fight and hostilities and all."

Christie moved toward the phone, her back to Mickey; she made a face to equal her son's expression. This was not the night she particularly cared to hear an earnest, gratuitous, friendly but professional evaluation of her son's emotional life. She interrupted the third ring, determined to cut short Violet Taylor's soft, breathy onslaught.

"Detective Opara?"

She couldn't immediately place the voice: it was female, brisk, and businesslike.

"Yes?"

"This is Mother Superior Catherine Therese. This is the first chance I've had to return your call. How can I help you?"

She had completely forgotten the call to the Mother Superior. She already had the information. But she couldn't tell the woman that. Christie sat on the arm of a chair and slowly let her body slide into the seat. She held the phone on her lap and closed her eyes. The weariness, which had been held back by tension, seemed to flood her. She went through the formalities somewhat listlessly.

"Well, Reverend Mother, in checking on Elena Vargas, I learned that Elena had a baby."

Mickey Opara, relieved that the telephone call did not concern his misdeeds, followed Christie's signal and went upstairs, where he was supposed to take a bath.

"I told you that I had a feeling we'd speak again, Detective Opara."

Yes. Christie remembered that now. "Yes, and I appreciate your calling me. I wanted to know whatever you could tell me about the child."

The silence lasted a few seconds and then she was told, "Detective Opara, you must surely realize that there is little I can tell you about Elena's child. These matters are kept confidential. This is essential, for all concerned."

"Yes. Of course." Automatic response, totally meaningless. Yes. Of course. *What matters are kept confidential?* For what *"all concerned"?*

Christie swung her legs around so that she was sitting on the edge of the chair. "What *can* you tell me about Elena's son?"

"Not much. That the child was born sometime in September of 1962 and . . ."

"Where was he born, Reverend Mother?"

The nun's voice was tighter, warier, possibly in response to her own sharpening sense of the change in Christie's voice. "Didn't Elena tell you?"

"No. Actually, Elena told me she had an abortion. I learned . . . from other sources, that Elena had a child. It is *very* important that I find out as much as I possibly can about this."

"Well, the child was born in the Wingate Shelter for Unwed Mothers, in Westchester County. At the end of three weeks—which is the routine time in such cases—the child was given up for adoption."

Professionally, smoothly, Christie held down any exclamation of surprise. "And after that time, she went to Puerto Rico for a while?"

"Yes. She went directly from the Shelter to the Island. She stayed with some relative for a few months. And then," the voice was weary, resigned, "she returned to New York City. And began her life with Mr. Enzo Giardino."

"Did Elena ever see her baby again?" Christie didn't really expect an answer, it was a throwaway question; but then, she didn't expect the long, heavy silence. "Reverend Mother?"

"I heard you, Detective Opara. I am trying to see where all this is leading. Trying to see the relevance this has."

Carefully, Christie said, "I'm not too sure myself, but I think that possibly a child's life might be involved. In a very real sense."

There was a sigh, a clearing of a throat, then, "About two years after her child was born, Elena sent a pregnant friend of hers to Wingate Shelter. I'm afraid that through inexcusable carelessness, and through totally misplaced loyalty, the girl was able to look at Elena's file. And thought she was doing a favor to inform her of the name of the adoptive family."

There was a long, hard cough and then the voice went low with an almost tough sound. "Detective Opara, Elena came to see me shortly after this incident. It was the last time I saw her. I believed what she told me then, and I believe it now. I will repeat it to you as accurately as I remember her telling it to me."

"About seeing her child?"

"Yes. She drove to the address her friend had given her. She saw the house, rode around, saw the school, the community where he would be raised, then sat in her car, across from the house. A car pulled up, a young woman got out and began unloading grocery bags. Elena saw a small boy—her son—beside the woman. He staggered with a heavy bag he had selected for himself and stumbled. The food went all over the place and the boy started to cry. Elena watched the young woman kneel down, wipe the child's face, help him gather things together. Then, she made up a smaller bundle which he could manage easily. The last sight she had of her son was as the child, carrying his package with one arm, trailing his mother into the house, his free hand clutching her skirt.

"Elena came to tell me not just this little vignette, but to tell me something far more important. Because she knew her friend's indiscretion had been discovered, Elena came to reassure me that

134

she would never go near her child again, nor interfere in his life in any way. That what she had seen she would carry with her always. And as I said before, I believe her."

Christie asked cautiously, "Reverend Mother, would you give me the name of the adoptive family? With my assurance that they will know absolutely nothing about Elena."

"You should know better than to have asked that. Our records are carefully protected now, Detective Opara, and nothing contained in them can possibly be made available to you. I've had a long and somewhat tedious day and three more of the same are coming up. Is there anything further?"

"No. No, thank you very much for calling."

Christie sat staring at the phone for a moment before replacing it on the table. Mickey came into the living room in his pajamas. The smell of hot water and soap surrounded him, moved about the room with him. His dark hair clung wetly to his neck and his face was red and glowing.

"Hey, Mom, I don't know how it happened, but about half of the water from the tub got onto the bathroom floor. It must have been a tidal wave."

Christie gestured toward the kitchen. "Go get the mop, Mickey. I'll be upstairs in a minute. And put your slippers on."

Mickey's singing, high and treble, trailed along the stairway, then reverberated against the tiled bathroom walls. Christie stopped halfway to the second floor and leaned against the banister.

If Elena's child had been adopted, then who the hell is Raphael?

13

The Squad Room had a special quality, an electric tempo that was apparent the moment she walked in. It was only eight-thirty, and Christie had arrived early to type her notes, but there was nothing early-morning about any of the men. They were deep into their work, and a collection of stained coffee cups and cardboard containers lined the long gray table across the front of the room.

Detective Pat O'Hanlon put his coat on and, with a smooth turn, caught Christie's coat and placed it on his hanger.

"Still raining out there, Christie?"

"On and off. What's doing, Pat?"

O'Hanlon shrugged, noncommittal. "Things might start moving pretty soon. Have to see a man about a ship. See you, Christie."

Tom Dell, neatly tailored and carefully groomed, came to check the coat rack. He rearranged a few hangers. "I don't want any wet coats leaning against mine. No offense, Christie."

"The boss in, Tom?"

"Since five A.M." He turned back to his copy of the *Daily News*.

Christie reached for the telephone, caught it before the second ring. "D.A.'s Squad, Detective Opara. Hold it a minute, Marty. Hey, Tom, is Stoney around?"

"With the boss. Is that Ginsburg? I'll get Stoney."

Marty was speaking to someone at the other end of the connection. Christie looked around the office. Bill Ferranti was pecking away at the typewriter and Sam Farrell squinted over his notes. Christie could see it wasn't a final report. They looked very transient themselves, ready to grab their coats and disappear into mysterious directions on secret assignments. Christie began to feel slightly annoyed. She listened carefully, then heard Marty whistling in her ear.

"Hey, Marty, what's doing anyway?"

Stoner Martin barely nodded at her as he took the receiver from her hand. "Yeah, Marty. Right. Are you with Dudley now? Good. Mr. Reardon said to stick with him. You checked out homicide already? Okay. Yeah, Pat brought the pictures in from the lab. No, he left already, I think." Stoner raised his brows at Christie, and she confirmed what he had said. "Yeah, O'Hanlon left. No, I won't be down there. I gotta meet in an hour with a guy. Right, kid, stick with it."

Christie had to move quickly to catch up with Stoner Martin. "Hey, Stoney, would you tell Mr. Reardon I want to see him? It's very important."

He turned and regarded her blankly. His eyes were red-rimmed and his face looked drawn. "Not now, Christie, okay?"

Sam Farrell stood at the coat rack and dug into the pockets of a black coat, looked surprised when his hand came up empty. Carefully, he examined the label. "Gee, these dark coats all look alike. I could have sworn this was mine."

"Hey, Sam, what's doing? What's all the action this morning?"

Farrell located his own coat, dug into a pocket with his injured left hand, winced and carefully extracted the notes he sought. "Damn thing still hurts," he said quietly. "Oh, Christie. Yeah, it's pretty bad. This narcotics case is moving. There were three homicides last night. That's how come we're all in action around here."

Bill Ferranti handed her a copy of their interim report and told her, "Two informants were found shot this morning at about 3 A.M. One of Marty's and one of Pat's."

Quickly, she scanned the report. It contained the brief facts relating to the discovery of bodies. Cause of death in both cases: one .38 bullet at the base of the neck of each victim, fired at close range. Each body had been found slumped over the steering wheel of a late-model, high-priced automobile. One victim had been found in Queens, two blocks from the middle-class, attached brick house where he lived. The other had been found with legs dangling from the partially opened door of his automobile which had been parked on the service road of the Belt Parkway in Brooklyn.

The rest of the report was a check list of what the detectives would do in continuing their investigation: obtain yellow sheets on each victim from the Bureau of Criminal Identification; record of employment; associates, business and personal; last-known activities; union affiliations, if any; social club memberships, if any. Routine check out.

Christie handed the report to Ferranti. "Sam said three homicides. Who was the third?"

Ferranti shook his head, removed his spotless eyeglasses and rubbed at them with a fresh linen handkerchief. "That was a rough one, Christie. A girl. Rough."

Sam Farrell extracted a copy of the report, folded it into a wad and stuffed it into his jacket pocket. "Yeah, that was a mess, from what we hear. Stabbed." His bandaged index finger pointed at his chest and throat. "Gee, maybe forty, forty-five times. Hell of a way to go. Marty's down on that now."

Christie stiffened. Marty was with Dudley. Dudley the Dude. "What girl?"

"Name of Sondra or . . . Celia. Yeah. She was one of Bill Dudley's sources. Hey, yeah, that's right, you met her, didn't you, Christie?"

Christie nodded, then, impulsively she reached out and caught Farrell's arm. "My God, Sam, why? Why were they all murdered?"

Farrell's eyebrows shifted up his forehead. "Well, they can't have it both ways, I guess. These two guys who were giving bits and pieces of information to Pat and Marty, for instance. Played it too cozy for their own health, I guess. They told the fellas that the market in narcotics has tightened up lately. Very, very tight." Farrell disregarded the dead informants. The only thing important about them was the information they had relayed. "We checked with the Narcotics Bureau, local, state and federal. We all been getting the same word: the market's been deliberately dried up, so that when the stuff arrives, it will cost, but plenty.

This isn't any penny-ante stuff, Christie. This will run into millions and millions. The feds have been getting word from the West Coast too, like Frisco and L.A. and San Diego. Even from Seattle. Plus what we've been getting here and from Jersey and a couple of southern ports." He blinked, noticed the expression on her face. "And, well, these guys who've been feeding the information, I guess they must have got too careless. But anyway, from all we've learned, the information has been pretty accurate. Stands up so far."

"But the girl, this Celia. She was just . . . a very sad girl. She didn't tell us anything about the narcotics operation. She was just very pathetic."

"Well, she's just very dead now."

Bill Ferranti frowned. "Christie, we're going in the field now. Want me to send some tea up from the luncheonette?"

"No. Thanks, Bill. It just doesn't make sense. All the killing. The girl, particularly."

Detective Bill Ferranti was a kind and a sensitive man. He nodded his agreement. "None of it makes any sense when you get right down to it. All this killing, all this violence. Sometimes, this job makes me sick."

The office seemed unnaturally quiet after the men left. The phones didn't ring; Tom Dell sat quietly laboring over the gas and mileage report he was required to submit each day relative to the use of Reardon's car. Christie walked to the window, looked down at the wet gray streets. Rain was coming down again in uneven, windblown slashes.

"Hey, Tom, when do you think I might get in to see Mr. Reardon?"

Dell rubbed his chin, made a clicking sound deep in his throat. "I'd advise you to wait, Christie. Things are getting pretty tight."

Christie scanned the morning newspaper. The murder of the two men was reported briefly and described as typical gangland killings. The girl's death was sensationalized and covered in carefully lurid detail. The picture of Celia Kendall was obviously several years old and bore little resemblance to the girl Christie had met. It could have been the picture of any of a hundred girls with aspirations for a glamorous career: the tall, buxom body was vulgarly displayed by a too-small bikini; the face, featureless, turned archly, chin resting on a raised shoulder. The caption read: "Former starlet brutally stabbed." Starlet. She had probably reached Hollywood, gotten inside of one studio. Christie tossed the newspaper on the desk and walked quickly down the corridor to Casey Reardon's office. She tapped twice and entered without waiting for a response.

"Mr. Reardon, could I see you for a minute? I have something that might be important."

Reardon and Stoner Martin turned from the windowsill. There was a collection of papers along the sill and Stoner was jotting down notes on a lined legal pad.

"Not just now, Christie. We're up to our ears." He turned back, his finger stabbed a line of print. "I want this guy checked out. You got Treadwell in the field or what?"

"He's over in Narcotics."

"Yeah. Well, let's get some additional people. We're too damn shorthanded around here. Get the precinct detectives in on this. Call Captain Morrison and tell him—" Reardon turned abruptly. "Christie, what do you want? Can't it wait?"

Christie took the photographs from the envelope clutched in her hand and spread them across Reardon's desk. "Mr. Reardon, I think we might have something here. *Really* something. Take a look at these."

Reardon whistled between his teeth, leaned forward and scowled at the photographs which were totally meaningless to him. "Well, what is it?"

"Well, that's *supposed* to be Elena and her son. But it isn't really. That's the part that's important."

Casey Reardon drew his dark red eyebrows close together. He roughly massaged his eyes for a moment, then, eyes still closed, he told her, "Pull this together for me, Christie. Make it fast and to the point, okay?"

"Right. Elena had a child. A boy. First she told me that she'd

140

had an abortion, but I had a feeling that . . ." Christie felt the pressure of the glazed amber eyes and she tried to pull the information tightly together. She waved her hand rapidly, dismissing the details of her investigation. "Anyway, Elena Vargas had a son. And the important thing is that Enzo Giardino thinks that *these* are pictures of her and her son. But they aren't. That's what Elena wanted him to think. *Her* son was adopted. This boy is some kid named Raphael. Probably one of her cousin's children. In Puerto Rico."

She didn't need Reardon's expression to tell her she wasn't making much sense. She took a long, steadying breath, then said, "Enzo Giardino gave me those pictures yesterday. He said I was to give them to Elena and that it was a 'friendly' gesture on his part, but of course, the threat was implied. That's obvious. But Elena is a lot smarter than Giardino gave her credit for and . . ."

Reardon covered his eyes with his hand and shook his head as though to clear it. Then, he held his hand up to her. "Hold it, right there. Say that again, because I'm not sure I heard you right the first time."

Stoner Martin turned from the window and both men stared at her. Finally, they were listening. Christie felt excitement race through her. She *had* latched on to something. "Okay. The point is that Elena wanted Giardino to think that this boy," she pointed, "the one in the picture, is really her son but . . . "

Reardon's voice was clear and District-Attorney-sharp now. "No, skip all that. Who did you say gave you those pictures?"

"Enzo Giardino. He said that it was a 'friendly' gesture, but . . . "

"Hold it a minute, okay? *Enzo Giardino* gave *you* those pictures of Elena?"

"Yes. Well, he's out on bail isn't he? I mean, I assumed he was out on bail."

He nodded. "Yeah. He's out on bail. No, just wait and answer my questions. When did you see Enzo Giardino? And where?"

Christie slowed down with difficulty and despite several interruptions, she told Reardon about Giardino and the pictures.

She tried to tell him about her conversation with the Mother Superior and the fact that Elena's son had been adopted, but Reardon seemed to tune out. He kept going back to Giardino and his car.

"Was anybody else in the car with you. Besides Giardino?"

Christie's mouth pulled down. "Yes. Well, not in the car actually, but outside the car. Some little creep named Tonio. He's a real Neanderthal type; terrible beady little eyes and . . . "

Reardon slumped into his chair. "Holy Christ," he said.

Stoner Martin lit a cigarette and didn't realize he already had one going until he put the match into the ashtray on Reardon's desk.

"Well, can I tell you the rest of it now? You see, I think we might be on to something. If we can find out who Elena's real child is, we can use that information to our advantage. I think she'd tell us anything we wanted to know, you know about Giardino's operation and the ledger and all. . . ."

"You know something, Christie?" Reardon said quietly. "You need a keeper. Jesus Christ. Stoney, did you ever hear of anything like this?" He turned back to Christie and his face was angry, his words ridiculing her. "What the hell is the matter with you? You got into a car with Enzo Giardino . . . "

"Well, I had my gun in my pocket. And I didn't get into the car until that Tonio character was gone." She bit the inside of her cheeks and matched his anger. "I felt we were evenly matched."

Reardon started to speak, stopped and gnawed on his thumb, then reached for one of Stoner's lit cigarettes. He rarely smoked and didn't seem aware of what he was doing. He spoke to Stoner. "She thought they were evenly matched."

Her hands clenched the back of the chair and she tried to control her anger. "I happen to think that I've found the key to Elena. That's what you told me to do, wasn't it? If you would just *listen* to me for a moment . . . "

Reardon stood up abruptly and reached for a folder from the windowsill. He leaned across the desk and thrust the folder at her. "Open it. Go ahead, sit down and open it and take a good long look at those pictures."

They were photographs of a nude woman. Her body was covered with small wounds and from each wound, a long, dark rivulet of blood ran downward to join a thick, heavy pool on the carpet beside the body. The head was thrown back and a mass of dark hair covered most of the face. There were a series of punctures along the throat, the breasts, the stomach, the arms and thighs.

It was Celia: not as Christie had seen her, not as the news photographs had shown her.

She looked up at Reardon when he spoke. "That's the girl we spoke to, Dudley's contact. In a matter of hours, we should have enough evidence to pick up that . . . what did you call him? . . . that 'Neanderthal little creep,' Tonio." He gestured impatiently at Stoney, who handed him another folder which he tossed to Christie. "Here. This is 'Tonio-the-creep' LoMarco. Take a look at his arrest record." He leaned forward, pulled a yellow sheet from the folder and read, "Assault and robbery, 1961: dismissed. Rape, 1961: dismissed. Assault with intent to kill, 1963: mistrial." He glanced up from the paper. "A couple of key witnesses 'disappeared' while that case was on trial. And so on and so on. Fifteen arrests in all, one conviction for a misdemeanor. And Tonio LoMarco is as clean as a newborn baby when compared to Mr. Enzo Giardino. Twelve separate arrests for homicide, and not one conviction. Ten arrests for various and sundry felonies and misdemeanors: no convictions." Reardon's hand moved roughly across his forehead, down his face, along the back of his neck. "And you got into a car with him; you felt you were 'evenly matched.' "

Christie put the photographs of the dead girl back into the folder and placed it on Reardon's desk. She ignored the almost contemptuous tone, ignored everything he had just told her. "But all of that is beside the point. The point is that I think we've finally got something we can use. To get Elena to talk."

"Christie, as of right now, you are off this case. Go on home. Take care of your cold. Go on sick leave, but go home. Right now."

"You have to be kidding. What about . . . what about the pictures? And what I've found out and . . ."

Reardon gathered the photographs of Elena and the boy and put them into the envelope. "Here. Take them."

"But . . . what about Elena?"

There was a short, sharp whistling sound and Reardon's voice was tight. "Forget about Elena. She doesn't know a goddamn thing. Look, Elena was a red herring, to throw us off. We wasted enough time on her. We've got other things going in this investigation, Christie. Elena was just one facet and we drew a blank with her. Giardino's been playing games with us. Now just do what I tell you and forget it."

Christie absently felt the contours of the envelope, her fingers outlining the thickness of the photographs. He was wrong. She shook her head. "No, Mr. Reardon. We can't just drop it now. You *told* me to find something we could use with Elena. And that's just what I did and . . . "

Reardon hit the surface of his desk with the flat of his hand. "Okay, now you listen. This is a direct order, Detective Opara. *You are off this case.* As of right now. You go home and stay there until you are notified otherwise. *You got that?*"

Christie clutched the envelope so tightly that she could feel the photographs bending and cracking under the pressure. She could see Reardon's face through a shimmer of hot, heavy tears and she blinked rapidly. "Yes, sir, Mr. Reardon. Whatever you say, sir."

She left the office quickly without looking back but she grasped the doorknob outside the room and slammed the door hard.

14

Christie sat in the phone booth and pressed the dime between her thumb and index finger. If it had been anyone else's lead, Reardon would have followed through on it. It was a good lead, carefully developed. Damn Reardon and his peculiar moods. Elena had been his idea in the first place. He was the one who had made such a big deal about her. It was impossible to figure him out. One minute he. . . . Well, that was his problem.

She held the dime poised over the coin slot for a moment, then dropped it in, waited for the dial tone. She was not about to abandon her part of the investigation. Carefully, she dialed the number. After four rings, an unfamiliar voice answered.

"Bureau of Special Services, Detective Rhodes."

"Is Detective Krupp there?"

"Hold it a minute." She waited, listened intently to the background office sounds.

"Detective Krupp."

"Hey, Hank, boy, am I glad you're in. This is Christie Opara."

"Hey, Christie, how's things? Listen, kid, you just caught me. I'm on my way uptown."

"Are you going by subway? Look, I'm right down the street. Can you meet me for about ten minutes, Hank? It's important. The coffee shop on Canal Street, okay?"

Christie leaned against the cold plastic seat and carefully stirred a small amount of milk into her tea. Henry Krupp had an ageless face: he had probably never looked really young and would probably never look really old. He was a grandfather four times over, yet his face was unlined, his hair dark, his body lean and his curiosity sharp. He had been Christie's regular partner for the two years she had worked in the Bureau of Special Services and they had worked well together, carefully building and maintaining the special mutual respect and trust essential to a smoothly functioning investigative team.

"I'm sorry to have to rush you, Christie, but I figured this wasn't for reminiscences."

"Right. Hank, I need some information. Something very tight."

Krupp continued pouring sugar into his coffee and nodded. "Okay. What?"

"I need the name and address of a family who adopted a child." She tore a page from her spiral notebook. "Here's all the information I have. I assume the adoption took place in Westchester County."

Krupp stirred his coffee and shook his head. "That's practically impossible. Chris, couldn't the D.A. do this with a subpoena or by application or something?"

"Hank, I haven't got time to go into details. This is a very touchy area and would get tied up going through channels. I need it right away. Like yesterday morning."

Krupp reached for the slip of paper and studied it. "I get the feeling that this is off the cuff." She nodded. "As I said, Christie, this is next to impossible."

Christie smiled. "That's why I came to you, old buddy."

As soon as Christie touched the iron to the shirt, she realized it was too hot. A wide yellow burn mark outlined the shape of the iron. She glanced at the label on the shirt: Dacron. And the iron was set for cotton. She tossed the damp shirt back into the laundry basket and checked the next shirt: polyester and cotton. She set the indicator to the proper heat and waited for the iron to cool off. The kitchen was filled with small shirts, hanging from various cabinet knobs and the backs of chairs. There was a neat pile of freshly pressed blouses and cotton turtleneck sweaters and jeans on the kitchen table. Christie was surprised at how much work she had accomplished. Her mind hadn't been on the laundry.

She was filled with words she *should* have said and with words Reardon *had* said and with too many other things. Among them, a fact Reardon might have forgotten, but she hadn't. She was a first-grade detective. It was a rating she had earned solely on merit and that was how she was going to keep it. What other first-grade detective would get dumped off a case just when things started to open up? And he had been complaining about being shorthanded. Was using precinct detectives. But had told her to go home. And had been so nasty about it . . .

There was a faint stirring in the laundry basket, then a rapid series of movements. Christie lifted a damp shirt. Sweet William was asleep, stretched comfortably on the pile of clean clothing. His back legs jerked rapidly in a series of running motions, then stopped, and his large, vacant green eyes snapped open.

Christie knelt and petted the cat, then lifted him carefully and placed him on the tiled floor. "Sweet William, you really do smell pretty sour. You're going to smell up all those nice clean clothes." The cat stared at her, then pushed against her legs. Christie took a large bath mat and spread it in the corner of the room. "Come on over and sleep here." She dove for the cat as he leaped into the laundry basket. There was a deep rumble along his throat. "You better not be growling at me, dumb-dumb, because I'm not going to take growling from anyone else today. Especially not you." She settled the fat animal on the mat; he stretched, locked his eyes shut and within a minute he was back into his dream. The stubby back legs began their pursuit again.

Christie licked the tip of her finger, then touched it to the iron. There was a faint sizzle. She reached for the shirt, then changed her mind. The heck with it. She'd done enough for now. She put the ironing equipment away and began collecting clothes.

Mickey's little shirts looked starchy and fresh. He had gone to bed early, falling asleep the minute his head hit the pillow. She had done a lot of thinking about Giardino and his remark about her son. Where Mickey was concerned, she would take no chances, but she was convinced it had been a throwaway remark. To scare her. Giardino had nothing whatever to gain by threatening her or her son. But still, she was glad that she had arranged for Mickey to spend the weekend out on Long Island with her brother, Christopher, and his family. It would work out perfectly. Christopher was coming into the city early Saturday morning to have his youngest son's eyes checked. He'd pick Mickey up on the way home and Christie would bring him back Sunday night. Nora was going to Boston for the weekend to visit her sister's new granddaughter.

And if Casey Reardon thought she was afraid of Enzo Giardino or that creepy little Tonio . . .

Christie carried the freshly ironed clothing across the kitchen and toward the hallway. The hangers cut into the palm of her right hand and she couldn't adjust them. She balanced the large stack of folded clothing against her body and pressed her chin down on the top of the bundle. The telephone rang as she reached the stairs.

Nora called out at the second ring. "Want me to get it, Christie?"

"Would you please, Nora? I'm loaded down."

Nora met her at the top of the stairs. "It's Hank Krupp. Here, let me take those things."

‍· Christie snatched a piece of paper from her dresser and cradled the telephone against her shoulder. "Hank, did you get it?"

"Sorry to call so late, Christie, but it's the first chance I've had. Listen, you working on that narcotics thing? I didn't realize who Elena Vargas was when I saw you this morning."

Christie dug in the drawer of her night table for a pencil or a pen. All she could find was a fuchsia Crayola crayon. "Hank, I'm working on bits and pieces. You know: a bit of this and a piece of that."

"Okay, Christie. I got what you wanted."

It was a clear, bright, hard, clean winter day. Christie turned the heater down to low. When it was set on high, a scorching blast raced up her legs in one concentrated stream and the rest of the Volkswagen was frigid. The Westchester roads had been plowed and sanded and the accumulation of snow surprised her. What had been rain and sleet in the city had been heavy snow in the suburbs. Christie exited from the Thruway carefully, then pulled up outside of a diner to study her map. County Meadow Road was off the main street, not five minutes' drive away. It was five after eight and, if she had calculated correctly, she had plenty of time.

Christie went into the diner and ordered a cup of tea, then asked the waitress, a pretty young girl whose long hair kept slipping free of the little starched cap, "Miss, could you tell me where the elementary school is?"

The girl's voice was early-morning thick. She adjusted her cap with a languid motion. "Depends. On which one you mean."

That was something she hadn't thought about: that there might be more than one elementary school in the area. "Well, I'm not too sure which one it would be. You see, my husband and I have been looking at a house on County Meadow Road. Our children are in the elementary grades. Which school would they go to?"

The girl nodded. "Oh, yeah, that would be the John Marshall School. Over on Allenby Place. The reason I asked is, see, the district line runs right along Main Road, but John Marshall is the school you want. On Allenby Place right off Parker's Lane. You going there now?"

"Well, I thought I'd like to take a look around. It seems like such a nice community, but I want to check on the school."

"Won't do you much good today. They're closed today. All the schools are closed today in Allenby. That's how come I'm working. It's good for me, cause I get to put in a whole day. Usually, I just work after school and on weekends."

"What do you mean, the schools are closed today?"

"It's county conference day. Like, all the teachers and the principals and the school boards and P.T.A. and like that, get together and discuss the curriculum." The girl added morosely, "Uh, only ones they don't include are the students and we're the only ones really concerned."

Christie pushed a quarter on the counter and left the cup of tea untouched. Swell. Great. She had been planning to sit outside the address on County Meadow Road until the boy left for school. Which would have been at around eight-thirty. Except there was no school today. Because of county conference day, whatever the heck that was.

There went the whole plan. The whole thing. Her hand went to the camera with the zoom lens. It would have been easy, routine observation. Spot the boy. Drive to the school and wait for him. Shoot a roll of film from an inconspicuous location. No one would notice her. She wouldn't be loitering around his house. It had been perfect. Now what?

Christie warmed the motor and sat staring vacantly. It was Friday. School wouldn't be open again until Monday. Three days lost. She couldn't afford the time. Not from the way the Squad seemed to be moving. She drove to the school. It was a huge, one-story complex of buildings set way back from the main road in a field of snow. And it definitely had a closed look about it.

Okay. So it wasn't going to be easy. If one plan doesn't work, you find another that does. Hank Krupp had taught her that. Carefully, she made a U-turn and followed the road signs.

The house on County Meadow Road was a neat, two-story colonial, white with blue shutters. There was a large snowman on the front lawn with straw hair and button eyes and a carrot mouth. It was a nice day. The kind of day made to order for a kid who didn't have school. If he wasn't sick or bedded down with a broken leg.

She drove past the house and parked half a block away. One lucky thing: it was an older neighborhood, complete with sidewalks and other parked cars. It would have been impossible to remain inconspicuous in a cul-de-sac. Christie kept the map in her hand so that if anyone became curious about her presence, she could study the map. She glanced in the rear-view mirror, her attention caught by the honking of a horn.

A large dark-blue station wagon pulled up directly in front of her subject's house. She turned and looked directly through the back window. The station wagon was filled with children. A boy darted from the house into the station wagon. Christie started her motor. She hadn't even glimpsed what color jacket he wore.

She kept a fair distance from the station wagon until they hit the main road, then kept one car between them. It occurred to her more than once that a bright red Volkswagen was not the ideal car for a tail job. The station wagon made two sharp right turns, then a left that led directly to a parking area bordering a frozen lake. Scattered along the edge of the lake were small green tents and little banners proclaiming what particular group occupied what particular area.

Christie glanced at the skaters and her heart sank: they were all dressed in Cub Scout uniforms and they all wore blue quilted jackets. About ten boys tumbled from the station wagon: their arm patches designated them as members of Den 4. Christie got out of her car and quickly surveyed the area. It was a hell of a day for a camp-out or skate-out or whatever. The lake area was alive with young boys, pink-faced, red-eared, carrying skates slung over their shoulders, lugging camping equipment, squatting over sputtering fires, shrieking, laughing, complaining, arguing, tussling. The air was filled with their voices and sporadically with snowballs, followed by complaints and wishful admonitions from the few adults present.

Den 4 was loaded down with equipment. The scout leader, a stout, bald man, was very red in the face. Each time he leaned into the wagon and came out with another pair of skates or another knapsack, he turned a little brighter.

Christie got back into her car, smoked a cigarette and watched her den's leader confer with someone who seemed to be, more or less, in charge. Then he led the boys to the location where they were to be settled. They dumped everything where he indicated, then all the boys turned and ran to the long, low wooden canteen building. Christie thought of joining them, but she had seen a steady parade of boys marching in and out of the canteen. She would wait.

Her hands moved absently over the camera and she closed her eyes: closed out all the little boys dressed in their identical uniforms. There was only one small boy she wanted to see: the son of Elena Vargas. There was a way to find him without anyone being aware of what she was doing.

There was a way. It would come. She had to relax and not let tension or anxiety block the cool, professional train of thought. In the diner. Something in the diner. She visualized the girl, the counter, the cup of tea. The newspaper on the counter. The *Allenby News*. One of those small, very local newspapers. Dedicated to reporting all of those small, very local news events. Like a Cub Scout Skate-Out on Lake Draco. At least, that's what the banner over the canteen proclaimed.

Christie saw Den 4 come back to their site. She flexed her fingers, dug her library card from her wallet and put it into her coat pocket. She slung the camera over her shoulder and took a deep breath. She waited until the man in charge was sufficiently besieged by complaining scout leaders, shivering mothers and vociferous, healthy young scouts.

She thrust her leather-gloved hand at him. "How do you do, sir. I'm Virginia Kilby. Of the *Allenby News*." She flashed her library card quickly, in confirmation of her words, then slipped it back in her pocket. "I'm here to shoot the troops!" She gave a sudden, arch little laugh. "May I start with you? You know, directing things?"

The man regarded Christie blankly for a moment, then, distracted by horseplay practically under his feet, he scolded several boys, warning them of demerits for their den. Finally, he turned to her. "Look, could you get around to me later? I mean, we'll be here, God, all day long. Get me later, when we're better organized, Miss . . . er . . . "

"Kilby. Virginia Kilby. And may I have your name?"

"Frisby. George Frisby. Excuse me, please. Now listen, you fellas, I'm not going to give you too many more chances . . . "

She started with the group of boys nearest to her: arranged them in a grinning, leering, face-making semicircle. The tallest boy held the banner proudly until just before she clicked the shutter. Then his face twisted into a grotesque leer. Charming child, Christie thought. She reached for her notebook. "Now, no one move. I'll go around the group and get you in order, so we'll know who you are. For the newspaper. In case we decide to print your den's picture."

"Here, here, now, just a minute. What's this all about?"

The leader of the pack, an intent, dark-browed man with the build of a wrestler, scowled at Christie, then at Den 4, who kept the places she had assigned them.

Her smile was quick and relaxed. "How do you do. I'm Virginia Kilby, the photographer. For the *Allenby News*."

The information did nothing to change the challenging expression.

Christie waved her hand to Mr. Frisby. "George Frisby knows all about it. Didn't he tell you?"

"George Frisby thinks that just because he's been appointed temporary leader of the area . . . he never told *me* about the photographs. Maybe he told the other leaders, but he didn't tell me. I'm going to straighten that guy out before the day is over. First, he tells us there won't be any snacking before noon. And did you see the kids marching on that canteen? Ah, the hell with it."

No other leader interfered with Christie in any way. Her fingers were stiff and numb by the time she got to Den 4. It seemed that she was taking the same picture, over and over again: the same semicircle, the same clowning, the same faces in the same uniforms.

"Okay, don't move now. Please stay exactly as you were until I write your names down."

Elena's son was the fourth boy from the left. He had light-brown hair, a fair complexion reddened by the cold, fine features and huge black eyes which had an unexpected upward slant, and long, familiar black lashes. He jabbed his elbow sharply into the ribs of the boy next to him. He stopped roughhousing only long enough to give Christie his name.

"Richard C. Arvin, Junior."

It was the only name that mattered.

She went through the motions: photographed two more dens, wrote down names. She spent the next hour taking candid shots of the skaters: she didn't even need the zoom lens. She shot right out in the open: Elena's son at the end of a crack-the-whip; hunched over his den's campfire; as he relaced his skates; as he glanced up, directly into the camera, smiling; as he picked himself up from a spill on the ice; as he looked, impatiently, over his shoulder for a friend.

She tossed the camera into the front seat beside her, warmed up the motor, watched the energetic boys for a moment, thought of Mickey, shuddered once, emptied her mind and drove home.

15

Edgar Katz was a lanky boy of eighteen who
had only recently grown used to his stiltlike legs.
He was beginning to overcome his adolescent stoop, despite his
mother's nagging.

"Put your shoulders back, you're going to be a hunchback,"
Harriet Katz informed her son.

Edgar ran a bony hand through his shaggy long hair and ignored his mother. "Christie, I thought you were putting me on
when you told me the pictures were for a guy in your squad."

"Edgar," Christie said, "I *told* you it was to surprise one of the
fellows. You didn't want to believe me."

When she had brought the roll of film to him the previous
night, she told Edgar that she had taken candid snapshots of the
son of one of the detectives she worked with: that it was to be a
surprise birthday present. The young amateur photographer had
regarded her with a surge of secretive enthusiasm, assuring her
he could be trusted in a confidential police matter. Finally, Christie told him that the roll of film contained pictures of a notorious
car thief at work and that the careful development of these pictures could lead to his immediate capture and incarceration.

"See, Edgar, you never believe when someone tells you something. You'd rather believe a make-believe fairy tale. Why would
Christie lie to you? Stand up straight. Christie, eat some of that
pie. You're playing with your fork." Mrs. Katz, mother of five,
automatically mothered everyone who came into her home. It
was easier to eat the pie than to protest that ten A.M. was a little
early for such a rich dessert.

Christie felt a mild, passing guilt at the stories she had told to

155

Edgar: that too was part of her profession. Tell a story, any story, as long as it is believed. Sometimes, she lost track of what really was true.

"Ed, you're really getting professional. The pictures are good."

Harriet Katz glanced at the photographs. "A cute little boy. This is the son of one of your partners? It's a shame they're all married."

"This is Tommy O'Hanlon. You met his father, Pat O'Hanlon, remember, when they stopped by a few weeks ago to take Mickey ice skating? That's right, you didn't see Tommy, he waited in the car."

The woman didn't really notice the face in the pictures. Her eyes watched for the stoop, the hunch, the motionless fork. "Did Edgar really do a good job? This looks a little blurred. You're not eating, Christie. They got you working even on a Saturday?" She shook her head. "They give you crazy hours. Not even weekends off. I saw Nora leave in a taxicab. She's going to Boston? She told me yesterday. And your brother came for Mickey before? Listen, if you're lonely tonight, come over and you'll have supper with us. Edgar, stand up. You look like you're shrinking."

16

It was four o'clock and nearly dark when Christie arrived at the hotel on Park Avenue. The sky was a somber, heavy, impenetrable gray. The brief spell of clear weather was apparently over and Christie felt an aching coldness across her shoulders. She watched a mink-clad woman come from the hotel, walk to the nearest lamp post and carefully deposit a tiny, blanketed poodle at its base. The little dog shivered for a moment before the woman carried it farther down the street.

Christie walked past the hotel, around the corner to the street entrance to the coffee shop. Now that she was so close, she felt a sense of caution. It would not be particularly pleasant to run into either Casey Reardon or Stoner Martin. Not at this point. She went into a phone booth, dialed the hotel desk and asked for Suite 16A. She wanted to find out who was on duty upstairs.

"Who's calling, please?" the desk clerk asked after a moment's pause.

"This is Detective Opara, of the District Attorney's Squad."

"Well, then, surely you know . . . "

"Look, could you just connect me with the suite."

"Well, I could but there's no one there."

"What do you mean, no one there?"

The desk clerk became cautious. "I am sorry, but I'm not at liberty to give out any information over the telephone."

Christie hung up abruptly, walked through the coffee shop and emerged inside the lobby of the hotel. It was warm and elegant and quiet. There was a group of well-dressed men seated in a discrete cluster. They rose soundlessly as a beautiful woman, dressed in a candy-satin, figure-revealing gown, came toward

157

them from the elevator. She was trailed by a pasty-complexioned, tall thin man who kept his eyes on the carpet.

"Sit down, fellas, sit down, sit down. Let's get the conference over with, okay? I got a dinner engagement."

Christie recognized the woman as a very well-known film star. And the pasty-faced thin man as her husband. She didn't think he was her dinner date.

The woman with the mink coat entered the lobby, the little dog huddled against her. "Jack, would you have Henry take Boo-Boo out for a walk in about an hour? Boo-Boo has some 'unfinished business' to attend to, right darling?" She pressed her face against the little blanketed body.

The room clerk made a notation on his pad and nodded. His eyes fastened on Christie and his smile held. "May I help you, Miss?"

She held her palm out and showed him her detective's shield. "Did I just speak to you on the phone? I'm Detective Opara."

"Why, yes. But . . . where did you pop up from?"

Christie ignored his confusion. "Why isn't there anyone in Suite 16A? Look, I've been upstate for the last few days and haven't been in touch with my office. Where's Elena Vargas?"

The room clerk looked around, then leaned forward. His lips barely moved as he spoke: he was being confidential. "Why, so far as I know, Miss Vargas was . . . I believe the word is 'bailed' out. At any rate, her lawyer came this afternoon and they left together. The detective, I believe it was Mr. Farrell . . . the gentleman with the bandaged hand? . . . he stopped at the desk and said that your squad wanted the suite held for the time being but that Miss V . . . wouldn't be staying there. I don't mind telling you that I am relieved. This is hardly the type of hotel that encourages 'guests' of that type."

The burst of laughter from the other side of the lobby was loud and female and dangerously close to hysteria. The room clerk closed his eyes for a moment, then whispered to Christie, "We could do without *her* too. But her studio keeps a number of rooms on a permanent basis. What can we do?"

158

"There isn't *anyone* up there now?"

He turned, indicated the key hanging on the board behind them. "If you want to go upstairs, you may, of course."

Christie shook her head. "No. No, thanks very much."

As she passed the group, Christie had a better look at the movie star: she was loud and slightly drunk but, Christie noted with some slight disappointment, she was even more beautiful than in her films.

It was seven short blocks downtown and three long crosstown blocks to Elena Vargas's apartment. Christie walked rapidly, her hands deep inside her pockets, her eyes straight ahead. She noticed an occasional umbrella, but the snow was light and scattered and the air had warmed a bit. A taxicab jumped the light, edged close to the sidewalk and sent a spray of black slush against her legs. Christie brushed at her boots and coat with tissues, then felt a cold lump of ice press inside her boot against her ankle. She balled the wad of tissues into a tight missile which she tossed into a wire wastebasket on the corner of the street.

The lump of ice was a cold dull wetness against her foot by the time she reached the tall, gleaming white brick apartment house where Elena Vargas lived. This might be the only opportunity she would have to speak to Elena alone. The doorman had his back turned toward the entrance. He was speaking on the intercom telephone and didn't see Christie as she entered the building. Music, the same as she had heard in the lobby previously, swept through the large expanse softly. The elevator was waiting for her touch on the button and the door slid open. She hesitated for a moment, then remembered, and touched the square over the number nine.

Christie slid her fingers inside her shoulder bag and felt the contours of the envelope containing the pictures of Elena's son. She would have to handle this meeting precisely right, yet she still could not anticipate how it would go. It would just *have* to go: she would play it by ear, instinctively. Absently, she unbuckled the change compartment on the outside of her pocketbook and looked down in surprise. The envelope of pictures that Enzo Giardino had given her, and which Casey Reardon had tossed back at her, was still there. She redid the buckle as the elevator door opened.

Christie blinked at her reflection in the small, square mirrored peephole, but it was difficult to see more than the outline of her face. She heard the echo of chimes through the interior of the apartment, then the soft click as she was observed through the two-way mirror.

The door to Elena Vargas's apartment opened swiftly and Tonio LoMarco stepped to one side. His eyes were bright and his thin lips pulled back into an unpleasant smile.

"Come on in, Detective Opara."

17

Casey Reardon let the telephone ring one more time, then smashed the receiver back into place. He searched randomly through the morass of papers on his desk, then glanced at his watch. He depressed the button on the intercom. "Stoney, come on in here."

Stoner Martin knew the answer before he asked his question. "Still didn't reach Christie?"

"No. Where the hell could she be? We've been sitting on that phone most of the day."

"Well," Stoner said reasonably, "you did tell her to take off. Maybe that's what she did—took off."

"You her mouthpiece or something?" Casey demanded brusquely. He rubbed the back of his neck. "Sorry, Stoney. Damn it, she should have called in. Give her number a ring periodically, right? Now, what have you got for me?"

He reached for the typed papers, scanned them as he listened to Stoner's verbal report.

"That's Pat O'Hanlon's report from his waterfront contact. There seems to be a definite pattern. Sam Farrell's over at the Bureau of Narcotics and their information jibes with what we've been getting. The word is out along the waterfront that something 'special' is due to arrive within the next few days. They've got a grapevine like you wouldn't believe. A couple of heavies show up during shape-up. They just 'show up,' wait quietly, don't even expect to work. But it puts the hiring boss on notice. When the time comes, he'll know exactly when to assign them, and where to assign them, without a word being exchanged. No questions asked, no answers given. These guys show up a couple of times a year and work a couple of days each time. They might work just one ship or two or ten. On anything from fragile stuff to imported cars. But when they *do* work, nobody bothers them."

"Does the Narcotics Squad have anybody on the docks? Besides informers, I mean—their own men?"

"They have two: one guy is a real rough character. Actually was a dock-walloper before he came on the job. The other guy is kind of quiet, minds his own business, does his day's work. But both of them have been getting the same vibrations. The general feeling is that something big is going to happen pretty soon."

Stoney leaned forward, ran his hands quickly through the papers on Reardon's desk. "Here, this one. This is a rundown from the Port of New York Authority, Customs Division. Relative to the number of cargo ships due to arrive in New York harbor this coming week." His long dark finger slid down the page. "Approximately forty-two, carrying approximately a zillion and two tons of cargo from ports in Spain, Italy, Morocco, England, Ireland, West Germany and France. Not to mention what cargo might have been picked up prior to the last port of departure. Cargo listed here ranges the whole scale: automobiles to perfume. And this doesn't cover airfreight, which is covered in another report." He searched briefly, pulled out the proper neatly typed information.

Casey Reardon rubbed his fingers into his aching eyes then squinted through the blurred irritation he had caused. "In other words, unless we know where the hell to look, it's a needle in a haystack."

"That's about it, Casey. The customs people will be working like crazy because they've been alerted, but hell," his hand swept over the desk, "with all this material coming in . . . without some good information, as you said, a needle in a haystack. Or lots of needles in lots of haystacks."

Reardon leaned back in his chair, stretched his legs and carefully placed his feet on an opened drawer. He locked his hands behind his head. "Okay. Now, tell me again. What's funny about Elena Vargas?"

162

The detective cupped his hands over a match, inhaled deeply on his cigarette, closed his eyes momentarily against the smoke. "One: too much money. Her own bank account, in the five figures. Two: no trade. She's not earning and Enzo Giardino is not known for his generosity. Three: Giardino is also not known as a great lover, either sexually or sentimentally. What it adds up to is that there is no known reason for him to be keeping Elena Vargas."

Reardon said, "Except that she is somehow vital to his operation. If this goddamn ledger—or alleged ledger—is in Puerto Rico, and if it is the only complete rundown on the whole operation, that means Elena Vargas should be making a trip to Puerto Rico. And very, very pronto."

"Lucky for Ferranti. I wish to hell I spoke Spanish. Why I ever studied German in college I will never know."

Bill Ferranti, fluent in Spanish, had taken the nine P.M. flight to San Juan the previous night. He confirmed, by telephone call that morning, that he had been met at the airport by a top investigator from the San Juan Police Department and by the agent-in-charge of the F.B.I. regional office. Reardon's phone calls to both of these men had been brief and explicit and both had promised complete cooperation.

"Where's Opara's report?" It was always a source of wonder to Reardon that Stoner could immediately find the right papers. "Did Ferranti take a carbon of this with him?"

"Yeah. He'll call again at about eight or eight-thirty tonight. He's located the village where Elena's cousin lives. The locals gave him quite a bit of assistance. By the time he contacts us tonight, he should have some pretty concrete information."

There was a loud bang and thump, followed by a hiss and blast of hot air from the radiator. It hit Reardon's neck. "This goddamn heating system should have been overhauled years ago. We got the maintenance men coming up here any time this winter?"

Stoney shrugged. "They've been notified. It'll have to wait until Monday. We're the only ones who work weekends."

"How's Dudley doing on this little bum, LoMarco?"

"He's working with homicide. LoMarco has about sixteen witnesses who'll swear he spent the night of Celia's murder with them at a card game. There's one possibility though. A weak link. Some guy with a warrant on him from Texas, relative to an old homicide. They're working on him. Depends on what scares him most, LoMarco or Texas."

Reardon reached up impatiently. "Give me one of those damn things, will you Stoney?" He lit the cigarette, handed the matches back to the detective. "Back to Elena. She could still be a red herring. Or not. Damn it. It's the 'or not' that's got me. We could take her all the way to Puerto Rico and back and still not come up with a thing. Or she could be it." He stared through the cigarette smoke for a moment, then rubbed at his eyes. "What was Opara rambling about? About Elena's 'real' kid being adopted. She didn't put anything about that in her report, did she? Why the hell didn't she stick around long enough to bring her reports up to date?"

"As I remember it, boss, you more or less threw her out."

Reardon's eyes hardened into a glassy stare. He stubbed the cigarette out, glanced at his watch and lifted the receiver. The phone rang seven times before he replaced it.

"Stoney," he asked thoughtfully, "if you were Opara, where would you be?"

"Well, I think I'd take my kid and go away for a few days. Anywhere, just to get out of town until Enzo Giardino forgot my name."

"Yeah," Reardon said tersely. "That's what *you'd* do if *you* were Opara. *But you're not.*"

18

Elena Vargas leaned casually against the long walnut stereo unit and ran her tongue around the rim of the glass in her hand. She admired the way Christie Opara dismissed Tonio with a quick, withering look but it was obvious she had expected to find Elena alone.

Enzo Giardino did not seem as physically large as he had in the back seat of his Mercedes, but his face, revealed by the clear light in the room, was harder and more angular.

"I asked you, Detective Opara, what you are doing here?" His tone indicated that he was not accustomed to repeating questions.

Christie shrugged and her shoulder bag slipped to the floor. She picked it up awkwardly. Everything about her felt clumsy and awkward and, automatically, she let that feeling replace the deep grinding fear she had to hold down. And the almost overwhelming anger at her own stupidity: she never should have walked into this.

"Well, Mr. Giardino, I tried to see Elena at the hotel but they told me she wasn't there anymore. I was off yesterday, and nobody tells me anything. I mean, I'm away from my office for one day, everything changes but nobody notifies me."

It was her own voice, but lighter, higher, younger. She didn't risk a glance at Elena; she had to maintain the tempo she was building. She fumbled at her pocketbook. Tonio swiftly placed himself between Christie and Giardino. Wordless, he stood, eyes level with hers. Christie leaned to one side and spoke to Giardino.

"What's he afraid of, Mr. Giardino? I was digging for the pictures you asked me to give Elena."

165

"Tonio!" LoMarco stepped aside but his face was a rigid, totally emotionless mask, his eyes fixed on Christie. "You came here just to give Elena those pictures?"

Christie held out the envelope. "Yes. I've been carrying them around with me since the other night. . . . "

"What pictures?" Elena asked.

Giardino held his hand up, held back her words. "Now, you tell me, Detective Opara, why would you do that? Why would you bother to bring the pictures here?"

"Well," Christie said, "if they were *my* pictures, I'd want to have them." She glanced at Elena. "So, I figured that Elena would want to have them."

"No," Giardino said softly, "no. There is more to it than that. Tonio, go and sit down, you make me nervous. What did your Mr. Reardon say when you told him about the pictures? That I gave you these pictures for Elena."

Automatically, the responses flooded her: mix in enough truth to keep it plausible; don't lie enough to make it obvious.

"Well, Mr. Reardon said I was an idiot for having gotten into the car with you. He can be a very nasty man when he sets his mind to it." The three of them stared at her, waiting. Christie took a deep breath and sounded girlish and young, not only because she strove for that effect but because her nerve was beginning to fail and she kept going, quickly.

"Okay, here's what you want to know. Reardon said the pictures were just a part of some plan or other you had for us to think that Elena was more involved in your activities than she is. That we were supposed to think you were trying to intimidate her, but that I have been more or less wasting my time." She took the pictures out of the envelope and held them toward Elena. "He threw them back at me and practically threw me out of the office." Elena did not move. Christie felt a long, cold stream of perspiration down the center of her spine. "Now, *you* would be wasting *your* time, Mr. Giardino, by asking *me* anything about what Reardon is doing, because I know as much about that as . . . " She stopped suddenly. She was going too fast; too far. Beyond a certain point, she knew she couldn't be

166

convincing. She turned to Elena. "If they were pictures of *my* son, Elena, I'd sure want them."

Elena turned to Giardino. "When did these come, Frank? Why didn't you send them to the hotel?" She reached, her eyes met Christie's for a brief moment, then studied the photographs.

Giardino snapped his fingers at Tonio, who went to the bar and mixed a drink. "I thought you might like to have them, Elena. You haven't seen Raphael in a while. They change so rapidly, boys his age, and you don't want to forget him." He sipped the drink and nodded his satisfaction to Tonio.

Elena whispered something in Spanish, her face down as she studied the pictures. "You didn't have to do this, Frank," she said. Her eyes had brightened, her voice went low. "You think there is something wrong with my memory, eh, Frank, so you have to remind me, with these." She held the photographs up before him. "Ah, does my *memory* worry you Frank?"

"Shut up, Elena!" His hand swung back and Christie thought he was going to strike the girl, but Elena stood, unmoving, head held high.

"You don't talk to *me* like that, Enzo Giardino. You talk to that little *animal* over there, like that." She turned to Tonio and snapped her fingers. "Here, Tonio. Run and fetch. Open and close! Go and stay! Stand and sit! To *him*," she said directly to Giardino, "you say shut up, but not to *Elena Vargas!*"

Christie held her breath, tried to calculate not only what would happen next but what she would do next. Tonio regarded Elena stonily, nothing registered, nothing showed.

Giardino's jawline worked: there was a pulling and a tensing and his sallow face seemed darker. His effort at control was obvious, the words he spoke were not the words he wanted to speak.

"Elena, don't you think Tonio has any feelings? Those are not nice things to say about him."

Elena moved to Tonio, stood directly in front of him. "Do you have feelings, animal? Eh? What kind of feelings? What gives you your kicks, baby?" She leaned her head back, so that her throat was exposed. "Wouldn't it be fun, Tonio?" With her index finger she jabbed along her throat and into her breasts. "Bam,

bam, a little at a time. Look at him, Enzo. Look at his face. Nothing gets to him except . . . "

Christie's thigh slammed into a table. She had been moving, carefully edging around them so that there would be nothing between her and the door. But Elena's performance had been so extraordinary, had held her attention. The lamp pitched forward and Christie caught it before it hit the floor.

They all turned to her, as though she had been forgotten. Enzo Giardino seemed filled with rage, but a rage deeper than any Christie could have caused him. She sensed this; he turned on her because he could not, for some reason, turn on Elena.

"Ah, you. You detective." His voice was filled with scorn. "You're a filthy little liar, that's what you are. Out there," he moved a thumb over his shoulder, "out there they make you feel like a big shot, eh? They give you a gun that shoots real bullets and a shiny little badge. You didn't come up here to give Elena those pictures, so don't think I believe your crap about that." He slowed down, seemed to regain control of himself. He took a careful swallow from his glass and turned to Tonio. "You make the drink just right, Tonio. Just right." His eyes, half closed, hooded, moved slowly from Tonio to Christie. He jerked his head toward the door. "All right, little big shot. You go now."

Christie moved uncertainly, then stopped and looked directly at Enzo Giardino. "Sorry to have bothered you, Mr. Giardino. Goodbye, Elena."

She heard the fingers snap behind her but didn't look back: she couldn't look back. Tonio reached the door before she did. He opened the door and stepped back.

"Thank you, Tonio," Christie said.

Then Enzo Giardino was at the door and Tonio was in the hallway with her. His voice was a low hissing sound. "Tonio will ride down in the elevator with you."

Christie shook her head. "No. No, that won't be necessary."

Giardino's face, in the shadows, was haggard and hollowed by some terrible hunger. "Yes," he told her softly. "It *will* be necessary. It's a long way down to the street. You never know what kind of creep might be prowling around a large building like this. *Tonio will take care of you.*" The door slammed shut and Christie heard the chain lock slide into place.

The hall was long and narrow and low ceilinged. The musty odor of cleaning fluid rose from the carpeted floor. The light was dim and under the relentless soft music which emanated from unseen speakers there was virtually no sound.

They were in an isolated, insulated, heavy-aired tubular chamber. Tonio stayed to her right and Christie paced herself so that he was slightly ahead of her. He pushed at the elevator button. Christie looked for an exit. She would be better off racing down the nine flights of stairs than getting into an elevator with Tonio. *Tonio the creep.* Maybe there would be other people on the elevator. Maybe . . .

The elevator was empty. Christie heard herself swallow but her mouth and throat were dry. Tonio pushed a button, but she couldn't see which button. Her eyes went to the button marked "B." Maybe he'd pushed the basement button. Maybe. Maybe not.

There was no room to move. Anything she tried to do, he could block. God. Reardon was right. She was an idiot. She did need a keeper. She needed Casey Reardon, right now.

Tonio LoMarco leaned against the elevator wall, folded his arms across his chest and watched her. There was a glow in his bright eyes and they moved rapidly over her body. His lips parted and he licked at them. It was the most animation he had displayed. His hands dropped to his sides and his fingers flexed. His eyes moved slowly over her, lingered, moved on. He nodded slightly, pulled away from the wall and moved his feet apart. It was a fighter's stance: knees easy, body alert but at the same time relaxed. His head went down a bit, so that when he looked at Christie, it was from beneath his brows, wary and threatening.

"Hey," Tonio said, gravel voiced, *"you ever seen a stiletto?"*

His right hand moved slowly, reached inside his jacket and held. But his eyes moved, rapidly flickered: excited, glowing, stupid monkey eyes intently searching her face for something.

Not the pictures but the face of Celia came to her. Distorted by terror, punctured throat and body, round terrible wounds;

169

stilettoed, by Tonio and Tonio's stiletto. He is looking for my terror. It is what he needs. It is what he wants. She could not let herself think of where she was or what could happen; just of who she was and what must not happen.

Christie pushed herself forward so that she was standing clear, three feet from Tonio. Slowly, deliberately, instinctively refusing his need, she hunched her shoulders forward, balanced with her feet slightly apart. She lowered her head and looked directly at Tonio. Her voice was a surprisingly perfect imitation of his, low and gravelly.

"Nah. I never seen a stiletto. Ya got one ya wanna show me?"

Tonio's small eyes froze. A slow red flush burned upward from his cheeks. He suddenly rubbed the back of his hand across his mouth. "You son of a bitch of a broad," he said. "You son of a bitch of a broad." He rubbed his fist compulsively into the palm of his hand. "What makes you think you're gonna leave this elevator alive?"

"What makes you think my partner isn't waiting for me in the lobby?"

The elevator stopped and the door slid open. Tonio half turned, blocking her way. He breathed in short, loud, hard grunts and there were beads of perspiration along his upper lip. Christie held her pocketbook by the long leather loop, dropped it suddenly. Tonio's eyes went down to the unexpected sound but Christie's eyes stayed on his. She crashed her fist into the soft spot just below his jaw, felt the terrible rasp in his throat. She kicked at him, felt her boot contact some part of him.

As he went down, Tonio's hand reached, caught at the edge of her coat, then grasped at her ankle. Christie swung her pocketbook and hit the back of his head. He pulled at the pocketbook, almost brought her down, but she yanked away from him; had some fleeting impression of blood.

She didn't look back. She ran, straight through the lobby. She felt herself become an explosive force; slammed into some people, a man, a woman; the fragrance of perfume, the sound of outrage pursued her. Her shoulder hit the heavy glass door. She heard the doorman call after her, but all the sounds were lost in

170

the sudden assault of cold wet night air, the slippery sidewalk. Her feet ran too fast for her body to fall. She hit into something, a street sign, then careened against two men, felt the impact of hard metal against her thigh as she smashed into a wastebasket and became entangled in a morass of newspapers and debris.

Christie felt her breath hurt inside her chest with a deep shocking pain. She couldn't gasp the air in deep enough to fill her lungs. There was a force holding her back, but not a nightmare force. It was a human force, a hard strong hand on her shoulder. She spun about, tried to pull herself free.

"Christie! Christie, for God's sake. Take it easy kid, it's Tom Dell."

She nodded her head up and down, but was voiceless. Dell pulled her against him, led her to the car which was parked across the street from Elena's apartment. She leaned her head against the car seat, closed her eyes for a moment and tried to concentrate on regulating her breath and her heartbeat, but Tom Dell was insistent.

"Christie, what the hell happened? Where'd you come from? Come on, Christie, talk."

"Tonio. LoMarco. In the elevator. No. Wait, Tom. Wait." She held his arm. "Don't go after him. Let me catch my breath. Let me think a minute."

She held his arm, nodded at his questions.

"You okay? He hurt you?" Then, assured she was not injured, Dell asked in a puzzled voice, "When did you get there? Christie, I've been here for the last three hours. Jesus, I never saw you go into that building. I've been on a stake-out and I never saw you."

It was one of the things that happens: you can sit for three hours, never taking your eyes away from a particular door. And then you can sneeze, or reach down to adjust the radio, or bend over to light a cigarette, or blink too long. And all the effort put into the three previous hours suddenly becomes worthless.

Christie tightened her hand sympathetically on his arm, but she had her own reasons for telling him, "Tom, I think maybe we ought to keep it that way. I've never been here and you never saw me. Let me catch my breath and we'll talk about it, okay?"

171

19

Casey Reardon swallowed a mouthful of cold, dry hamburger, washed it down with some lukewarm coffee. Two buttons on his telephone lit up at exactly the same moment. He motioned to Stoney. "I'll take the direct, you take the extension."

Wearily, Reardon listened to the State Commissioner's investigator relay his latest information. "Hold it a minute, will you? I've got some notes on that somewhere. . . . " His hand moved restlessly across his desk and pulled out the paper he sought.

Stoner Martin leaned in from the doorway. "Casey, I think we'd better switch calls."

"Huh? What do you mean?"

"Enzo Giardino is on the extension."

"*Enzo Giardino?*"

"Yeah. And he wants to talk to you."

"Hold it a minute." He spoke tersely into the telephone. "Listen, John, something just came up. I'll get back to you as soon as I can. Right." Then, to the detective, "Get on the extension in the Squad Room. I don't know what the hell he's up to, but I want you to listen in."

Reardon waited a moment, then jabbed the button on the phone. "This is Reardon."

Giardino's voice was hard and cold, a careful monotone which could not seem to quite control the slight trace of accent that kept intruding. "I don't know what you think you accomplished, Reardon, but I'll tell you this. You don't push me around. You don't push my people around. I'm calling my lawyer now, see, and if he says so, we're going to get a warrant out on your girl. For as-

172

sault. How would you like that, huh? It wouldn't look so good, huh? Tonio wouldn't touch her with a ten-foot pole, unless I tell him. Tonio wouldn't spit on the sidewalk unless I told him to and I told him nothing but to ride down in the elevator with her."

Reardon rubbed at his eyes and tried to follow the rapid, rambling words. He tried to interrupt, but Giardino apparently hadn't heard him.

"Tonio's going to need stitches in his head, Reardon, and he didn't do nothing. Nothing to her. She didn't need to slug him and we're going to get her locked up. How'd you like that, huh?"

Casey Reardon pulled the receiver from his ear for a moment and actually stared at it. The voice continued the furious, repetitious barrage of words and they were directed at him, and it was undoubtedly Enzo Giardino, but he didn't know what the hell Giardino was talking about.

Reardon waited for a pause, then calmly said, "Hold it a minute, Enzo. Would you like to start at the beginning and tell me exactly what you're so upset about?"

The thin control snapped and Giardino's voice broke. "What I'm upset about? *You keep that Opara bitch away from Elena or what she did to Tonio's gonna seem like nothing!*" There was a loud crash in Reardon's ear, followed by a softer replacing of a receiver.

Reardon was still holding the phone when Stoney came into his office.

"I didn't hear what I think I heard, right? I'm just tired. I mean all this . . . this paper work and this lousy stale food can make a guy punchy, right? You didn't hear the same thing I heard. Did you?"

Reasonably, Stoney said, "Well, at least we know where Opara's been."

Casey Reardon walked to the window, pulled it open, let the cold air hit his face. He took two deep breaths, turned and reached for Stoney's cigarette. He pointed to the telephone. "Get Tom Dell on the car phone."

His voice, as he spoke to Tom Dell, was very calm. "Tom, I'm not going to ask you anything much. Not right now. But I assume that Christie Opara is with you?"

There was a quiet, respectful, "Yes, sir."

"Fine. Put her in the first cab you see and send her to the office. I want her here within the next ten minutes. Think you can manage that?"

"Yes, sir."

"That's fine, Tom. Just fine." He carefully replaced the receiver.

20

Christie felt a small trickle of moisture glide down her back and she knew it was caused by tension rather than the heat of Reardon's office. Her fingers were stiff and inflexible as she ran them along the back of the chair. In the short time it took for the taxi to deposit her in front of the office building, she prepared several different openings, but it took one quick glance at Casey Reardon's face to drain her of words. He barely nodded at her arrival, continued a quiet conversation with Stoner Martin, then stood, engrossed by Stoney's telephone conversation with someone at the State Commissioner's office.

Stoney replaced the receiver. "That brings us up to date, Mr. Reardon."

"Okay, fine." He glanced at his watch. "How about taking a coffee break, Stoney. Then bring back a couple of containers."

"Right."

"Well," he said finally looking up at her, "you've been a busy girl, haven't you?"

She sat down, but he motioned her to her feet. His face looked very earnest and matched his voice: almost boyish. "No, no, get up for a minute. I know you have a lot to tell me, Christie, but there's something I want you to show me. To clarify. Something that's got me puzzled."

"What's that?"

Reardon rubbed the back of his neck and kept his face down as he walked toward her. "Well, from what I understand, you were in an elevator. In Elena Vargas's apartment house. And Tonio LoMarco was in the elevator with you." He spoke very softly, almost gently. She didn't have a chance to question his source of information. He reached out for her, pulled her by the arm. "Come over here a minute. Let's see. About how big was the elevator?"

He wasn't really asking her a question. It was as though he was speaking to himself, but it was obvious what he was doing even if his purpose was obscure. Reardon slid two chairs from in front of the desk, paced off an area. "Was it about this size?" He moved his arm, indicated the partial square.

"The elevator?" Christie shrugged. "I guess that's about right, why?"

"Well, from what I understand, there was something of an altercation in the elevator. Right?"

"Yes, and . . ."

"Just let me get this straight in my mind." His hand covered his eyes. "You and LoMarco were in this elevator. Okay. Now, what I want you to do is *show* me what happened. If you just *tell* me, it won't be as clear. Give me a graphic demonstration of what happened."

"Don't you want to first know . . ."

He interrupted and the first edge of hardness came into his voice. "No. First I want you to *show* me what happened in the elevator. Any objections?"

"No, no objections," Christie answered warily. She turned, positioned herself. "Tonio was . . . over there, I guess." Reardon nodded and moved. "And then, when we reached the main floor, the door slid open and . . ."

Reardon moved his hand. "The door would be here? To my . . . to LoMarco's right? Okay. Now what?"

"Well, the door opened and . . . well, he had said some . . . some threatening things to me on the way down and I . . . had reason to believe that he wasn't going to let me get off the elevator. In fact, he moved to block the door and . . ."

"Like this?" Reardon moved his body to the right and Christie nodded. "Okay, now what did you do? In order to get off the elevator?"

"Well, I distracted him. I dropped my pocketbook and he looked down at it for a second and then I . . . hit him in the throat and knocked him down and got out of the elevator."

"There wasn't much room to move, was there? You use judo or what? Something they taught you at the Police Academy?" He sounded mildly impressed.

"I guess so. I mean, it happened so quickly. It was an automatic response. You know."

He shook his head. "I don't think I can see it. How you could have knocked him down in such a small space. Go ahead, Christie, show me. Look, I'm Tonio LoMarco. And I've just said some 'threatening things' to you, okay? Now the elevator door is opening and you know that I'm not going to let you get off." He turned and blocked the imaginary exit. "Come on Opara, don't worry. You won't hurt me."

His voice was insistent; for whatever reason, he wanted her to demonstrate her escape from Tonio. Christie took a deep breath, shrugged, then dropped her pocketbook, her eyes on Reardon's.

She lunged. And then, everything went wrong. She was propelled by her own momentum, spun about by Reardon, tripped by his foot. She landed on the floor. Hard. She groped for something to grab onto, to pull herself up by. Reardon reached down, grasped the lapels of her coat and yanked her to her feet, then shoved her into the chair.

"United States Marine Corps style judo," he said, his face close to hers. "Weren't you lucky that Tonio-the-creep wasn't an ex-Marine?"

For a moment, she didn't comprehend what he had done, but his anger was open now. "You did that *deliberately*. You . . . you deliberately dumped me on the floor!" She grasped the wooden arms of the chair and tried to pull herself up from the chair, but Reardon's hands forced her shoulders back.

"You stay put until I'm finished with you." He relaxed his grip and his voice softened. "You damn fool. You goddamn little fool, you're lucky you're still around to be dumped on the floor."

Christie started to speak, to answer him, but she was overwhelmed by anger and humiliation and, more than she had realized, by stored-up fear. She covered her eyes and kept her face down. "Damn it," she muttered. "Damn it, damn it." Finally, she looked up and spoke very slowly. "Don't you *bully* me, Mr. Reardon." He leaned back against his desk and folded his arms. "I won't be *bullied* anymore. Enzo Giardino bullied me and Tonio bullied me and even people I don't know, making phone calls about me and about where I was and what I was doing and where I was going." Her hand clenched into a fist and she tapped it on the arm of the chair. "And . . . and now *you're* bullying me and I won't be bullied anymore."

Reardon walked around his desk, took a box of tissues from the bottom drawer. He leaned forward, placed the box near her, then sat in his swivel chair. Christie ignored the box, dug in her pocketbook for her own tissues, blew her nose and wiped her face.

"Are you finished?" he asked quietly.

"Yes."

"All right if I ask you a few questions? I mean, you won't feel like I'm bullying you, if I just ask a few questions? I'll stay on this side of my desk, so you won't feel intimidated or anything."

Christie tried a long, hard stare and a slow blink to let him know that his soft sarcasm was a waste of time. "I *don't* feel intimidated. I *refuse* to feel intimidated any more."

"Well, that's fine, Christie. Wouldn't you be more comfortable if you took your coat off?"

She pulled the coat closer around her. "I'm perfectly comfortable, thank you."

He ran his index finger over his lips for a moment and studied her. She had slid down in the chair, her face was pale and taut; she hadn't expected what he had done to her. He could see her eyes, unnaturally bright and shining, moving restlessly over the papers on his desk, blinking too rapidly. She had been cut way down, to little-girl size; she had to climb back now to claim her professional status.

Briskly, he said, "Suppose you start by telling me where the hell you've been for the last two days. And why you haven't called the office."

"You told me to stay away. To go on sick leave, so I . . ." She stopped. It was standard procedure to check with the office when on sick leave and to leave an alternate phone number if you were away from home.

"All right," Reardon said, "we'll discuss proper procedure another time. Bring me up to date. I assume you've put your time to some good use."

She told him all of it, carefully and thoroughly. Reardon studied the photographs of Elena Vargas's son.

"Are you positive that this is Elena's son?"

"Yes. Positive."

He turned one photograph over: on it, in a neat, small handwriting, was the boy's name and address. "How the hell did you get to him?"

She shot the answer back to him. "Through a confidential source."

Reardon caught the challenge beneath her words; he merely nodded, then asked, "Is it a source you trust completely?"

Without hesitation, she told him, "Absolutely."

"Okay. Good enough." He looked up, and his voice softened. "Christie, for Christ's sake take your coat off."

She stood up, glanced around, undid the toggles. "Well, it's gotten a lot warmer. Yes, I think I'll take my coat off now."

Christie glanced over her newest report, signed her name on the last page of each of the three copies, collated them, stapled them and headed for Reardon's office just as his voice summoned her from the intercom on Stoner Martin's desk.

Reardon was standing with his back to the office; he leaned forward and his forehead pressed against the cold windowpane. It was Stoney who asked her questions this time.

"Christie, we've been kicking around the information you've gotten the last few days. A couple of questions: one—are you *sure* this kid is Elena's son?"

179

Her eyes flickered to the back of Reardon's head; there was an unruly thick lock of hair that needed smoothing. Her attention returned to Stoney. "Yes. It's Elena's son."

The detective nodded. "Okay. Now this is *crucial*. Are you positive, *absolutely positive,* that Elena Vargas knows that this boy, this Richard C. Arvin, Junior, is her son?"

Reardon turned from the window. Both men watched her intently. Christie felt a small doubt, not really a doubt, but a possibility: the words *absolutely* and *positive* were too rigid, too unyielding. She closed her eyes for a moment to shut out their close examination of her. "Yes," she said, finally, her eyes on Reardon. "Elena Vargas *knows* that Richard C. Arvin, Junior, is her son."

Still, Stoney questioned her. "Christie, one more question. Do you think that Elena Vargas knows where this ledger, or the information we need, is?"

"Yes." She answered too quickly; stopped. "I don't know, Stoney. Maybe. Yes, I think she does."

"Okay," Casey Reardon said, "which is it? Yes, no or maybe?"

Christie sat down and ran her fingertips along the edge of his desk. The wood was warm and gleaming and smooth. She didn't notice that Reardon had moved, that he was leaning against his desk, almost directly in front of her.

"Hey," he said quietly, "you're doing some thinking, right? Do it out loud, Christie. Stoney and I have been kicking things around out loud all night. Let's hear what's on your mind."

"Well, Elena. I don't think Elena is what I originally thought she was. The way she talks to Enzo Giardino. The way she spoke to Tonio LoMarco. She'd have to be crazy or something not to be afraid of Giardino and LoMarco. And whatever she is, Elena isn't crazy. And she isn't afraid of them, either."

"Which leads you to believe . . ."

Christie bit her lip. "That Elena is very valuable to Giardino. That she is . . . necessary . . . to his operation. Not as a woman, a female. But as a key part of his operation. That she knows where this ledger is. And that she might be the only one who does know." It was impossible for her to read the expression on Rear-

180

don's face. Wearily, she asked, "Did I say something good or bad?"

Reardon didn't answer but he and Stoner Martin were aware of the fact that everything Christie Opara had just said more or less confirmed what they had concluded.

"Christie, why would Giardino trust Elena so completely?" She hesitated, uncertain of his reaction. "Come on, you're doing fine."

"Well, Giardino trusts her because he thinks he has his finger on the boy, Raphael, in Puerto Rico. Elena wouldn't cross him because of the boy. She's made certain that Giardino is convinced the boy is hers. Raphael is probably the child of her cousin."

Reardon reached for the photographs of Richard Arvin. "And we know and Elena knows that *this* is her real son. And if we got hold of Elena and showed her these pictures, and told her that if we didn't get what we want from her, we'd mail these photos to Enzo Giardino . . ."

Christie chewed on her thumb nail for a moment, then sighed. "Yes, but Elena would know it's a bluff."

"What do you mean, a bluff?"

"Well, she'd know that we wouldn't *really* . . ."

Casey Reardon's face was a hard, unfamiliar mask; his mouth pulled tight and his eyes, beneath the thick red lashes, were pale and cold. *"The hell we wouldn't."*

He walked quickly behind his desk, pulled open a drawer, slammed it, reached into another, found an envelope. He snatched at a pen, wrote on the envelope, then looked up impatiently at Stoner. "What the hell is the address?"

"Forty-four Terrace Drive, Hilton, New Jersey."

Reardon finished addressing the envelope, found a stamp in his top drawer. "All ready to go. The rest will be up to Elena."

He reached for the photographs at the same time that Christie did and his hand held hers. "Detective Opara," he said sharply, "exactly what did you have in mind when you went to all the trouble of tracking this kid down?"

"But . . . we wouldn't . . ."

Reardon pushed her hand away, gathered the pictures and put

181

them into the envelope. "We'll see how it goes." He cut to Stoner. "You reached Ginsburg and Dudley?"

"They're getting warrants on LoMarco: one for the murder of the girl and one for the assault on Christie. Their card-playing Texas man has decided to talk, plus the fact that they've gotten a lead on the weapon and have come up with some bloody clothing of LoMarco's. The blood matches that of Celia Kendall."

Christie was puzzled. "What was that about a warrant for assault on me?"

Reardon stood up, tightened the knot on his tie. "To protect you. The bastard had to have some stitches in his head at the end of his elevator ride with you. Some strong-arm guy he is, getting clobbered by you," he added caustically.

"But why the warrant? I don't get it."

"If we don't have a warrant to cover you for splitting his head open, he just might have *you* locked up."

"He couldn't do that. There were just the two of us in the elevator and it was self-defense . . ."

"Stoney, will you explain the facts of life to this character."

"Christie," Stoney said, "Tonio LoMarco could supply ten witnesses who would all swear on their mothers' graves and their wives' honor that you sneaked up behind him and hit him with a candelabra while he was praying in church. With a warrant, we'll get the facts on record."

Before he left the office Reardon gave her a long list of notations. There were reports she was to prepare, messages she was to relay, telephone calls she would receive. The last notation concerned Tom Dell.

Christie looked up cautiously. "Mr. Reardon, about Tom."

He glanced at his wrist watch. Stoney should have a cab at the curb by this time. "What about Tom Dell?"

"Well . . . Tom didn't know I was in Elena's apartment, because even if he was looking right at me when I entered the building, he wouldn't have recognized me. Not from where he was sitting. And not without expecting me. Which of course he wasn't."

182

Reardon stood motionless for a moment; his eyes flickered over her face, caught the nervous deep intake of breath. Compulsively, her fingers tapped lightly on the keyboard of the typewriter. He moved his head to one side. "Go on, why wouldn't Tom have recognized you?"

"Well, I had this cape over my head." Her hands traced a vague, shapeless form in the air. "It was a big plastic thing, a rain cape, and I pulled it over my head when I went into the building."

"Why did you do that, Christie?"

"I didn't want the doorman to recognize me. Because, well, frankly, I thought you might have occasion to see him and he might mention it to you, you know, that I had been there. And I figured that if things worked out, I'd tell you about it anyway. And if they didn't, well," she shrugged, "you'd never need to know."

There was a streak of carbon smudged along her chin; the terrible tension that had registered on her face earlier was gone, was replaced by an excited animation now that all her solitary work was being incorporated into the Squad's plan of action. He was touched by her attempt to cover for a fellow squad member. He reached out, lifted her chin gently.

"Christie, let me give you a little advice, okay? Never volunteer an excuse unless you're asked. If you are asked and have to wing it, keep your story simple, believable and open-ended. If it involves another person, either be very sure he knows about it, or else, just keep quiet. Right?"

She felt her face go hot; she made a short, clicking, self-disparaging sound with her tongue against her teeth. "I guess you think I'm pretty stupid sometimes, don't you?"

His hand traced the contour of her face. "Yeah," he said tersely, "sometimes."

183

21

 he manager of the Arden Hotel was beautifully groomed and everything about him, including his voice, was carefully modulated. "But Mr. Reardon, the point is that even if these items *are* missing from the suite, we would not have the occupant arrested. There are ways that these things are handled."

Casey Reardon sensed it was time to crack the quiet confidence of Mr. Peter Eldridge. His eyes moved rapidly over Mr. Eldridge, who sat forward politely in his chair. "Wait a minute. Did I understand you to say '*if*' the items on that list we gave you are missing from the suite?"

Mr. Eldridge's hand moved slightly. "Well, as I say, I haven't had an opportunity to inventory . . ."

"*We* have prepared an inventory. You're holding it in your hand. The list of items missing from Suite 16A totals merchandise in excess of two hundred dollars retail value. They have been missing from the suite as of yesterday, when Miss Vargas checked out."

"But why would Miss Vargas, or anyone else for that matter, walk off with"—he glanced at the list Reardon had given him— "four heavy glass ash trays with gold-plated insignia; one hotel courtesy hair dryer; one French provincial telephone; four complete sets of linen? Et cetera. Surely, we do have experience with souvenir collectors, but this list, under the circumstances, seems highly unlikely."

"How the hell would I know? Maybe the girl is a klepto."

Mr. Eldridge tried a smile. It was almost pleasant and touched every part of his smooth face but his eyes. "Mr. Reardon, please don't misunderstand me. Assuming . . . no, I'll go further, accepting the fact that your list is accurate, and even that Miss Vargas did steal these items, we would not prosecute. Particularly under the circumstances of Miss Vargas's . . . stay . . . at our hotel. You must realize that we would not want the sort of publicity that would ensue from such a situation."

Reardon stood up. "Oh, I understand completely, Mr. Eldridge. The Arden doesn't want any unsavory publicity, right?"

Eldridge nodded brightly.

"And you sure as hell don't want any scandal, right?"

The smile pulled uncertainly at the corners of his mouth. "Scandal? What do you mean?"

"Well," Reardon said, "it would be a hell of a scandal if it became public knowledge that several well-known, solid-citizen-type gentlemen frequent the Arden periodically for various reasons pertaining to their own particular peculiarities. Which of course is nobody's goddamn business. Except the newspapers are always hungry for that kind of item. We wouldn't want that known, right?" He slid his hands into the pockets of his coat and turned to Stoner Martin. "What else we got, Stoney?"

Stoner Martin dug his toe into the thick carpet and carefully traced a circle in the shaded nap before he looked up at Reardon. "You mean besides the middle-aged homosexual shenanigans? Well, we have the every-other-Wednesday-night, all-night poker game that takes place regularly in Suite 12C, involving six public officials."

Eldridge's voice went higher. "But . . . but that's just a friendly get-together. A friendly game of cards . . ."

Stoner shook his head decisively. "Uh-uh. Stakes are too high for a friendly game of cards. One suicide last month when the stakes got altogether too high. Of course, the suicide did take place in a summer cottage in Pennsylvania. But the motive came from Suite 12C of the Arden Hotel. Are you with us, Mr. Eldridge, or did we lose you somewhere along the way?"

"Nah, we didn't lose him, Stoney. Peter is going to sign a complaint for the arrest of Elena Vargas on a grand larceny rap. And as I told you before, Peter, it's a case that will never get any publicity and will never even come to trial. All we're asking you for is a little formal cooperation. As a good citizen, interested in seeing justice triumph, you won't do less than your civic duty. Will you, Mr. Eldridge?"

22

Elena Vargas glanced around the familiar hotel room, pulled the soft warm fur against her cheeks and moved her face slowly inside the mink coat. She enjoyed the sensuous pleasure of the touch of silky animal hair. She closed her eyes for a moment and listened to the voice, rather than the words, of Casey Reardon. Always telling, telling, telling. Elena opened her eyes and wondered what it would be like with Reardon.

Ralph Marshall's voice was low and deep and cultivated. He spoke slowly and deliberately as though he wasn't certain he was being fully understood. "Mr. Reardon, we both know that I will have Elena released by writ within the next few hours. This whole arrest, arraignment, reinstatement of protective custody"—his large, manicured white hands turned upward in a studied gesture—"this is all nonsense at best and intentional harassment at worst."

"Why don't you run down to the Tombs and hold hands with Tonio LoMarco, Counselor? Or don't you reach down that low?"

The attorney smiled bleakly. "Mr. Reardon, Miss Vargas is my client and I am here to protect her rights. Had I been present at the arraignment, she wouldn't be here at all. Bail would have been set, provided, and a hearing date arranged. Now, I have attempted to speak with the so-called complainant, Mr. Peter Eldridge, but it appears that he has disappeared. Would you be so kind as to advise me where I might find him?"

Casey Reardon moved a Life Saver from one side of his mouth to the other. He regarded the well-groomed, middle-aged man before him carefully. Meticulously custom-tailored, handsomely

187

gray-haired, radiating well-cared-for good health, encased in an aura of subtle, expensive cologne which surrounded him inside an almost unapproachably protective capsule, Ralph Marshall hardly resembled a syndicate attorney. The facts flashed through Reardon's mind: Ralph Marshall, fifty-two years old; personal worth in the mid-six figures; a home in one of the best New Jersey suburbs; winter home in Palm Beach; recently acquired large tract of land for development purposes in the West Indies; member of four prestigious gentlemen's clubs; graduate of an Ivy League college and law school; father of four grown children; grandfather of seven young children; senior partner in a law firm which specialized in handling investments for clients who, though barely literate, had been systematically buying into and gaining control over huge essential service industries. Through the years, Ralph Marshall had guided, suggested, advised and steered these particular clients through the intricacies of the investment world. Through his endeavors on their behalf, they had mutually profited.

Marshall stood perfectly at ease under Reardon's scrutiny. "Well, I see that you're not going to cooperate, Mr. Reardon. That, of course, is your privilege. Elena, I shall be back shortly. You don't have to open your mouth, my dear, you don't have to say a word." He leaned forward and his dry lips brushed Elena's cheek. Elena's eyes, black and bright, stared past him at Casey Reardon.

"By the way," the attorney said, adjusting his topcoat carefully, "it seems to me that you have failed to observe proper procedure. There is supposed to be a female police officer present when a female is being detained. All I've seen are men."

Reardon jerked his thumb over his shoulder. "There's a female detective in the outer room. She's just arrived. That makes it safe for me to be in the same room with Elena, right?"

Elena moved slightly inside the coat. "Ah, but safe is not fun, Mr. Reardon." She caught the slight distasteful pull downward of his thin lips. "Ralph, stop huddling around me like a mother hen and get your writ and get me out of here. Ralph is not used to this kind of thing," she told Reardon. "He handles investments and it disturbs him to have to become involved with people. But you see, Richie Burns is in the Bahamas and Mr. Giardino trusts Ralph *almost* as much as he trusts Richie."

Her voice was soft and playful but she knew how to place it. The well-groomed face tightened; the lips pursed together; the attorney's sky-blue eyes flickered for just one quick moment and revealed contempt. Elena caught it all.

"You're not in the same category with Richie Burns, are you, Ralph? He doesn't like to be mentioned in the same breath with Burns, Mr. Reardon, but they are the same after all." Elena laughed a sharp brittle sound. "Ralph, stop looking so alarmed. I will sit here and flirt with Casey Reardon for the next hour or two until you come back to free me from all of this, okay?"

The attorney gave a short, semi-bow, first toward Elena and then toward Reardon. He did not put his hat on his head until he had left the suite.

Christie Opara moved her toes but could feel absolutely nothing from the ankles down. She carefully stepped on the toe of one boot and tried to pull her foot out but gave up the effort when Casey Reardon came into the room. He nodded at her briefly, then, one hand on Stoner Martin's shoulder, he received whatever information he needed, gave whatever instructions he thought necessary. Sam Farrell appeared briefly, his collar turned up, his ears a bright red. His conversation with Reardon was also whispered, hurried, had the appearance of urgency.

Christie leaned against the hardwood chair and wondered what Reardon had told Farrell: where he had sent him; what Stoner Martin was being told. There were always additional scraps of information, some parts of the whole that were never revealed to her completely. There was always some aspect of every case on which she worked that was not made totally available to her. She had relayed the short, cryptic messages to O'Hanlon and Treadwell as they had phoned in. Jotted down messages from several other men: always incomplete scraps of information that only Reardon fully coordinated. And the phone call from Bill Ferranti; from San Juan.

Reardon turned to her brusquely. "Christie, what have you got for me?"

"All your messages were delivered. Marty Ginsburg called. He and Dudley picked up Tonio LoMarco at some girl's apartment in midtown. He had a stiletto on him; Marty's at the police lab now and Dudley's taking care of the booking and interrogation." She changed the pacing of her words now. "And there was a phone call from Bill Ferranti. From San Juan. In Puerto Rico."

Reardon pulled at his mouth impatiently and nodded. "Yeah, what'd he have?"

"What did he report from San Juan? In Puerto Rico?"

Reardon's eyes filled with color: honey held to light, tinged with a darker color around the edges. "Detective Opara, I *know* where San Juan is. What was the message?"

"Aside from the fact that the weather was warm and clear and the people very helpful and cooperative? Well, he said that he's located a bank account and safe-deposit box in Elena's name; one account in the name of Raphael Garcia, her nephew. The local authorities helped him quite a bit: they examined the contents of the safe-deposit box. Some bonds, some insurance policies with the boy as beneficiary. The rest can wait for a written report. And he'll call the office tomorrow at noon. Or can be reached at his hotel if something comes up that involves anything in *sunny San Juan.*"

Casey Reardon exhaled with a slow, thin whistling sound between his teeth. Confronting him was everything about Christie Opara that both irritated and interested him: her complete determination to reveal her exact feelings, or perhaps her inability to disguise her feelings about a particular situation.

"Who should have gone to San Juan?" he asked her softly.

"It was *my* lead. *I* should have followed it up."

She had answered without hesitation and with total honesty. No other member of the Squad would have complained to him directly about a trip assigned to someone else. Considering the circumstances of the past few days, Reardon shook his head in wonder. She had more goddamn nerve than anyone he had ever met. He had a strong urge to shake her, but instead he smiled.

"Well, Christie, I tried getting you on the phone for the last two days. There was no answer and you didn't call in . . . so . . . "

"You mean," her mouth fell open as she considered the implication. "Were you going to send me to San Juan? Were you *really* going to . . . "

Reardon shrugged. "Ya'll never know now, will you?"

"But you wouldn't have, anyway. Would you?" Her face had a stricken look and she struggled with the possible loss of a trip into the warm and sunny climate. "I mean, actually . . . "

Reardon reached out and lifted a small white thread from the shoulder of her blue sweater. "Look at it this way, Christie. You should really consider yourself as one very lucky girl."

"Lucky? To have missed a trip?"

He shook his head. "No, lucky to have missed being murdered sometime during the last couple of days. By Enzo Giardino. Or by Tonio LoMarco." He turned her toward the room where Elena waited and his hand rested lightly on her neck for a moment. Very softly, he added, "Or by *me*, Detective Opara."

The tension she had managed to hold down beneath the façade of irritation hit Christie when she saw Elena Vargas. Her hands trembled as she lit a cigarette and she turned quickly in search of an ash tray.

"Well, Detective Opara, now we are on your grounds again." Elena sounded amused and unconcerned.

Christie watched Reardon for some signal, but he wasn't ready. There was a phone call for him and he took it in the outer room.

"Isn't this getting just a little silly?" Elena asked.

Christie walked to the window without answering. There was a cold draft of thin, sharp air along the windowsill. The street, far below, was as black and shining as a frozen lake: an endless, ugly winter. An occasional gust of wind blew rain and sleet against the windowpane.

"Okay, Christie, come on over and sit down." Reardon's voice was firm and businesslike.

"Well, Mr. Reardon, now what?" Elena moved her small body deeper inside her mink coat. Her eyes moved from Reardon to Christie.

"It's all going to be up to you Elena. From here on." Casey Reardon removed the photographs from the envelope and carefully placed them on the cocktail table in front of Elena, then leaned back in his chair. "Go ahead. Take a look."

Elena sighed, made it obvious that she was merely humoring him. She carefully slid the coat from her shoulders. The bright-orange jersey dress was a startling contrast to the darkness of her skin. She ran her delicate fingers through her short, crisp black hair and reached casually for the photographs. She looked through them quickly, then raised her eyes. "So? A little Cub Scout." She glanced from the photographs to Christie. "Is this your son?"

Slowly, Christie shook her head. Her voice was hollow and thin, but she knew Reardon wanted her to answer. "No, Elena. That's not *my* son. It's *your* son."

"*My* son? This boy . . . "

It was between the two of them. No matter what anyone else had done on the case, no matter what knowledge Reardon had obtained, no matter what information all the various detectives and special agents had garnered, this was between Elena and Christie, and both girls realized it.

Elena tossed the photographs to the table. They fell, some on the table, some on the floor.

"What kind of fool do you take me for?" she asked Christie. Her hand moved vaguely. "That is not my son."

In the silence, she studied their faces: Reardon's, hard and unmoving, and Christie Opara's. There was something implacable in Christie's face, something that frightened Elena. She stood up, reached for the photographs and flung them at Christie. "This is

not my son. This little fair-haired boy, in his gringo uniform."
She whirled to Reardon. "Listen, Reardon. Listen, you bastard,
what are you trying to pull?"

Christie calmly gathered the photographs together, extended
them to Elena. "Look at him, Elena. Take a good look."

Elena turned her back. "No. It is a stranger. I will not look at
the pictures of this child. He is nothing to me."

Are you *absolutely positive* that the boy is Elena's son? that
Elena will know it is her son? The deadly words forced Christie
to speak. "Elena," she said insistently, "his name is Richard C.
Arvin, Junior."

The girl's body went rigid. They did not need to see her face,
it was all there: in her shoulders, which pulled together, her
hands, which clutched her elbows and hugged her body as
though to protect herself against an onslaught of blows.

Reardon stood up, turned her around. Elena Vargas's face was
the sick yellow color of fear; the black eyes, beneath the long full
lashes, were dull and flat and empty. The lipstick, perfectly
matched to the bright dress, was all wrong for the drained complexion. Reardon reached for the photographs and held them to
Elena.

"Take a careful look, Elena." There was something terrible
and inflexible in Reardon's voice. "The games are all over, kid.
Take a look at your son."

She stared without seeing for a moment, then focused on the
pictures. There was a low sobbing sound from deep within her
throat and Elena doubled up into the chair. Christie stared at her
own hands; she did not want to see either Elena's pain or Reardon's coldness.

Elena found the one really good close-up: the small young
face, grinning right into the camera. "His eyes," she said softly.
Her finger traced the dark slanted eyes, then tentatively touched
her own. "These are my eyes?"

Christie nodded. "Yes. He has your eyes."

"But he is so fair. I did not realize he was so fair."

Reardon suddenly snatched the photographs from Elena's

hand. She half rose, her hand reaching out. "No, please no. Let me look at him."

Carefully, Reardon extracted one photograph, turned it over to check that it was the one he wanted. He tossed it to Elena.

She retrieved it from the floor. "But this one isn't clear. It's blurred. Please . . . "

"Turn it over," he told her shortly.

Elena studied the small neat writing on the reverse side of the photograph then looked up blankly.

Casey Reardon's voice was the voice of a stranger: cruel and relentless. "His name, his address, his date and place of birth, the date of his adoption, the name of his adoptive parents, their address. And the name of his natural mother."

Christie cut through her own sense of shock at Reardon's lack of feeling. "Mr. Reardon, let her look at them a little longer."

In response, he took the photograph from Elena. "She's seen enough to know that this is her kid." He put the photographs into the envelope, sealed it and tapped the envelope against his open palm. "You have information we want, Elena."

Slowly, she moved her head from side to side. "I know nothing. *Nothing.* I've told you that over and over again."

"Yeah. I know you've told me that." He held the envelope before her eyes. "It's addressed to Enzo Giardino. It's stamped and ready to be mailed. There's a mail slot in the hallway. You want to talk to me, or what?"

For a moment, the words did not seem to penetrate, made no sense, and then the reality hit her and Elena lunged.

"Uh-uh." Reardon stepped back easily. "Not that easy, Elena. We *deal* now: we make a trade. *The kid for the information.*"

Elena turned to Christie. Her voice was a whisper, hoarse and frightened. "Detective Opara, you found him? You found my son for this . . . this trade?"

Christie stubbed out her cigarette and avoided Elena's eyes. "Mr. Reardon, couldn't you give her a minute or two to pull herself together? She hasn't seen her son in almost seven years. Give her a little time to . . . "

Reardon cut her off harshly. "You know, Detective Opara, this is one of the times when I *do* think you are stupid. Elena's had all the time she's going to get. Once this letter is dropped down the mail slot in the hall, Elena, it's on its way. I've wasted enough goddamn time on you. We making a deal or not?"

Elena breathed deeply and tried to regain some composure. She tried to measure the words against the man: it was too blatant an attempt at blackmail. Her lips attempted a smile and she took her last chance. "I don't think you would do it."

Reardon stood perfectly still for several seconds then turned abruptly. "The hell I won't."

It was not his quick movement across the room, nor his words; it was Christie Opara's reaction. Her face crumpled into a look of disbelief, she cried out a word, a sound, and threw herself after Reardon. It was Christie's face and Christie's reaction that sent Elena racing, in total, absolute terror, after them.

The hallway was long and narrow and Elena crashed against the wall, grasped Reardon's arm. He pushed her away from him. Christie caught his elbow and Reardon stopped for an instant, his face turned toward her.

"Get your hands off me, Opara." But Christie's hands held, tried to work upward, reaching for the envelope, which he held over her head. "Christie, I will bounce you right down the hall. Let go!"

But she persisted, tried to stop him, threw her body against him with a desperate force; for one fleeting instant, she saw his face clearly: his lips were parted in surprised amusement, a familiar mocking expression that confused her. Then his shoulder slammed against her cheek and she fell back against the wall.

Both girls watched incredulously as Reardon inserted the envelope into the mail slot and held it by the corner. He breathed heavily and spoke softly. "Okay. We're here, Elena. No bluff. Don't try me, because your kid means no more to me than your cousin's kid, Raphael, means to you."

"Oh no," the imitation of Elena's voice told him, "you don't understand about Raphael. You don't understand."

195

"I understand perfectly. He was a substitute. To protect your own son. *You* set the whole thing up, Elena, not me." Reardon eased the envelope several inches down into the mail slot.

Elena leaned against the wall. Her head fell back and her face, turned up toward the dim light, registered total defeat. "Oh, no. Please no. Detective Opara. Tell him. Tell him."

Christie glared at Reardon. "Elena will tell you everything you want to know."

Elena's head bobbed up and down in confirmation. Her eyes were locked tight against the sight of the envelope in the mail slot. She shuddered at the unexpected pressure of Reardon's hand on her arm.

"I'll keep the photographs for the time being," he said quietly. "Come on, let's get back into the room before someone calls the house dicks."

Elena Vargas sipped the coffee without tasting it, then put the cup back on the saucer. She took a bite of sandwich, chewed automatically, swallowed. Nothing had flavor: everything was flat and dull. Her beautiful dark mink coat was a collection of dead animal bodies. And Casey Reardon, lithe and strong and energetic, the electric excitement radiating from him, was just another man, now that she had agreed to be used.

And Christie Opara. Elena raised her eyes. Just a little girl after all. Her wide-open face bore traces of shock and disbelief and betrayal. Had she really not seen brutality before?

"Do either of you girls want anything else?" Reardon asked them.

"No, thank you, Mr. Reardon." Christie avoided looking at him.

He reached forward and lit Elena's cigarette for her. He had won, could afford this politeness now. "Okay, Elena, whenever you're ready. Where is this ledger we've been hearing so much about?"

She glanced at Stoner Martin who stood quietly in the doorway. Smoke from his cigarette curled upward in spirals over his head. They all waited.

Elena stretched her arms before her. Her color had come back: she was reconciled. "Oh, Mr. Reardon. No one, not even *you*, guessed? How about you, Detective Stoner-Stoney Martin?" She stood up and crossed the room. She reached out and her fingers lightly touched the dark, handsome face. Her lips moved, made playful, suggestive sounds, then she removed his cigarette from his mouth, replaced it with her own. She inhaled deeply on Stoner's cigarette and turned. "Not Christie Opara? Didn't you guess? She is your best detective, Reardon, isn't she? Or your bravest. Or your dumbest, maybe. To walk into my apartment with Enzo and Tonio. A baby, this one."

Reardon's voice was firm. "Okay, Elena. Let's get to it."

"Get to it? But, Mr. Reardon, that is so funny. You don't know how funny that is. You are right *at* it. Right at it, stud, all the time, right in the room with you, moving in front of you, playing with you." Her hand lightly caressed his face. "Touching you." She turned to Christie. "Macho, this one, eh? Much man. But this one," she indicated Stoner Martin, "this one much more so, eh, Stoney." Her voice changed suddenly, the playfulness gone, anger and contempt and defiance filling the room. Her hands moved along her body and she said to Reardon, "*Me*, you stupid bastard. *Me*."

Elena glanced around the room, spotted a newspaper. "Here. I will show you." She opened *The New York Times*, turned to the real estate section. Her eyes raced over the print, then she flung the newspaper at Reardon. Her finger pointed to a section. She closed her eyes tightly. "Stores: Nassau and Suffolk. Central Avenue and 236th Street. Oliver. 20' x 80' plus basement and out building; suitable for women's and children's wear; call 212-HE 6-1130. Floral Park: renovate this solid 900-square-foot building yourself; handyman's special; ideal location machine shop. Hauppage: 14,000 feet commercial; ideal location; suit any type retail or service business."

The dark eyes snapped open. "Well, do you get it now, Casey Reardon? *I am Enzo Giardino's ledger!*"

197

23

Elena's voice droned on and on until the words became a hum devoid of meaning. Christie reached down and turned off the tape recorder, but she could still hear Elena's voice, speaking from the tape recorder in the outer room, stopped from time to time by Stoner Martin, whose fingers quickly caught up with her words on his typewriter.

She rolled the paper up on her typewriter and read what she had typed. Places, names of places, and people and numbers; codes, aboard which ship departing from which port, arriving on which date; in the hold of what ship, packed carefully into a predetermined location, among thousands of tons of legitimate goods, carefully planted, sixteen pounds of uncut heroin; nineteen pounds of uncut heroin; twenty-five pounds of uncut heroin. Hundreds and hundreds of pounds of uncut heroin, destined to arrive over a period of the next five days. On its way, not to be recalled, on its way to handlers, distributors, hundreds of thousands of dollars' worth of narcotics, millions and millions of dollars' worth of narcotics.

Christie stood up, flexed her fingers. She had been typing steadily for nearly four hours. Reardon had set her to work on the hotel typewriter, a flimsy, tinny portable, as soon as the first tape had been completed, then had moved Elena into another room with a second tape recorder and now into a third room.

There had been a steady procession of people in and out of the suite: the attorney with his writ, his face collapsing, his foundation of certainty deserting him when Elena told him, coldly, "I have requested that Mr. Reardon hold me in protective custody since I have reason to believe that my life is in danger."

"But what will I tell Enzo?"

Elena's answer had been bitter and pungent and to the point.

Then, the endless stream of officials involved in the investigation: Reardon's men, briefed rapidly, sent on their way. State Investigations people, checking out certain facts; Federal men from Internal Revenue checking their particular aspect of the case; F.B.I. agents, sharing and comparing notes with Reardon and with the others involved. The hotel suite had become a communications and information center, and still, in another room, Elena rambled on and on, stopping to explain wearily the various codes, the various, intricate routings that had been worked out and fed into her extraordinary brain.

Casey Reardon came into the room and Christie sat down, her fingers on the tape recorder rewind switch.

"How you doing, Christie?"

"Fine."

His voice was light and excited. "I'll take what you've typed already. Are you following the numbering sequence you worked out with Stoney? I don't want to get these mixed up." She nodded, without looking at him. "Jesus, we are *really* in business. She's giving us more than we even began to suspect."

"That's nice."

He reached down and hit the off switch on the tape recorder. "Okay. What's the matter with you?"

She raised her brows. "Is there something the matter with me?"

"You mad at me because I shoved you in the hall? I didn't hurt you, did I?" He reached for her face but she pulled back. "Ah, come on Christie, didn't you ever play good-guy bad-guy before?"

"Is that what we were playing?"

"Think about it for a minute," he told her. His thumb jerked toward himself, his index finger pointed at her. "Bad-guy, good-guy. Elena watched you a hell of a lot closer than she watched me. She reacted to *your* reaction, not to what I said."

It made sense, yet Christie felt there was still something lacking in his explanation. It was a perfectly acceptable technique but there was a difference in the way Reardon used it.

He answered before she could state her objection. "I didn't set it up in advance for one very good reason. I didn't think you'd be able to carry it off." He grinned. "Honey, I'll go so far as to credit you with being one hell of a good detective, but I don't think you'd ever be good as an actress. For instance, right now. You should be playing the role of competent detective, agreeing with the boss that he had the right instincts on that particular score. Instead, you're glaring at me like a sore-headed twelve year old who's been kept out of part of the game. Come on, baby, grow up."

"That envelope *might* have slipped from your fingers," she said. "It just *might* have and . . ."

Casey Reardon tapped the edges of the papers together without taking his eyes from her. "You know, Christie, sometimes I wonder why the hell I feel that I owe you explanations of any kind. You just keep typing, Detective Opara. And make sure you don't miss a thing. Every word coming out of Elena's mouth is worth its weight in heroin."

Gray light shone between the half-opened slats of the venetian blind. Christie squinted at her wrist watch. It was a quarter to six. She was supposed to be off duty until the afternoon tour. The loud, impatient knocking on the door could only be Reardon.

"Just a minute," she called out. "I'll be there in a minute."

She switched the lamp on and gazed around the small hotel room. The Arden might be one of the most exclusive hotels in New York City, but its lesser rooms were unattractive and cramped. Christie smoothed her dress on over her slip, zipped it hurriedly, left her shoes off. She glanced at herself in the mirror through half-closed eyes. Beautiful. Her hand was moving through her hair as she opened the door.

Reardon stepped back and allowed Elena Vargas to enter the room. "You awake, Christie? Elena wants to see you."

She nodded.

"I'll be in the suite down the hall. You want coffee or anything, call room service."

Elena seemed diminished, as though now drained of all her secrets she had become physically smaller.

"Sit anywhere," Christie told her. "You have a big choice, the floor, the chair or the bed."

Elena sat on the chair, waved away the offered cigarette. Christie turned the light higher, pulled up the venetian blinds. "Another beautiful gray New York day. Tell me something, Elena, why did you ever leave Puerto Rico?"

The dark head moved. Her voice was thin and raspy, used up. "It was not the Puerto Rico of the posters. Not for me, when I was seventeen. Surely you know that."

"I'm sorry. Look, Elena. I'm about as exhausted as you are. What did you want?"

Elena's fingers moved over the arms of the small upholstered chair. The nail polish was cracked and chipped. "I've talked so much. My throat is hoarse. Please. Tell me about him."

Christie pulled at a torn bit of cuticle on her index finger. Pulled too hard and felt a needle of pain. Her wrists and fingers ached from the hours of typing. She felt too tired for pity.

"You tell me first about the other boy. About Raphael, who Enzo Giardino thought was your son." It was an accusation; soft-spoken, but an accusation.

"I did not deliberately seek out Raphael. It did not happen that way. Maybe you should know about it. When I returned to New York, I went to work for Enzo Giardino." Her hand brushed away details. "It is all really very simple and ordinary. I was what you said: a whore. But I had this very interesting trick with the brain." Her finger tapped her forehead lightly. "Total recall, or instant memory or whatever it should be called. And I used to amuse Enzo by showing off this . . . this talent of mine. He was as good to me as a man like that can be. When I asked to go and visit my family on the Island, he sent me. Many times." Elena leaned back, moved her shoulders and head, to relieve the stiffness of the long night. "And eventually, this trick with the memory became important to him. No one would know about the operation but him. No one could steal his records. I would be his record and only he and I would know this. And to guarantee the integrity of this living ledger, he let me know that Raphael's life

201

would be at stake. You see, not even Enzo Giardino himself had access to the entire operation: he had to rely on me. That was the whole point: nothing written." She stopped speaking for a moment, her hand rubbed her throat. Her eyes were dark again and steady. "Tell me, Christie, would *you* have told Enzo Giardino that he was mistaken, that Raphael was *not* your son?"

"You *used* a child, Elena, you placed his life in jeopardy."

Elena stood up, walked to the window, stared down for a moment. She turned slowly. "And still you *judge* me, eh? Well, you tell me then, Christie Opara, what the difference is between us? *You used a child, too. My child.*"

"No. It's not the same. His life was never in question. Reardon wouldn't have . . . " She pressed her lips together.

"But you didn't know he wouldn't have! I watched *you*. If *you* believed he would have sent those pictures to Enzo, then *I* believed. *And I saw your face.* You can conceal nothing."

"No," she said, "it was staged. The whole thing in the hallway. We planned it beforehand. I never believed he would have . . . "

Elena slumped into the chair. "It doesn't really matter anyway. You believed, I believed. It doesn't matter any more."

"Tell me about Raphael."

Elena was puzzled by Christie's insistence, by her need to know. "Can't you see?" she said. "He never was in danger, because I never would have revealed Enzo's secrets. *You* are the one who has put him in danger. It is something I never thought could happen. Raphael was born four weeks after my child was born. I was present at his birth and I held him in my arms and he filled the terrible emptiness." Without realizing it, Elena cradled her arms across her body. "He was my godson and I went to see him many times, and each time, I pretended to myself that he was my child. I loved him, my Raphael."

"Did you ask Mr. Reardon about what precautions were being taken to protect him now?"

Elena nodded. "He told me that there is a detective from your office there now. He called this detective last night. There is a bank account, in my cousin's name, in trust for Raphael. This de-

202

tective—the quiet Italian with the white hair—he found out about the bank account even before I told Reardon. You people are very good at finding out secrets, aren't you? Raphael will be taken care of; Reardon would not tell me more. I will have to rely on him."

"If he said the boy will be safe, you can believe it."

"And now," Elena said, a touch of pleading in her voice for the first time, "will you tell me?"

Christie sat on the floor, her back against the side of the bed. She felt the black eyes, hungry and anxious.

The boy was tall and handsome; he glowed in the special way of a well-loved and happy child; he was bright and friendly.

"Do the other children like him? Does he seem to have many friends?"

Christie told her yes. To all the questions Elena needed to have answered, Christie told her yes.

"Then, I did the right thing after all, didn't I? To give him up?"

Christie pulled herself up from the floor. Her back was sore and ached. "Why are you asking me, Elena? You said I've judged you too much. You're right, so don't ask for my judgment now."

The response surprised Elena. "So, out of all this, you've learned something, eh, Christie?"

"I don't know. I don't know anything about anything at this point, Elena. I'm too tired."

Elena bowed her head, dug into her pocketbook and extracted the envelope of photographs of her son. She thrust them at Christie without looking at them. "Take these please. I never wanted souvenirs. I had made a vow never to see him again. I never will." Her face was anxious and she leaned close to Christie. "You will destroy them? When all this is finished?"

Christie nodded. "No one will ever see them, Elena. You have my word."

Elena stood up. "Yes. I believe you." She turned and walked quickly across the room, pulled the door open. Her voice, still hoarse and tight, tried for a tough, playful brightness as she looked Marty Ginsburg over carefully. "He pulls his stomach in

203

every time I come close to him, this one. But actually, Ginsburg, heavy men are the best."

Marty rubbed his nose and studied his shoes in a great effort to keep his eyes from Elena Vargas.

When she faced Christie again, her face was a dark hard mask. She regarded the pale, fair-haired detective curiously. For a moment, it did not seem possible that this thin, almost innocently ignorant girl could have brought about the total destruction of the world Elena had carefully built and inhabited for so many years. Elena was overwhelmed by a sudden need to strike out and to destroy Christie Opara. And her only weapon was words.

"Let me tell you something, Detective Opara." Elena moved back into the room, jutted her hips forward, her breasts pushed against the smooth orange fabric of her dress. She felt the fullness of her body revealed and apparent and her eyes contemptuously traced Christie. She spoke in a mean whisper. "That Casey Reardon: he knows what to do with a woman. He is a bastard, that we both know. But he knows how to make a woman's body come alive." There was a small, hard smile on the full lips and the dark eyes narrowed. "That *you* do not know, because he has *never* made love to you."

Elena felt some small pleasure in the totally revealed pain she had inflicted. She turned, walked into the hall and her hand reached for Ginsburg's arm. She made a harsh, vulgar, clicking sound with her tongue and dismissed Christie from her life.

24

Casey Reardon ignored Christie's request for just a cup of tea and carefully scanned the menu. The waitress was bright and cheerful, too happy and wide awake for six-thirty in the morning. Christie wondered what shift she worked. The only other person in the hotel coffee shop was the counterman and he looked appropriately sullen and morose.

"You should eat a good breakfast, Christie. Gives you a start on the day." Reardon reached across the table and took the cigarette from her lips. "Too early for that poison. I know you'd rather be sleeping right now, but I wanted to bring you up to date."

"Really. Why?"

He tapped the unlit cigarette on the surface of the table, turned it end on end. It was hard to give her anything. It was even harder to understand his need to give her something. His hand touched the rough stubble along his jaw and chin and he tried to keep his voice reasonable. "Well, let's say because you did a really fine job and that you played an invaluable role in pulling this case together." The tough, wary expression crossed her face and he pretended not to notice. "By the way, I guess you'll be relieved to know that the memo . . . relative to your demotion . . . won't be sent through."

"Gee, Mr. Reardon, you mean I'm still a first-grade detective?"

Reardon put the cigarette in his mouth, struck a match and inhaled. "You never felt for one minute that your grade really was in jeopardy, did you?"

Christie shrugged slightly. "I know my capabilities. You wouldn't want me to be guilty of false modesty, would you, Mr. Reardon?"

Carefully, deliberately, he stubbed out the unwanted cigarette. There was nothing he had said, no word or gesture or expression of his, that led to the tension between them. "Okay, Christie, what is it? What the hell is bothering you? Are you still sore because I shoved you?"

"What's a shove between friends?"

He tried to hold his responsive anger back, but her coldness was getting to him more than he thought possible. It had been a long hard night, but the revelations which poured out of the tape recorder had kept them all wide awake and alert. Elena had known more than they had anticipated. She had confirmed wide areas of their own investigations and had opened other, unexpected areas.

It was the sense of excitement he had wanted to share with Christie, the realization that all the fragmentary pieces had fit into a larger puzzle, that all the hours and anxieties and fatigue were worthwhile, were leading to something really valuable.

He leaned back and studied Christie thoughtfully, tried for an objectivity he did not really possess where she was concerned. Across the table from him was the tomboy face: the same face that had confronted him in the hallway, at the mail slide. Come hell or high water, she would hold her own: outweighed, outdistanced, outranked, she had actually been ready to grapple with him because she was convinced that he was going to mail those photographs to Enzo Giardino, and in the one fleeting instant, he had recognized the complete integrity of her determination.

"Is it about the photographs, Christie? Did you really believe I would have mailed them to Giardino?"

Her face changed, softened. "I don't know whether I thought that or not. I guess I did, for a second or two."

"But what the hell, I told you why I played it that way. I'm a good actor. Give me credit."

"Well, that's not the point." She turned her face, bit her lip. "What is the point?"

She glanced at her watch without seeing the time, over her

shoulder toward the waitress who would bring them food she did not want, out the window, toward the empty street. Reardon felt a tightening along his throat because a casual question had unexpectedly become important to both of them.

"You didn't answer me, Christie."

"I'm not going to answer your question. You figure it out for yourself. You know what? I'm not at all hungry. I'm more tired than hungry and I think I'll just go back upstairs and . . . "

The waitress arrived as Christie was trying to extricate herself from the booth. She sat down, watched as the woman placed the food before them. She winked and nodded and smiled and made little pleasant sounds and poured Christie's tea and left a carafe of hot coffee beside Reardon's filled cup. "It's nice to see people with some good sense," she told them. "My mother always told me there was nothing like a good hearty breakfast to get you going in the right direction." She followed her words with a hearty laugh. "Well, I don't know what direction she meant for me to take, but just look at me now!"

Christie pushed the scrambled eggs around the edge of her plate, stabbing with her fork. "There is something I'd like to know," she said, her eyes on the eggs. "A while back, when I first was assigned to the case, I heard . . . " She stopped for a moment, tried to be careful.

"You heard what?" Reardon's voice was sharp, District Attorney to witness.

"Well, that something more was involved in this case. For you, personally. Than just . . . breaking up an important narcotics ring."

Reardon dropped the piece of toast back to his plate. There was no point in asking where she'd heard the rumor, from whom. He wanted to break the mood between them, not continue it. He swallowed some coffee, then motioned toward her food. "All right. Eat something and I'll tell you about it, okay? Come on, like a good girl. Haven't you read the papers for the last few days?" He snapped his fingers and his voice was more familiar to her than it had been: mocking and sarcastic. "Gee, that's right.

You've been so damn busy playing private detective all by yourself, you haven't been in touch with the rest of us. Well, you see, Detective Opara, the Great Master of Us All, up on the top floor," Reardon said, referring to the District Attorney of New York County, "called three of his top assistants in about a month ago. Being the charming gent he is, our Master advised us that he had finally decided to call it quits and give the rest of us an opportunity to fill the great, and doubtless unfillable shoes. This being an election year, the kindly fellow decided that one of us would be appointed in the very near future so that by election day, the fortunate appointee would have had a chance to establish himself as the incumbent, very likely to be elected to the post come November."

He poured more coffee into his cup, sipped it, then continued. "The announcement was made public last week. Little Tony Otis, supervisor of criminal torts, was named as successor. Tom Smith and I were told we were out of the running just before the public announcement." Reardon shook his head and exhaled between his teeth. "Now if you could tell me why the hell I'm bothering to explain all this to you . . ."

The tomboy was gone; the tough, wary, angry face was replaced by a suddenly vulnerable young girl who had been following his every word and who suddenly looked as though she had been somehow assaulted.

"*Now* what the hell is the matter?"

She put the fork down and raised her chin. Her eyes were shimmering. "But when you asked me . . . when I loused up with Elena that first night . . . and then when I came into your office . . . you asked me if I *deliberately* loused things up. Do you mean that you considered, even for a moment, that for some reason I might have been trying to ruin your chances for the appointment?"

"Christie, it is in the nature of the job we're both involved in to be suspicious. Of everyone and everything. Even without justification of any kind for our suspicions."

"But, I *wouldn't* have. You should have known that. I *wouldn't* have."

"Let me put it to you this way, Christie. I would have asked that question of any member of the Squad who had muffed an important assignment. Any and every member. It seems to me that it's always been a sore point with you—your feeling that you want to be treated like any other member of the Squad, right?"

"Well, yes but . . . "

Finally, Reardon's anger came through. "Damn it, Christie, there's always a 'but' with you. Let me put it to you this way. You've indicated some pretty damn rough suspicions as far as I'm concerned. I didn't get all red in the face and insulted and indignant and outraged, did I? I just accepted the fact that it is in the nature of the job we do to have suspicions. Now just shut up and eat your goddamn eggs."

Reardon attacked his scrambled eggs which were cold and greasy, with great concentration, reached for some toast, which was dry and hard. "You really spoiled a nice breakfast, you know that, don't you?"

"I thought you were going to bring me up to date. About the case."

He finished the coffee, then poured the remaining few drops from the carafe. "Well, just for your information, approximately fifty percent of the information Elena gave us about the narcotics shipment we already had."

"That makes fifty percent new information, right?"

"Yeah, but I thought you might like to know that some other people besides you have been working." He relented. "That's not to take any credit from you, Christie. You really did a hell of a job. And if you say yes, you know, I'll dump this coffeepot right on your head."

"And what about Elena? What happens to her now?"

"Oh, Elena has a long, long way to go. We spent the entire night on the narcotics thing. The beautiful part of the whole thing is that there is no way to call back any shipment, no way for Giardino or any of his people to notify anyone involved. We'll be on top of it from the minute the stuff starts hitting ports. Which will be tomorrow, by the way. Everyone on our side has been notified. Hell, we've been photostating copies of the tape transcriptions and distributing them to all agencies involved. Funny thing is, with all she told us, it will still be tough to nail Enzo Giardino on a narcotics rap."

"But why? He's the number one man, right?"

"Yeah, but the network is so loose that no finger points directly at him. But that's where our girl comes in handy again. Elena's got the goods on Enzo Giardino about ten different ways: murder, extortion, grand larceny. Not to mention hijacking, stock manipulation and that old reliable demon of the mob boys, income tax evasion."

"How about Tonio?"

"Ah, yes, Tonio the creep. We've got him cold. Combined with some damn good legwork by Marty Ginsburg and Dudley and what Elena told us and the lab workup, we'll send Tonio away for a long time." Reardon's hand went to the clump of hair at the crown of his head. "Boy, there is nothing truer than that old saying: only a woman knows how to really get you. And Elena knows how. And how!"

It was true: Christie studied Reardon's face and knew it was true. Elena knew how to leave her with an unexpected wound. His thick orangey eyelashes shadowed the honey-colored eyes which were not seeing her now. It was a strong face, marked with deepening lines across the forehead. There was no trace of the cruelty she had seen and been frightened by. His short, tight smile was amused, puzzled.

"Well, what's on your mind?"

"I guess I was wondering about Elena."

There was no reaction, no flicker, and she knew, as a certainty, that Elena had lied to her.

"Listen, Christie," Reardon told her earnestly, "don't worry about Elena. She's had one hell of a ride. Been everywhere, done everything, had the best, first class all the way. Now she has to pick up the tab. She was smart enough to know there were risks involved. She's smart enough to play straight now. Someday, all the big magazines and publishers will be offering her a million bucks for her memoirs. With her total recall, all she has to do is

put it on paper. She won't even need to split with a ghost-writer."
He signaled the waitress, paid the check and stood up.

"Oh, Mr. Reardon. Elena gave me these photographs. I gave
her my word that I'd destroy them, but I guess I should hold off a
while . . . "

Reardon's face froze. "Oh, Jesus. I just remembered something.
Come on, Christie. Move."

She followed him rapidly through the lobby and into the elevator. He stabbed the button for the fifteenth floor, glanced at
his watch and tapped his knuckles impatiently until the elevator
came to a halt.

He looked carefully up and down the length of the hallway
and whispered, "Think anybody's around? Be careful, Christie,
we could get locked up on a federal rap."

There was a sudden boyish enthusiasm as he put his finger
over his mouth and gestured for her to follow him silently. He
pointed to the mail slot, then quickly clamped his hand over her
mouth.

"Don't make a sound. We get caught and we're in big trouble.
I'm not kidding, Christie."

He ran his finger under the warning engraved into the metal
placket over the slot, which informed the public of the dire conse-
quences faced by those who tampered with the United States
mail. There was an accumulation of letters and postcards rising
about six inches above the open slot. They rested on an almost in-
visible piece of celluloid which had been inserted about four
inches below the slot, through a fine line cut into the glass of the
mail chute.

Reardon carefully pried the celluloid free and tapped the glass
until the mail fell down the chute. "That's good. It'll make the
seven o'clock collection and we didn't commit any crime."

Christie touched the glass with her fingertip. "You can't even
see the cut. How did . . . "

Casey Reardon cupped his hand around his mouth. "Forget
what you seen, kid. Them Feds are tough. Five-to-ten on the
first offense. You won't turn me in, will ya?" He pulled her arm,

led her to the fire exit. "Come on, we'll walk up the flight of stairs. Good exercise."

The iron stairs and concrete landing of the fire exit added to the coldness. The area was dimly lit by small electric bulbs which flickered inside of wire mesh cages.

"Watch your step," Reardon told her. He reached out for her arm. "You fall and break your leg here, I don't know how the hell I'd explain it." His hand tightened on her arm as they reached the first landing. "Hold it a minute, Christie."

She turned, faced him. The boyishness was gone, the playfulness. His voice was low and serious now.

"Why did it matter to you, Christie? What difference did it make to you?"

"Because it matters to me . . . very much . . . what kind of a man you are. And . . . "

Reardon leaned down and kissed her very gently, his mouth scarcely touching hers, just pressing lightly and withdrawing. Her eyes caught the flicker of a bulb and were shiny, not definitely blue or green or gray, just flashes of brightness. He leaned his elbow against the tile wall, his hand at the back of his head. His right hand traced empty patterns along her shoulder and neck and face, along her eyebrows, through her hair, down her ear to her chin. His smile was unfamiliar, relaxed, unguarded.

"You know what this reminds me of?" He gestured, indicated the atmosphere of the hallway. "My first girl. A long, long time ago. Standing in her hallway, on the landing. You look like her, Christie." His hand moved to the back of her neck, naturally, warmly, and she moved her face against his arm. "You don't *really* look like her of course. But like the memory of her. Do you remember the first time a boy kissed you?"

Christie smiled and nodded. "Yes. We were playing ring-a-levio. I had a great hiding place behind the shoemaker's shop. Bobby . . . Bobby somebody or other . . . " Her eyes closed, strained for the memory. "Bobby found me and instead of rejoining the game, we started poking around in all the junk back there. There were all kinds of scraps of leather and . . . " She smiled. "I

212

don't know why I'm telling you this." Reardon told her to go on. "Well, I was trying to figure out what we could do with the scraps of leather and Bobby started getting very tense. Usually, he'd argue about anything I suggested first. And vice versa, of course."

Reardon nodded. "Where you were involved, of course."

"Well, he just kept agreeing with everything I said and I was getting a little suspicious. Then, all of a sudden, he just reached out with both his hands and held my head. I think his hands were on my ears. And smack. Right on the mouth."

"What did you do?"

Christie grinned. "I belted him. Right on the nose. Poor Bobby."

"That's my girl. How old were you?"

"Ten, eleven. But you don't have to feel sorry for him. He belted me right back. Then we got back into the ring-a-levio game and never mentioned the kiss."

"That was little girl, little boy stuff. How about when you were a big girl?"

Christie shook her head. "Uh-uh."

"I wasn't prying, Christie. I was just trying to place you. To find you in time. You're a puzzle to me, Christie. Why does that seem to surprise you?"

"Oh, I don't know. Because I guess I don't really think you consider me very much of a mystery. I guess I don't think you even *consider* me, very much."

"You know damn well that isn't true." Reardon pulled away from the wall. "I *consider* you, all right. Too damn much, in too damn many ways. I'm trying to put all the Christies together: I haven't seen all of them yet, right? It's incredible, what do you do, push buttons or something? You programmed? There, your chin is going up, eyes turning green: Christie number . . . what? three? four?" His fingertip moved along her lips. "Now, the smile. What the *hell* does that smile mean? Are you taunting me? Go ahead, now you nibble on your finger: button number . . . six: little girl. There's one I haven't seen clearly yet, Christie. Just glimpses, just hints, but then she disappears. Gets lost behind the little girl-tomboy-competent detective covering. It's the most pro-vocative Christie of all."

She shook her head. "I don't know what you mean. I don't have the slightest idea of what you're talking about."

"The hell you don't."

Casey Reardon pulled her to him and his mouth was warm and her hands slid inside his suit jacket and their bodies held together. She began speaking, her voice almost lost against him.

"You know why it mattered to me, Casey, don't you? Because I shouldn't have believed that you would have . . . because I shouldn't have believed you would have betrayed a child and . . ."

"Hey. Hey, Christie, come on now." He sat on the top step and pulled her beside him. "So that makes two of us who aren't per-fect, right? I didn't think you could have carried off the bit with the pictures; I even questioned your loyalty in the beginning of the investigation. I didn't have enough confidence in you. And I should have." Very casually, he threw it off. "When you love someone, you should have confidence in them, right? And you should have had confidence in me, right? So we were both wrong."

"Yes. I should have. And for the same reason."

Reardon sat very still, his hands clasped over hers. "Christie, it is very complicated with us. I wish to hell it wasn't. It's not just physical, not just chemistry. I'm not making any assumptions, am I?" She shook her head. "We both know there can't be any prom-ises made and kept. Not any public ones, anyhow. Maybe some private ones. Christie, I've tried to keep it from reaching this point. Because of you. Because of the particular girl you are . . ."

Christie Opara's face was calm and still and serene. There was nothing guarded or hidden about her expression. "But we're at this point, aren't we?"

Reardon stood up, reached into his jacket pocket and extracted a key with the hotel placket attached to it. He extended it to Christie. "I have a room on the tenth floor. No one upstairs knows about it. And it wasn't calculated," he added quickly, defensively, surprised by himself. "I just thought I might need to catch a few hours of uninterrupted sleep somewhere along the line."

"Why are you giving the key to me? You can open the door, can't you?"

His hand tightened on her shoulder and he shook her lightly. "Oh, hell, Christie. It would be so damn easy. Right now. And don't you tempt me, or dare me, or whatever the hell that expression on your face means. You take the key." He squinted at his wrist watch. "I have to leave for the F.B.I. office in about a half hour. I'll be back in the hotel by ten, the very latest. That'll give you a little time. To think. Damn it. You really use that smile, don't you? Are you listening to me? Do you know what I'm telling you?"

The smile moved across her mouth and she nodded. "I know what you're saying."

"When I come back to the hotel, I'll go directly to my room. If you're not there," he said shortly, "the key will be in the suite. Leave it on the coffee table, near the flowerpot or whatever that goddamn thing is."

"What about if I *am* there?"

Reardon studied the grin and reached with both hands, deliberately placed them on her ears and gave her a fast, hard kiss. "If you *are* there, Christie, don't play games with me." He dropped his hands, shook his head. "There goes your chin up. Are you daring me, or something?"

"Who, me? 'Never make a dare, never take a dare.'" She frowned for a minute. "And what do you mean 'don't play games with me'?" She did a close imitation of his tone. "Why not, Casey? Games are fun."

He turned her toward the staircase and pushed her lightly. "*I'll* let you know which games are fun. Come on. Up to the sixteenth floor."

They stopped at the top landing but didn't touch. They could hear voices coming from the hotel hallway. Waited a moment, then Reardon reached for the doorknob, felt her touch on his hand as he pulled the door open. He caught a quick glimpse of her face as the light of the hall caught her: it was young and flushed and happy. And beneath the radiance, he sensed a seriousness.

Stoner Martin and Marty Ginsburg emerged from the suite; Stoner waved a paper at Reardon, then waited patiently for him to walk down the hallway.

"I guess I still have some time to catch up on my sleep, Mr. Reardon," Christie said. "I guess I'll go to my room."

"Right," he said.

"Christie." He hadn't meant to call her back, but she turned, expectantly. Tensely, he asked, "Christie, will you be there, in my room, when I get back?"

She shrugged and pitched her voice low. "Ya never know, Mr. Reardon. Guess you'll just have to wait and see."

Reardon watched her walk down the hall, stop at her door and glance back at him.

"Fresh little bastard," he said softly to himself.

》》 If you've enjoyed this book and would like to discover more great vintage crime and thriller titles, as well as the most exciting crime and thriller authors writing today, visit: 》》

The Murder Room
Where Criminal Minds Meet

themurderroom.com